CYPRUS KISS

Murray Bailey

Also by Murray Bailey

Ash Carter Thrillers:
Singapore 52
Singapore Girl
Singapore Boxer
Singapore Ghost
Singapore Fire

The Egyptian series:
Map of the Dead
Sign of the Dead*

Dare You series:
I Dare You
Dare You Twice

Stand alone:
The Lost Pharaoh
Black Creek White Lies

* previously entitled Secrets of the Dead

CYPRUS KISS

Murray Bailey

Heritage Books

First published in Great Britain in 2021 by
Heritage Books

16797610123

copyright © Murray Bailey 2021

The moral right of Murray Bailey to be identified as the author of this work has been asserted in accordance with the copyright, Designs and Patents Act of 1988.

All rights reserved. No part of this publication may be reproduced, stored in a retrieval system, or transmitted in any form or by any means, electronic, mechanical, photocopying, recording, or otherwise, without the prior permission of the copyright owner.

All the characters in this book are fictitious and any resemblance to actual persons, living or dead, is purely coincidental.

ISBN 9798742522911

Cover image © Ian Coles Photography
Cover design by Blue Dog Designs

Heritage Books, Truro, Cornwall

For my wife, Kerry, my Aphrodite

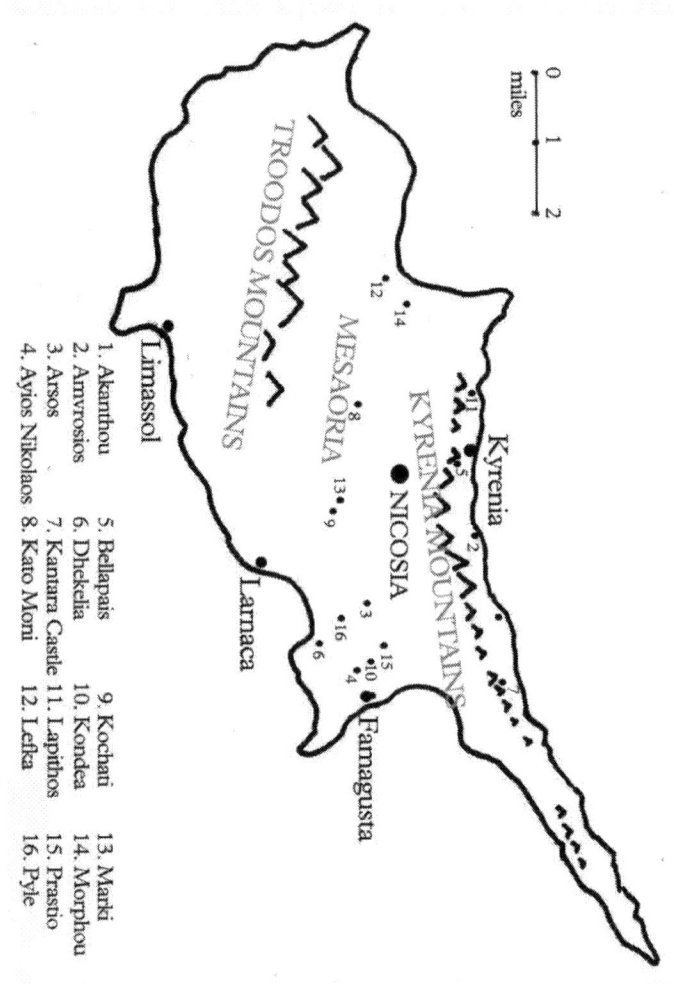

Cyprus 1948

PART ONE

"Don't bother the snake and it won't bite you."
- Cypriot Proverb

ONE

Johnson looked at the photograph for a long time, although he wasn't really looking, he was thinking.

"So where is Lieutenant Carter?" he eventually asked the investigating officer.

The younger man shook his head. "We can't find him, sir. His office is closed and no one's seen him since Friday evening."

"Since the murder, you mean."

"Yes, sir. He's just disappeared."

This didn't look good for Ash Carter. The man had been an irritant, poking his nose into matters that shouldn't concern him. Personal things. Carter hadn't got his way and had now taken matters into his own hands.

"An innocent man doesn't run," Johnson said, more to himself than for the benefit of the investigating officer.

"No, sir."

Johnson looked at the photograph again. A very pretty young woman. A black-and-white photograph, not professionally shot, but good, none the less.

He said, "Tell me about the case again."

"The victim was at the Kings Head. At nineteen fifteen he said he was going outside to meet this girl. According to one witness, the meeting had been pre-arranged the previous week."

"What about outside? Tell me again about the man who saw them together."

"Right. They—the victim and woman—were seen meeting. They walked through to the adjoining road, beside the pub and across the road behind. There's an alley between buildings and they went down there."

"And that's where he was found?"

"Yes, sir, less than fifteen minutes later. Dead. A single, effective stab wound. The attacker must have known what they were doing. It was an assassination, clear and simple. A second witness led me right to the address. There's no doubt about it, sir. We know the killer."

Johnson thought about the younger man's words. He had a tendency to make assumptions. He wasn't a trained investigator, not like Carter. Should he, Johnson, take over or should he influence and guide from the wings? Johnson cleared his throat. "You haven't dealt with a murder investigation before?"

"No, sir, but—"

This wasn't just a murder. The victim wasn't just anybody.

"But what, man?" Johnson said. Tension pulled across his chest like piano wire, and he knew his Scottish accent would be more pronounced. He paused and breathed. "This is a big responsibility."

"I can handle it, sir. I've attended court-martials before."

Could Johnson risk it? On the other hand, could he risk getting directly involved? Would his own connection be exposed and brought into question? Again Johnson cleared his throat.

"This isn't like a court-martial. This is big. The goddamn murder of one of our own." Johnson realized he'd raised his voice, but the younger man didn't flinch. Maybe he was up to it.

The junior officer nodded. "Understood, sir."

"This needs to be watertight."

"Yes, sir."

"Good man." Johnson returned the photograph to the investigating officer and dismissed him.

Just before the door clicked shut, another man entered Johnson's office. His cheeks twitched as though he was holding back a smile.

"You've heard." Johnson said, as the other man made himself comfortable in the chair opposite.

"Everyone's talking about it."

"Could it be a problem for me?"

Finally the man released his smile. "You worry too much, Jonny. Ellis was a problem and now it's gone away. If anything, I'd say it's time for a celebration."

Neither spoke for a moment, their eyes searching one another's before the other man stood and poured two fingers of single malt Scotch into cut-crystal tumblers. He handed one to Johnson.

The major knocked back his drink, felt the burn all the way down then sucked in air and enjoyed a second burn. He nodded and held out the empty glass for another shot.

Finally the tightness in his chest was evaporating.

The murder of a military policeman. It looked very bad for Lieutenant Ash Carter. Very bad indeed.

This wasn't going to result in a prison sentence. Oh no. The only reasonable outcome would be the death penalty.

TWO

Three weeks earlier

Only my fifth day in Cyprus and I'd already found trouble.

"You're chicken," the big man said. Beside him were three others, all of whom looked eager. They had the kind of fixed expressions and clenched fists that spoke volumes.

I'm six two and rarely had men square up to me like this, but the three cronies were all solidly built, all over six foot. And the big guy was probably six five.

I said, "We don't want trouble." The "we" in this case included the girl I'd come out with: Penny Cartwright. She edged behind me and I used my arm to guide her so that we had a wall at our backs.

The big guy said, "We're gonna whip you."

The men took a step closer.

"We?" I said. "Can't take me on your own?"

The man laughed. The three cronies laughed.

"Ash," Penny whispered. "Let's run."

I could hear the fear in her voice. They could too, and it made the big man grin even more.

"Fun's over, lads," I said as calmly as I could. "We'll leave now."

I gave Penny a nudge, and we stepped sideways.

"You're a yellow-bellied chicken," the big guy said. "And your tart is fair game."

"Excuse me?" I said, stopping. I smiled at him. "What did you say?"

"Next time I see her, your little floozy is mine."

I reached for Penny's hand and felt it shaking.

"This is ridiculous." I could hear the strain in my own voice now. *Stay calm*. Fighting when angry could lead to mistakes. My first boxing coach back home taught me that. He was the toughest man I've ever met—and he had to be. A Liverpudlian living in Manchester. Two towns that hated one another, so whenever a thug from Manchester heard Sammy speak, he would go for him. Sammy taught Queensbury boxing rules in his gym, but he would also give lessons on street fighting.

"Because your opponents might not know the rules," he said. And of course, he was right. The skills had immediately come in handy in Palestine, my first posting as a Royal Military Police, Special Investigations Branch officer.

"We'll take turns," said one of the goons.

"She'll love it," said another.

"Because she's a fair-game slut," the third one said.

How had we got into this crazy situation? Penny had invited me to the cinema in Larnaca. She was a typist assigned to our small SIB unit that had just transferred from Palestine. We hit it off and she was being nice to a new arrival. This wasn't a date. Although I admit she was pretty. Five eight in heels with raven black hair, which she wore tied back. She said that her bright eyes and a dark complexion came from her mother, who was half Indian. She was two years older than my twenty-four and had a confidence that belied her status. At least in my limited experience.

The film we'd seen was called *Down to Earth*, a strange musical comedy that would have been an easy way to spend a Saturday night if it hadn't been for the four hooligans who now confronted us.

Everyone in the army is used to catcalls and tomfoolery at a cinema, but this wasn't an army screening. It might not have been *The Rex* but there was a reasonable-sized audience—a mix of locals and military. Each time Rita Hayworth appeared on screen, men wolf-whistled so loudly that no one could hear the dialogue or songs.

The Greek gods in the show were mocked, and the leading man prompted missiles to be thrown at the screen.

It hadn't just been the four thugs who'd been rowdy, but they had been only two rows behind, and when an ice cream tub sailed over Penny's shoulder, she turned and I heard them laugh.

She'd politely asked them to settle down and, in response, had received a wet paper ball in the face.

That's when I'd stepped in. I'd turned, raised a hand and asked them to calm down.

The big guy had nodded, but as soon as I was looking away again, something struck me on the back of the head.

"Enough!" I'd said, glaring at them. "You've had some fun, don't spoil it."

"You challenging me?" the big guy said.

"No."

"Right now," he said, shouting above the latest musical number. "You and me outside now."

"After the film," I said.

"You're chicken!"

"If that's what you want, then yes, I'm chicken."

I turned and sat and heard them laughing. Penny put her arm through mine and smiled. Yes, she had a lovely smile too.

"That was the big-man thing to do," she whispered.

"I'm glad you think so," I said, expecting that the men would forget the challenge when we came out in another half an hour. Or they'd turn their attention to something else—beer, probably.

But no.

Here they were, not only confronting me but insulting Penny—threatening Penny.

"OK," I said.

The big man blinked. "OK what?"

"Let's do this."

THREE

Penny moved away and the four men stayed focused on me. I had a wall behind me, which might not seem the sensible thing because I couldn't turn and run, but coach Sammy had explained that keeping the opponents in front of you was more important than having an exit strategy.

When faced off, the Englishman's natural response is to fight one-on-one. "It's basic cowardice," Sammy said. "Men attack in packs when they know they can win. The others join in when you are down or have your back turned. So guess what? Don't show them your back and don't go down."

Good advice.

So, facing four men, I expected the big one to make the first move, and he did. He had one man on his right and two on the left. I prompted his attack by deliberately looking at the man furthest on the left.

Give him a target.

The big man stepped in and swung a right-handed roundhouse. More exaggerated than a right cross; too much power and stupid.

A roundhouse isn't a wise first punch. Not against a trained boxer. It's slow and telegraphed. But I'd done nothing to warn him that I could box. He went for a show-boating punch when he should have jabbed.

At the last second, I inched out of range, let him continue with the momentum, and then stepped inside what should have been a defence. He had none and was now an easy target.

When you're in the ring, staying calm means you can think, and most good boxers feel like time slows down. You see, you predict the moves, you see your target and you pick your counter.

Without gloves, the wise man chooses a soft target like the throat. One punch there and he'd be down and gasping. However, I could do serious damage and he'd be hospitalized, maybe never breathe easily again.

Maybe he deserved it. Maybe he didn't.

I used my stronger, faster left hand and drove it into his neck, just below his right ear. Enough muscle to save him, not enough to stop the jarring shock.

The big man hadn't finished his flailing first punch when I made satisfying contact. His rotation continued, he lost balance, and he went down like a Messerschmitt in a tailspin.

I wish I'd had a camera to capture the faces of the other men. They'd clearly never seen their leader dispensed with so easily. Three open mouths, three pairs of bulging eyes and uncertainty. Hands unclenched, half clenched, and Adam's apples bobbed as they swallowed.

"Next?" I said.

No one moved except the big guy on the floor.

"I thought not," I said. "Now apologize to the lady."

Penny got three apologies. The big man levered himself to his feet, shook his head to relieve the ache in his neck, and dusted his trousers.

He didn't apologize, but his humiliation was enough.

"OK, you can clear off. And don't try it again. If you give anyone any more trouble, I won't pull my punch next time—and I won't stop at one. Got it?"

They got it.

Three relieved men turned and tried to saunter away as though it was their choice. The big man looked at me hard, shook his head, and then a second later joined his buddies.

Penny put her arms around me. I could suddenly feel the tingle of adrenaline in my hands and the tremble in my chest, but if she noticed, she didn't say.

★

We'd only planned for the cinema, but it didn't seem right to take her home just yet and she must have felt the same.

"Let's go for a drive," she said.

It had been a scorching day and the sun was now leaving purple and orange streaks across the sky. At eighty degrees Fahrenheit, the temperature was now comfortable and getting better.

I collected my Land Rover from outside the SIB office on Pine Street, and we drove, roof off, along the long, sweeping coast.

With the wind in her hair, Penny relaxed, and I smiled over at her in the rapidly fading light.

"You all right?"

She smiled back. "Stop just up here."

I pulled off the road onto a promontory overlooking the sea.

"I love this spot."

I switched off the engine and enjoyed the dying light and hum of cicadas.

"I didn't know you could fight," she said. "I wouldn't have been so worried if I'd known. Are all SIB men like that? Can Captain Wolfe box as well?"

"No," I said. "But he can take care of himself. You learn how to do that pretty quickly in Palestine."

"But the Emergency is over now, right?"

"The British Army's left, if that's what you mean. But I sense there'll be trouble for a long time yet."

"What's it like? How does Cyprus compare?"

"Totally different. Mandatory Palestine was a war zone. A war between the Arabs and Jews, for taking their land, for arriving in their droves—thousands a week. And a war with the British, who both sides hated."

"And Cyprus?"

"Too early to say."

"But we don't have a war here."

I smiled and stretched my legs out, hands behind my head. "No, you don't. So far, it's been the first break I've had in two years."

"Two years in Palestine? Before that, where were you?"

"Officer training in Sandhurst and then specific SIB training in Mytchett Hutments. First posting, straight into the thick of it."

"So, Lieutenant Ash Carter, what is the Special Investigations Branch doing in Cyprus?"

I was surprised by the direct question. She knew we couldn't talk about it. As a secretary, she had been privy to some communications, but our orders were secret.

Then she laughed at me. "I was joking! I know you can't tell a civilian."

"I can't tell anyone," I said. "Except that we have our new posting in Larnaca."

The embers of the dying sun had vanished, and the clear skies were lit by more stars than a man could count.

"The sky is so clear here," I said, changing the subject.

"I love it—most of the time," she said.

"Best and worst?" I asked.

"Well, you saw the worst, back there. Young white men."

"Army," I said, recognizing the type despite their civilian clothes.

"Undoubtedly. They can be quite racist."

I didn't think Penny's heritage was that obvious. Her smooth brown skin could have easily been cultivated on a sandy beach.

"What about the best?" I asked.

"The views, the weather—when it's not too hot—and the food."

"The food?" I asked, suddenly feeling hungry despite an early dinner. Perhaps the adrenaline from the fight had stirred my appetite.

"Come on," she said. "Let me direct you to a quaint tavern I know. It's in the middle of nowhere, and patronized by locals, but—come to think of it, perhaps that's why I like it so much. We'll be the only Brits."

Fifteen minutes later, driving across dusty roads that seemed more suited for animals than cars, we arrived at a village and a tavern with eight tables arranged outside.

Fortunately the staff spoke English, and we soon had plates of food that we shared. It was far better than what I'd eaten in the Middle East.

I don't drink alcohol, and I was surprised to find that Penny didn't either. Mine was mainly for health reasons, hers because of family history. I could tell she didn't want to talk about it, so I didn't press her.

The journey back made me regret eating so much. Each jolt threatened to reveal the contents of my stomach. So at a junction, I stopped for a moment and turned off the lights.

Warm dry air filled my lungs, and we enjoyed the panoply of stars for a while until my stomach settled.

"I love the song of the cicadas," she said quietly. "Most people either tune them out or hate them, but for me, they're beautiful."

I didn't feel so strongly, and wondered if that would change over time. Naturally, I'd heard them in Palestine, but I'd spent most of my time in built-up areas and just thought of them as the sound of the countryside. Here in Cyprus, their clicking never ceased.

"Can you hear their songs, Ash?" she asked as I relaxed and listened.

Then a gunshot shattered the peace.

Close by.

"My God!" Penny said, alarmed.

I switched on the headlights. Could I hear voices?

Starting the engine, I turned right, away from the road home. Then I stopped, switched off and listened. Another engine. A car had started and was driving fast.

What the heck was going on?

I fired up the engine once more and put my foot down. Then I braked hard. Just off the track, the headlights caught a dark shape on the ground.

Grabbing a torch, I jumped out and approached.

I feared the worst, and it was the worst.

The shape was a man. His legs and hands were tied, and he had a bullet hole in the side of his head.

FOUR

The police HQ in Nicosia was a long building just inside Paphos Gate, within a few hundred yards of Wolseley Barracks outside and to the west.

When I reported the body at the police station in Larnaca, they asked me to provide a statement—but not there. I needed to attend the only detective unit on the island and it was in Nicosia.

I travelled up on Monday morning and drove around the city before stopping outside the police HQ.

The capital and Larnaca had stark differences.

Larnaca was a jumble of buildings: a core that was the old town, and a sprawling area that was modern and mostly military. GHQ was based there, as were offices for the RAF and Royal Navy. The main airport was just outside. There was a port, although the main naval base was around the coast at Famagusta, which also served as the merchant port. Between Larnaca and Famagusta was the large army cantonment of Dhekelia, with Alexander Barracks and the Nightingale Hospital being the significant buildings. The south-east coast felt like a huge British military base.

In juxtaposition, Nicosia was a cosmopolitan walled city. Approximately circular, everyone referred to the gates as though on a clock face. The police HQ at Paphos Gate was at half past eight.

Outside the dark walls, boulevards and grand buildings shouted British colonialism as loudly as anywhere in the empire. Inside was a jumble of cultures, a few wide thoroughfares, but mostly twisting lanes crammed with offices and shops. In the heart was Saint Sophia Cathedral, with its twin towers visible from miles around, but there were about twenty other churches, basilicas and minarets serving almost as many religious sects.

Similar to most cities, I sensed business and urgency. This wasn't a relaxing place like the coast, with its glorious sea views and beaches.

Perhaps the detective sergeant I met should have spent more time away from the city, because he was anything but relaxed.

"So you're the one who found the body?" he said without introducing himself. He was tall—a shade over six foot and wearing a brown pinstriped suit. As cigarette smoke clouded his creased left eye, I wondered if he was younger than he looked, possibly mid-thirties. Which, like most men of a certain age, meant ex-military.

"Yes," I said laconically. Normally I might have made conversation about his service, but this guy didn't seem in the mood to make small talk.

"All right, I'll get someone in to write up your statement."

"I could write it myself."

He eyed me suspiciously. "Oh, you're a copper then?"

I wasn't wearing a uniform, since SIB officers rarely do, so I explained.

"Army. Lieutenant Ash Carter," I said, holding out my hand.

His shake was firm and strong. "Well, Lieutenant, I'm sure you could write a good statement, but just humour me if you would." Then he walked away without introducing himself.

A few minutes later I found myself talking to a stenographer. I described driving and stopping for a breath of air, hearing a gunshot and then possibly voices before a car drove away. I made no mention of being with Penny.

The sergeant hadn't asked any questions, and I was left wondering whether he had been too busy or was simply disinterested. However, I couldn't tell them much and he didn't return to see me off.

I travelled back to Larnaca and parked in the temporary shade of the pine tree copse outside the Pine Street office. I don't know who had occupied the office before us, but now it was me, Captain Bill Wolfe, and Penny Cartwright.

Working with Penny could have been a problem, and there was an unwritten rule about avoiding relationships with staff. However, she'd insisted the cinema night wasn't a date and then when I dropped her at home she'd suggested I omit her from the report and not mention it to Wolfe. I thought that worked well if we were to date again—and I was sure we would. Her parting kiss on my cheek told me all I needed to know.

Rules are made to be broken.

Penny glanced at me as I entered the room and merely nodded politely like she had on previous mornings.

The windows were open and my desk looked out at the pine trees. It would have been idyllic if not for the heat, and two fans spun frantically but did little in the fight against the warm air.

Wolfe also nodded a greeting.

He was a man of few words, and I'd first thought he didn't like me. But it was just his way. He had a broad Yorkshire accent which I suspect he exaggerated because of its harder sounding edge. He used it to bark orders and swear as aggressively as any regimental sergeant major I'd heard.

His placid face was hard to read, especially because of his large moustache that turned down around his lips giving him a constant air of disapproval. He had curly brown hair and his skin had bronzed more than mine in the sun.

I had an inch height advantage over Wolfe, whereas he had gained a few pounds around his midriff since we'd been stationed in the Middle East. However, I'd seen him operate and knew he could handle himself in a fight.

If our roles had been reversed, I would have asked him about the trip to the police in Nicosia, but he didn't mention it.

Wolfe and I were two of the last British soldiers to have left Mandatory Palestine as it transitioned to Israel. Men either shipped home or south to the *Canal Zone* or north to Cyprus.

Of the sixteen-strong SIB team in Palestine, Wolfe and I were the only ones on the Cyprus boat. We said goodbye to the challenging place that had been my home for two years, but we both knew it wasn't over. Cyprus had little need of the Special Investigations Branch, and I was sure there was much more to our role.

We had no specific orders, and when I'd asked Wolfe, he said that we should await instructions. He also told me I must be favoured because HQ would only trust the best with this job.

I wondered if he was being sarcastic, but then I'd seen him in action in Palestine and knew he'd earned respect. I was also a little jealous of his name. I'd changed mine to Carter when I left home—it was my mother's maiden name—partly as a snub to my father and partly because I wanted no favours. I wanted to progress on merit, not because of my father's connections.

I could have chosen an impactful name, like Wolfe, but then again it was the man rather than the name. At least I hoped so. Anyway, having a name similar to Penny's surname broke the ice between us and led to our date that wasn't officially a date.

Wolfe had given me the menial tasks of arranging for a telephone, finding an office cleaner, a translator, and arranging supplies. We'd normally have a batch of junior staff to handle such things, but I had nothing better to do and didn't complain.

At midday, a telephone engineer arrived and said he'd run a cable to the outside. He said it would take him another three hours before our phone would be installed and another day before it would be connected.

After a walk for fresh air, I came back in time to see a despatch rider deliver an *eyes-only* envelope for Wolfe.

The captain opened it, read the contents, resealed the envelope and locked it in his drawer.

I looked at him expectantly.

"Orders?"

"Yes." Wolfe played with his moustache, which told me he was mulling something over.

Would he tell me? I wouldn't claim to be his friend, but we had a fair relationship. Occasionally he played the *I'm your superior* card, but not often and not since we'd shipped out. I felt like we were in this together. Just the two of us on this semi-barren—and potentially boring—rock.

I said, "Penny, would you give us a moment please?"

Penny nodded and left the room.

Now that Wolfe and I were alone, I could speak openly.

"So?"

"It's as I suspected."

I shook my head. He'd given me no indication of his suspicions.

"This isn't about fuckin' Cyprus."

Again I shook my head. Why were we here then?

He let a smile flicker on his lips—at least I think it was a smile beneath that droopy caterpillar of a moustache.

He said, "The Middle East. You and me, Carter, we're covering the fuckin' Middle East. It's unofficial. We're not supposed to be there, but we're working for Intelligence and we tell fuckin' no one."

FIVE

"What does that mean in practice?" I asked Bill Wolfe after he didn't elaborate on our new role.

"I'm leaving tonight. And you're staying here."

"Oh." I was disappointed and didn't care that he knew.

He said, "Just for the time being. You'll get orders from HQ soon enough—or I'll call for you."

"And in the meantime?"

"Enjoy the sun."

I shook my head. "Bill—"

"I'm fuckin' joking. You're a smart man, Ash. Make use of your time here. Make contact with the various COs—and with the local detectives."

"But we aren't working Cyprus, you said so yourself!"

"You never know," he said, but it was bullshit. He was trying to find me work, keep me active so that I wouldn't switch off.

"Fine," I said.

He said, "I'll tell you what I can, when I can, OK?"

"Right."

"So tell me. How did it go this morning in Nicosia?"

That made me smile. He did care.

"I gave them my statement, but they didn't seem that interested."

"There you go," he said. "Your first job is to go back and get involved in the case."

"Like I said, they aren't interested."

"Ash,"—he shook his head—"make them interested. Wear your uniform and make it fuckin' formal."

★

He was right, the second time I visited the Nicosia police HQ, the desk clerk looked like he would have a heart attack when he saw me in uniform.

"The detective in charge of the murder on Saturday night, please?" I said, and watched the young man scurry away.

When he reappeared, the clerk breathlessly asked if I'd wait in a meeting room and offered me water. And so I did.

Most police waiting rooms are stark affairs with uncomfortable chairs. Not this one. The building was British Colonial, maybe a hundred years old, with the kind of features you'd expect in a stately home rather than a functional building. My chair had leather upholstery, and the pieces of furniture—a coffee table, lamp tables, desk and a bookcase—were of ornate mahogany.

I was reminded of a headmaster's study back home, and I choked back a laugh as an inspector came into the room with his hands behind his back. He could have been playing the headmaster, aged in his fifties with greying hair, round spectacles, a dark grey suit, tie and stern expression.

"Lieutenant Ash Carter?"

I held out my hand.

He raised his right hand to show me a metal claw, before shaking my hand, upside down, with his left.

Peering at me through his glasses, he said, "Military police? From Alexander Barracks?"

"Special Investigations Branch," I said. "Separate. We've set up an office in Larnaca."

He nodded like I'd explained everything. "I'm DI Dickins. I understand you found the body on Saturday night. How may I be of service?"

And so I told him that I was new to Cyprus, having been reassigned from Palestine. I was about to ask to join the investigation when he beat me to it.

I agreed that I would.

"You have the time? Marvellous. Let's jump in a car and visit where you found the body."

We took my Land Rover since it was more suited to the rough terrain than the car he offered.

"I wasn't impressed yesterday," I said as I drove south out of the town. "The sergeant I met—"

"DS Park."

"Very disinterested and dismissive."

"Ah."

I waited for more before prompting: "What does that mean, Inspector?"

"Call me Charles." He smiled at me. "Like the author, but Dickins is with an 'i' rather than an 'e'."

I nodded and wondered what it must be like to have an almost famous name. He probably explained the difference every time he met someone for the first time—after showing them his claw hand. He didn't seem embarrassed by either and was still smiling.

"So, it means that's what you should expect of DS Park," he continued. "Anthem's a good fellow, but—"

"But?"

"Well I originally thought he was bitter for not being promoted to inspector, but it's not that. It's frustration more than anything."

Dickins directed me off the main road and we headed east. I saw desiccated scrubland, red soil and stone walls. There were occasional olive groves and goat farms, but little else.

I said, "What did you mean about DS Park being frustrated?"

"Well, it was a local man—a native. Greek most likely."

"And locals deserve less protection than the Brits?"

"No, but it's hard to get them to talk to us." He waited a minute before speaking again. "You'll find there are three types of Brit in Cyprus: those who lived here before the war; those who are assigned here—civil servants mainly—and stay because they must."

"And the third group?"

"People who choose to come because they like it. That's Anthem. When he demobbed from the army he came here and joined the force."

I thought about Penny. She fitted into this final category.

"What about you, Charles?" I asked.

"Assigned. I've just started my second year of a three-year tour of duty." He laughed. "I was at Scotland Yard before getting this so-called holiday assignment."

"And is it a holiday?"

"Mostly. Certainly better than London during the Blitz."

"Most places were better than London during the Blitz."

He pointed with his hook. "Turn here."

We bumped along a track, creating a dust cloud in our trail. A shortcut, I realized, as we came out on the road I'd driven along on Saturday night. We turned left and stopped after a hundred yards.

He said, "So you heard the gunshot and then someone drive away."

"Not someone. There were at least two of them, because I'm certain I heard them talking."

"Not talking to the victim?"

"It was afterwards and conversational."

He nodded. "As you will have guessed, it was an execution. Single bullet to the head. The victim was brought out here—middle of nowhere—hogtied, shot and dumped."

We walked ten paces from the road and I saw a dark patch on the ground: the dead man's blood.

"Calibre of the bullet?" I asked.

"There will be an autopsy."

I nodded. So the coroner hadn't examined the body yet.

"What was this about?" I asked.

"The execution? Gang punishment most likely."

I had been checking the ground for clues—a bullet casing or footprint—and looked up, astonished. "There are gangs out here?"

"Ash," he chuckled kindly, and I was again reminded of a school headmaster, "there are gangs everywhere."

For a second I felt like he was patronizing and highlighting my immaturity. But Dickins saved my face by his next words.

"It may surprise you, but even among these poor communities, rivalries develop. It's nothing like what you will have experienced in Palestine."

"What's the—?"

"You have your Turks and Greeks. You actually have your true Cypriots and the ones from the mainland. I trust those the least."

"I was going to ask what they fight over. In Palestine, it's obviously land and religion. What's here—goats, olives, oranges and fish?"

"Could be. Could be anything. Humans are naturally tribal. It could be a family squabble, a village or a group of men. It could be over a girl, over turf, over money. It just takes two to disagree and—in this case—a gun."

"Have there been gang executions before."

"Of course, although not for a long time. We'll compare this one to the old cases."

"I got the impression from Anthem that it wouldn't be investigated."

He raised a hand. "Oh, don't get us wrong, Ash. It will be investigated. Reports will be written and filed. But—"

"But you don't expect to apprehend anyone because no one will talk."

We got back into the Land Rover and a thought struck me. "The ground was thoroughly searched?"

He looked at me critically.

"Just asking," I said apologetically.

He nodded. "Yes. Anthem and a couple of constables went over it with a fine-tooth comb."

"And found nothing?"

"That's right. Nothing on the ground and nothing on the victim. As you'd expect, there weren't any identification documents."

"You could do a house-to-house... show his mugshot."

"We could, but which houses? We could cover the whole island. He could be from anywhere and, even if he's not from the mainland and we find his village, the locals won't talk. That's how gangs work. That's how gangs thrive."

I shook my head. "What if he'd been a Brit?"

"Well, that's different because people would talk. Look, Ash, I know it sounds bad, but you learn pretty quickly out here that you can only do so much."

I didn't like it, and I didn't know whether DI Dickins was right or just jaded. Had he started with a different attitude? Had he been like this in his previous job?

Dickins promised to keep me abreast of developments and I gave him the contact details for the SIB office.

"Don't expect a call," he said.

"You can at least let me know the coroner's findings."

After he nodded, I said, "And to be honest, I'd appreciate it if you involved me in anything of interest."

I wondered if he was about to pat me on the head like I was a good boy, but he said he'd bear my request in mind.

He shook my hand again with his reversed left.

"No promises though, young man."

In my rear-view mirror, I saw him watching me drive away and wondered what he thought. Despite our age difference, had I just made an ally or was he privately laughing at my naivety?

SIX

Since I was in the capital, I had to visit Wolseley Barracks. It was a large base on the outskirts of Nicosia between Codrington Street and the Pedieos River, which ran to the west of the city. The barracks was home to the Royal Lancers, who were here more for ceremonial impact than anything truly military. This opinion was reinforced by the presence of the Army Music Corps. The whole thing was wrapped up by A-Branch—the administrative branch of the army—which illustrated the army's typically inventive naming convention.

Brigadier Squires, the CO at Wolseley, gave me a polite five minutes and told me nothing of interest. Nor did he show any interest in the presence of the SIB in Cyprus. Afterwards, his adjutant gave me a tour and then told me where to find Waynes Keep, over the river, which was the HQ for the First Guards Brigade, a mounted RMP unit.

Waynes Keep turned out to be an ugly white building with stables and a cemetery. The CO there was called Major Gee, a blond, good-looking chap with one of those mouths that turns up at the ends, giving him a permanent smile.

He gave me a boring history lesson, including how the First Guards dated back to the Duke of Wellington. Based on what I'd seen, I decided that the units based in Nicosia were all about braid, bureaucrats and bugles. If I wanted to organize a party for the governor of Cyprus, I knew where to come. Aside from that unlikely event, I figured my visits to Wolseley and Waynes Keep would be few and far between.

Gee invited me to have lunch with him, but I politely declined and sheltered from the heat of midday within the city walls. I found a café on a quiet, shaded street and waited until the worst of the heat passed.

People-watching seemed an easier way to spend a couple of hours than listening to the great and glorious history of the mounted police. Afterwards, I bought a tacky model of a church as a gift.

★

Driving south again, I went to Alexander Barracks and found myself introduced to Lieutenant Colonel Jim Dexter.

Dexter was CO of the 1st Battalion, Suffolk Regiment. Their unusual motto was Montis Insignia Calpe, which he'd explained originated from their barracks in Gibraltar. They had a proud history and were widely respected, even in Palestine where I'd originally met Dexter.

"I said you'd go far," he said, pumping my hand and grinning. He always had a ready smile and firm handshake for me.

"Looks like we've both come far," I said, laughing.

He shook his head. "It feels very strange—the regiment shipped here, just waiting. A holding place."

I nodded and he continued.

"That's why the barracks are by the sea. We can ship out fast. There's another at Limassol."

"I've not been," I said.

"Nice beach." He grinned, but I sensed his frustration at being put on standby for God-knows-what.

I handed him the gift I'd bought in Nicosia. Dexter hated ornaments; in fact, the only things he had in his office were official or military history books. He didn't even believe in family photographs. "Leave your personal life at home," he once told me.

He studied the model church with a mixture of horror and confusion on his face. "What is it?"

"No idea, I just wanted to see your expression when I handed it to you."

"Do I have to keep it?"

"Not unless you want to."

He chuckled then tossed the ornament into a bin.

"Now, what can I do for you, Ash?"

So I told him the little I knew and said I was just making contact. We chatted comfortably for a few minutes before a clerk popped his head in and said Dexter had another meeting.

The colonel nodded and turned his attention back to me. "Anything you need, you can always come to me."

"Thank you, sir."

"You know 227 Provost Company have a unit here at Alexander?"

"I saw the sign."

"You should meet Major Johnson. You might also call in on the wireless intelligence chaps at Ayios Nikolaos—it's close, on the back road to Famagusta."

He told me how to find it and I gripped his hand again.

"Good to see you, Ash."

*

With elbows on his desk, Major John Johnson looked at me kindly. We were in his house in the married quarters referred to as *the village*. The name belied the true appearance of the row of properties. They were single-storey, white-painted buildings that the Army classed as *Scale C* huts. Each had a large garden, picket fence and had been decorated with brightly coloured curtains, and there were bright flowers and climbers outside. Johnson had the end one, which was slightly bigger but still basically a large shed.

Johnson was the provost marshal, in his late forties, with well-groomed salt and pepper hair, bushy eyebrows, sad eyes.

I'd gone to his office at Alexander Barracks but his adjutant had insisted Johnson would be happy to receive me at his home.

"Kind of you to see me, sir," I said after introductions.

"Always good to meet the new boys." He had a soft Scottish accent that bordered on weary. He nodded as though thinking. "So you were with the 75 Provost Company chaps in Palestine. How was that?"

"Palestine was ugly. But if you mean the 75th, then they were good chaps. Although I also had dealings with the Suffolks."

He nodded again. "Good to have your friends here at Alexander."

In the corner of my eye, I saw a girl leave another room and go outside. I got the impression of long dark hair and tanned skin. From her size, I guessed seven or eight years old.

Johnson glanced her way and then back at me.

"We're a small company here," he said. "Most of the division is in Italy—Trieste."

"Sounds nice."

"First Guards Brigade is up in Nicosia."

"I visited them this morning. Met Major Gee."

"Right." Johnson sighed. "Don't have much to do with them."

"Bugles, braid and bangles," I said.

He gave a weak smile then said, "And the Suffolks are the band and drums, but you'll know that. That damned tune of theirs!"

"Speed the Plough."

"That's the one. What rot!" After a breath, he continued: "So why wasn't I informed?" He looked at me like an accountant wondering why the figures don't balance.

"Informed, sir?"

"Of your presence? Why didn't Command tell me SIB would be moving in?"

"It's just the two of us. A holding place," I said, using the same expression Dexter had used fifteen minutes earlier.

Johnson stretched his neck as though thinking. "So you'll report to me." It wasn't a question.

It was common practice to have a relationship with the CO of the local provost company. It made sense. We'd been part of 75 Company, and to Johnson's mind we should now be part of 227.

"Those aren't our orders, sir."

His sad eyes creased up. "Most unusual. Are you sure, Lieutenant?"

"Yes, sir."

"I'll need to check."

It wasn't an insult. He was senior and didn't need to accept my word.

I smiled. "Of course. And rest assured, we'll work closely with you—and report to you—where appropriate."

"Good. Make sure you do," he said, then offered me a velvet hand. "Welcome to Cyprus, Lieutenant Carter. Enjoy your stay."

I've met a number of provost marshals. They were typically bombastic, self-assured and sometimes arrogant. However, I'd never met one like Major Johnson before. He was also older than any I'd met, and I wondered if his weary demeanour was why he was still only a major.

As I left the house, the girl was outside hugging a big German Shepherd dog. I'd been right about the age. She had pretty eyes and an easy smile.

"What's he called?" I asked. "Your dog."

"Caesar. Daddy got him for me as an early Christmas present last year."

Caesar looked like a police dog. Not young. Maybe retired.

I said, "Do you walk him?"

"Sometimes, but mostly Uncle Graham. Do you work for Daddy?"

"No."

"Oh, I thought you were an MP, like Daddy and Uncle Graham."

"I am. Special Investigations"—I could see she wasn't sure—"like a police detective, only military."

"What's your name?"

"Ash—Ash Carter."

"Pleased to meet you Mr Carter. I'm Verity." She waved Caesar's paw. "Caesar is pleased to meet you too."

*

Jim Dexter had given me directions to the village called Ayios Nikolaos, but there had been no need. I could see the radio dishes from a mile away. There were low hills around Larnaca which Penny described as like a giant's sandcastles that had been flattened. I'd commented that they were rather green for sandcastles, but apparently I was seeing the country at its best—in spring. Soon the temperature would rise and the grass would turn brown.

On the hill beside three radio dishes was a cluster of huts. A sign read: Royal Signals, 2 Wireless Regiment. It was a small camp outside the equally tiny village. There I introduced myself to a first lieutenant called Vaughan who was courteous but wouldn't say much. He told me they were an electronic intelligence-gathering station. I told him my two-man unit had an intelligence role, but it didn't impress him at all.

So much for interdisciplinary support.

The low sun was in my face as I looped around, back towards Dhekelia. I hadn't intended any more stops but I saw a sign for 6DGU. Intrigued, I followed the sign and found a military police dog unit with three silver Nissen huts and a bunch of tents.

A board read: 6GDU Famagusta Sector. Behind it, I could see dogs in a long kennel, and I was amazed at the lack of noise. I counted six dogs, and not one of them barked.

Walking towards the command tent, I spotted a fenced-off area with obstacles, presumably for training. There were two men and a German Shepherd dog. One man appeared to be the handler. The second man wore a padded jacket and started running. He held something in his hand, possibly a rifle, more likely a stick that resembled a rifle. I stopped and watched for a minute as the handler shouted at the fleeing man before giving the dog an instruction.

"Jasper, takedown!"

In an instant, Jasper—which I assumed to be the dog's name—chased after the fugitive. It leapt and clamped its jaws around the man's outstretched arm, forcing him to drop the fake weapon.

The handler shouted for the man to get down on the ground, which he did. After a single shrill whistle from the handler, Jasper released the arm and took a pace back, watching and ready.

I was impressed at the display of control. By the handler and the dog.

And then I saw him. The man in the padded jacket got up and started walking towards me. Instantly recognizable. Unforgettable.

The big thug I'd punched on Saturday night.

SEVEN

I marched into the command tent. "Who's in charge?"

A skinny young private with acne was closest, and he jumped up and saluted because I was still in uniform. Behind him another man stood slowly.

"I am. Sergeant Major Ellis."

"You mean, Sergeant Major Ellis, sir!" I snapped. I don't normally pull rank, but Ellis was too casual and I was angry.

"Sergeant Major Ellis, sir," he said with more respect than I expected.

I nodded to the clerk. "Leave us."

The boy scampered out.

"What's up?" Ellis said, and I figured his casual attitude was too ingrained to last beyond one *sir*.

"Saturday night some of your lads were causing trouble in town." I told him about the incident.

He said, "Were you in uniform, sir?"

OK, I was mistaken. He *could* use the title more than once.

"I wasn't in uniform."

"So *he* wasn't to know. And the boys thought you were Navy."

"How the hell is that an excuse?"

"You know how it is—a bit of banter. They didn't mean much by it. It's not like it was serious."

"He's Royal Military Police," I said with emphasis on Royal. "He's a representative of the Crown. Causing an affray is a serious offence. I could put him on a charge and we both know what that would mean."

It would usually mean expulsion from the military police, probably demotion.

"You weren't in uniform. They weren't in uniform, and we're just a dog unit," he said.

I bristled, about to lose my cool, but then I thought better of it. "What's the big man's name?"

"Sergeant Payne." Then, before I could speak, Ellis quickly continued. "It won't happen again. It was just high jinks, that's all. I'll speak to the lads and they'll be pussycats from now on, sir."

Three times!

"Just see that it doesn't, Ellis," I growled. "No second chances whether they're in uniform or not."

I marched out of the tent and across scorched grass to my Land Rover. A group of men watched me go, and I could see the big guy among them.

It really wasn't like me to lose my cool, and although not over the top, I surprised myself. It wasn't until I reached Larnaca that I realized I was hungry and put the bad mood down to the heat and sugar deficiency.

★

It was late when I got back to the office but Penny was still working.

"Captain Wolfe has gone," she said. "I don't know where, but he said you did."

"Sort of."

The new black phone attracted my attention and I picked up the receiver and listened to nothing.

"Not connected yet," Penny said. "The engineer will be back in the morning. In Cyprus you'll find things don't always happen as quickly as you'd expect—or are promised."

I asked if she was hungry.

"I need to change," she replied.

"You look great as you are."

She looked dubious, but smiled, and five minutes later we were heading out of town and around the coast with the evening breeze in our hair.

We went east around Dhekelia towards Famagusta, but then turned, and Penny directed me to a quiet tavern which didn't have a view of the Mediterranean, but what it lacked in spectacle, it made up for with great food.

Afterwards, we continued around the headland, found a pretty spot and watched the sun set.

When we talked, Penny was careful to avoid work, which was ideal for her position supporting the SIB. It also suited my now broken rule, and we could pretend a separation of work and pleasure.

After a lungful of sea air, she said, "I keep thinking about Saturday night and those men."

"You get idiots everywhere—especially after a few drinks."

"I was scared. If you hadn't…" She linked her arm through mine and moved closer, like she was cold despite the warm evening.

"It won't happen again," I said. "They wouldn't dare."

She looked at me. "What do you mean?"

"I bumped into them."

"They had another go at you?"

I laughed. "No, no, no. I saw the big man today on my rounds. He's a dog trainer at 6GDU."

"Six—?" Her voice sounded strange.

"Guard Dog Unit. It's OK, I had a word with the officer in charge and—"

"Mike Ellis," she said quietly.

"What? Yes, his name was Ellis. Sergeant Major Ellis."

"Mike Ellis," she said again, and I heard barbs in her tone.

"You know him?"

She took a long breath. "I know him."

She'd tensed up, and I put my arm around her and waited. Eventually, she spoke.

"Mike Ellis is the man who raped my sister."

EIGHT

In the morning, I drove past where I'd parked the previous day at 6GDU and continued across the field to the command tent.

Ellis was there drinking tea and laughing with a couple of other men. I stormed in and told them to get out.

Ellis stood up. I saw something cross his mind before he spoke. Probably trying to second-guess the situation. "What can I do for you, sir?" he said calmly.

"Sarah Cartwright. Know the name?"

"She sounds familiar."

Sarah was Penny's younger sister, and last night she'd told me they'd come to Cyprus to escape the drudgery of home life. Home had been Stoke-on-Trent, an industrial town in the Midlands region known as the Potteries. Penny had applied for secretarial jobs after the war and got one in Cyprus. Sarah was twenty-one, five years younger than Penny and had joined her a year later.

"Prettier than me," Penny had said, and then after a hesitation, "She's got fair hair and blue eyes—can't tell she's got any Indian genes, unlike me. And she's more innocent. Despite her looks, she didn't really know about how boys can be. I tried to warn her."

They'd both dated young men and had more fun than they'd ever imagined. Until Ellis, that was.

"He forced himself on her," Penny told me. "She thought they were just fooling around at first, but then he started getting serious. He didn't stop. She asked him to stop but he forced her." Penny had broken down as she told me, and all I could do was hold her and listen to some graphic details.

She told me that it had happened four months ago and they'd spoken to no one about it.

"The military police, or if she's worried about us then report it to the civilian police," I said. "She has to report it somewhere, Penny. There needs to be a record."

"She's gone," Penny said.

"Gone?"

"Returned home. I tried to dissuade her but she was in too much of a mess."

I said nothing.

She said, "Well, we both went home."

"But you came back."

She took a breath. "I love it out here. So, yes, I came back and took the job working for you."

"OK," I said. "I'll deal with it."

So here I was at 6GDU, handling it on Sarah's behalf. Sergeant Major Ellis looked at me, his face full of innocence.

"You raped a girl called Sarah Cartwright."

"I never did!"

"Doesn't it bother you, Ellis? You forced yourself on a poor girl and took her innocence."

He barely suppressed a laugh. "Oh, that Sarah! She wasn't innocent. She was a bit of a tart."

"You raped her," I said, stepping closer. A further step and I could land a punch on his smug face. I thought about it, felt my hand twitch in anticipation.

He took a step back.

"Let's just take a seat and have a cup of tea and talk about this man to man."

I said, "You're guilty of a crime."

Now his cocky attitude melted faster than snow on a hotplate. He patted the air with both hands as if telling me to calm down.

"This is ridiculous. We dated, and yes, we had sex. I was probably a bit rougher than she liked, but I didn't force her. No way."

"She says you did. She's devastated, which tells me the truth of the matter."

He shook his head like it was on elastic. "Has she reported it?"

"To me."

"You have an official complaint?"

"From her sister."

He looked at me and slowly the truth dawned on him. "It was months ago," he said.

"Four—" I gave him the date.

"I'll have to take your word for it. Taken a while to complain then? You'd think if a girl was raped, she'd report it straight away, right?"

"Not necessarily. In my experience—"

"Sarah didn't complain, did she?" He nodded at me, his confidence returning. "If she did then you would have the report from her, not her sister."

I hesitated too long, thinking of my response.

He said, "This is about your little tiff with my boys on Saturday night at the cinema. I've had a word with them and it won't happen again. Let's just forget it shall we, Lieutenant? Come on, be reasonable."

I found my other hand tensing now and spoke through clenched teeth. "This is not about Saturday night. This is not about me, Ellis. It's about you."

He shrugged, and I imagined a right jab onto his nose. But it didn't happen. I couldn't. That would have given Ellis the perfect complaint against me. So I stepped back out of range to remove the temptation.

He said, "You're not letting this go, are you?"

"No, I am not."

"Fine. You'll want my superior, so pass on your baseless complaint to Major Johnson at the 227. He's at—"

"I know where to find the major," I said. "This is serious, Ellis. Wipe the smug smile off your face, because this is happening."

"Do your worst," he said, and then must have thought better of his attitude. "Look, I'm not being smug, sir. I just know there isn't a case to answer."

Johnson's office door was shut and his chief clerk held up a hand to stop me storming in.

"He's busy," the man said, then his eyes narrowed.

"Lieutenant Ash Carter," I said, hoping that would get me past Johnson's gatekeeper.

He stood at about my height and I noticed bright eyes beneath pencil-thin eyebrows. With a strong chin, I thought there was something both rugged and effeminate about his appearance.

"Sir, I'm sorry—"

I glanced at the name on his desk: Graham Crawley.

"You must be Uncle Graham," I said.

A frown transformed his attractive features.

"I've met Verity Johnson," I explained. "She told me you walk the major's dog."

He nodded curtly and then towards Johnson's office.

"He really is busy, Lieutenant."

"And this *really* is important, Chief."

He took a breath. "Look, let me check…"

He disappeared into Johnson's office and a few minutes later reappeared.

"He'll see you in five minutes providing it's quick."

I nodded my thanks and five minutes later entered Johnson's office. The delay had reduced my anger, which was definitely a good thing, and I was able to report CSM Ellis's crime without emotion.

"It's sad," Johnson said when I'd finished. "Rape is a terrible thing. The poor girl."

I wondered if he could empathize since he had a daughter.

But then he added: "If it really happened," and then I realized Ellis must have got to him before I arrived. He'd already told his version of events.

I said, "I have a statement from the girl's sister."

"You and I both know that's not the same thing. Where is this girl now?"

"She left the island."

"Ah."

I said, "I believe the sister. And Sarah Cartwright left Cyprus because of the incident."

He looked at me, saying nothing for a while. "Palestine was tough, wasn't it?"

We'd already had this conversation but I bit my tongue and just said, "Yes."

"You saw some terrible things."

I nodded and tried not to see the images of soldiers blown apart, or hear the screams of the dying. Was that Johnson's strategy? Distract me rather than confront the issue.

He said, "I was wounded in France. Not badly, but I was one of the lucky ones. You didn't serve during the war, am I right?"

"No, sir. It ended just as I started training."

He nodded, and I imagined him thinking that I didn't know what a real war was like. But maybe he wasn't, because he said, "We're all in this together."

"With respect, sir, I'm not sure what you mean."

"I mean we have a job to do. We're all soldiers at the end of the day."

I still didn't get his message.

"Look, Carter, treat it as a fabricated story. The rape didn't happen. You have no real proof, just hearsay."

"I believe—"

He cleared his throat, stopping me. "If you need it to look like it's being investigated, tell the sister that you've reported it to me. That'll keep the girl quiet."

I felt my blood pressure rise, but before I could explode, he held up a hand.

"But it's not about something someone did to a girl four months ago, now is it?" he said, his Scottish accent suddenly sounding more obvious. "Not really."

"Sir?"

"Look, Carter, I know about your little altercation with the boys from the GDU."

I inclined my head. "I wasn't going to bring that up, but they're lucky I don't bring a charge."

He raised an eyebrow. "From what I hear, you hit one of Ellis's men."

"Sergeant Payne. He threatened—"

"Who threw the first punch?"

"He did."

"Really? That's not what I hear and, to be frank, Carter, you appear unscathed."

I started to speak but he stopped me again. "Listen, you were caught in a brawl—unbecoming behaviour for an officer, don't you think?" He paused but wasn't expecting a response. "Your complaint now looks like a bit of tit-for-tat. You're new to the island and I'd like us all to get along."

I took a breath.

"Understood, Lieutenant?"

"Sir."

He nodded and smiled. "Good chap. Now let's get on with our jobs—and when the SIB has a real issue, I look forward to seeing you again."

*

My drive back to the office was filled with thoughts. If I had been the major, would I have responded any differently? Maybe not. Both he and Ellis were right about the evidence. It wouldn't stand up. However, I had reported the incident. Despite no formal action, at least Johnson was now aware of the accusation and Ellis couldn't get away with something like that again.

I wondered how to explain to Penny that nothing would be done. And then I pondered some of Johnson's words. He'd said some odd things like: "We're all soldiers at the end of the day." He was military police, for Christ's sake! Most of his job was about other soldiers—and we couldn't tolerate bad behaviour by other RMPs.

No, I wouldn't have responded in the same way, I decided. Not at all.

NINE

Penny took it very well when I arrived at the office. "I didn't expect anything," she said.

"I did. I thought I could help, and now I feel bad for raising your expectations."

"It's fine."

"Not really, Penny."

She sighed and I held her hand. I wanted to tell her I would keep trying, but that could make matters worse. Finally, I said, "I thought I could be your hero."

She smiled sweetly. "You *are* my hero."

I shook my head.

"Saturday night, remember? The way you handled that gorilla outside the cinema."

"He was a gorilla, wasn't he?"

"Knuckles practically dragged on the ground."

I laughed.

She said, "I like it when you laugh. You're normally so serious."

"Am I?"

"You're a nice man."

"Ouch!" I said. "That sounds bad."

She gripped my hand. "Not at all. I need a nice man. There are too many gorillas out in the wild." She looked up at me with big eyes. "And the way you defended my honour…"

Her lips twitched and I involuntarily leaned forward.

"OK, OK, we are at work!" she said, and then laughed at my alarm. "I'm sure you have plenty of work to do rather than flirt with me."

I knew I was blushing and busied myself with nothing important on my desk.

Thirty minutes passed before she spoke again. "Oh, I forgot to tell you, Lieutenant. The telephone is now connected, and Captain Wolfe has reported in." She slid across the room and handed me a piece of paper with an address in the Lebanon. He was just over the border from Israel.

"Did he say anything else?"

"Just gave me the address—his temporary base. We can't call him, because he doesn't have a telephone, but he'll check in now and again."

"Thanks."

I think she hovered at my desk for longer than necessary before returning to her own. She had a pink pencil case and seemed to fiddle with it.

"If you've nothing to do, I could murder a cuppa," I said.

"Oh, yes, of course. Sorry, I should have thought."

A short time later, I had a steaming cup of weak tea on my desk. We needed to have a conversation about letting the tea leaves steep, but now wasn't the time.

Penny drank water and still looked like she wanted to say something.

"All right, Penny. What is it?"

"Don't be cross."

"Why should I be cross?"

"I've handled one of your jobs." She swallowed. "I've hired the cleaner."

"Marvellous!" I said. Since Wolfe had given me the task, I'd done nothing, mainly because I wasn't sure where to start.

"You don't mind?" she said, relieved.

"You've saved me the effort—but next time check with me first."

She nodded.

"How did you find her—is it a lady?"

"Yes. She found us."

I frowned. "How did she know we were in need?"

"She didn't. Just called in on the off-chance. New office—new cleaner. She's native but speaks good English."

That might have solved my other issue. I needed to hire a translator, although just why we needed one, I didn't know.

"Greek or Turkish?"

"Greek."

"Great. Now the other criterion: is she attractive?"

Penny threw a pencil across the room.

"Yes or no, Penny?"

"Indeterminable age, and no, not attractive in my opinion."

I grinned. "Good, because one attractive young lady around here is more than enough for me."

*

Wolfe called as we were packing up for the day. I suspected he was just checking up on me.

"How's it going, Ash?"

"I'm enjoying the sun. How about you?"

"The same," he lied. No Englishman enjoyed being holed up in the Lebanon.

"Well, you know the telephone works. We now have a cleaner and translator and I've ordered supplies from the QM in Nicosia." I'd finally got around to working out what we needed and just placed a call to the quartermaster at Wolseley Barracks.

"Good. What's the cleaner called?"

I covered the handset and asked Penny.

"Maria," I replied after a moment.

"And the translator speaks Hebrew?"

"Er... no. She speaks Greek. I didn't—"

He cleared his throat. "I need Hebrew, written and spoken. Probably Arabic too."

"I'm not sure where I'll find a Hebrew and Arabic speakers in Cyprus, Bill."

"Use your head, Ash. A-Branch at Wolseley must have someone."

"Right," I said. "I'll ask tomorrow when I get the supplies."

He rang off, and I was left feeling like I'd let him down. I didn't have much to do while he was out in the field and I'd even got that wrong.

*

The following day, I drove up to Nicosia and loaded my vehicle with supplies for the office. Then I called in on A-Branch and asked for a translator.

It seemed that all the Arabic speakers had been shipped down to Suez. There was one chap who said he could speak it passably but not read Arabic, and so I requested his support in case of need. No one could help with Hebrew.

Since I was close, I called in at the police HQ and asked for DI Dickins.

He shook my hand, his left in my right. "How can I help you, Lieutenant?" He cracked his initial severe expression and added, "Ash?"

"I don't suppose you have anyone who can speak Hebrew?"

"What? No."

I smiled. "Seriously though, I was just passing and thought I'd ask you about the autopsy of the executed man."

"No surprises I'm afraid, if that's your hope. The bullet killed him. It was possibly a forty-five and fired against his temple. Bullet passed straight through, as you'd expect, blowing his brains out. No other injuries to speak of, just marks from the ropes on his wrists and ankles. Probably also had a gag in his mouth."

"Probably?"

"Traces of blue cotton. Can't imagine why else they'd be there."

"That explains why I didn't hear shouts or screams."

"Seems reasonable."

He took a long breath and I looked at him quizzically.

"Charles, what is it?" I could see he was struggling to admit something. "Charles?"

"I thought about what you said. Maybe I'm the one who's learned bad habits. Maybe the new man had a point."

I waited for him to explain.

A smile tweaked at the edge of his mouth. "You've probably heard people referring to the locals as wogs and anything they do as woggish?"

I had, and it was common in Palestine as well. Wog stood for Western Oriental Gentleman. Most Brits didn't appreciate how derogatory the term was, although I suspected it was a way of feeling superior. In Egypt, I'd heard they called the locals Gyps. Personally, I thought any such name was inappropriate.

Dickins continued: "It's ironic that the people of Cyprus, on the whole, view us with respect. We, on the other hand, get into the habit of treating them like second-class citizens. It's ingrained, and I had to take a long hard look at myself in the mirror."

I said, "So you're doing a house-to-house after all?"

He nodded. "I instructed DS Park and he's got men showing the mugshot of the victim. Just the nearby villages, mind, not the whole bloody island."

I shook his good hand. "Anything I can do, please let me know."

Foolishly perhaps, but DI Dickins's change of heart about a house-to-house made me grin. The sun was shining, the air was fresh and it felt damn good as I journeyed back south. The only bad thing about the visit was the translator. Then, maybe because of my good mood, I had a brainwave.

Four miles out of Larnaca, I detoured and visited 2 Wireless at Ayios Nikolaos.

Lieutenant Vaughan showed no surprise at my second visit. I judged him to be the kind of man who wouldn't have shown surprise even if I'd turned up with a Bengal tiger.

"Hello again," he said. "I still can't share information with you."

"Of course not," I said, but can you tell me if you have a Hebrew speaker here?

"I can and we do."

And so I asked whether he would be available should we need him. In strict confidence, naturally.

It was a long punt, but Vaughan agreed—providing it didn't take too much of the man's time, providing he wasn't pressured to talk about his work here, and providing we could review the arrangement on a regular basis.

*

I checked in at the office hoping to see Penny but she'd already left for the day. Just as I was about to leave, I noticed an envelope lying against the wall. It had come through the letterbox and been missed. A white envelope against a white wall.

Rather than our address, it just had a name, handwritten on the envelope. My name.

Intrigued, I slit it open and pulled out a five-by-seven colour photograph.

Colour photographs were rare, and I suspected this had been taken in a professional studio.

It was of an attractive young woman in an emerald-green dress. The colour highlighted two things. Firstly, her bright blue eyes and, secondly, her dark red hair. I judged her to be about twenty and was sure I'd never seen her.

Who had sent it to me and why?

I checked inside the envelope. Nothing else. Sometimes people write a description on the reverse of photographs, so I flipped it over and stared.

On the back were two words.

HELP ME!

TEN

I showed Penny the photograph when she arrived for work.

"Who is it?" she asked, holding it like she was looking for clues.

"I was hoping you'd recognize her, because I don't."

She frowned and shook her head. "She's very pretty."

"Those blue eyes and unusual hair..." As the words left my mouth I realized my mistake. Penny frowned at me.

I quickly recovered. "She's pretty, but you're prettier."

Penny laughed. "I was messing with you, Ash Carter. Yes, she is gorgeous."

I held up the photograph and looked from it to Penny. "Actually, ignoring the eyes and hair, there's a similarity. In fact, your tanned skin gives you the edge."

She laughed again. "Now you're messing with me!"

"And you have no idea who she is?"

"No." She took the photograph, looked at the HELP ME! and then the envelope.

"She knows you even if you don't know her," Penny said.

That was a reasonable statement. I was sure I'd remember that face, and certainly the hair if I ever saw her.

I shook my head.

"So why would some unknown woman want your help?"

I shook my head again. I'd wondered about that, as well as a more obvious question. Why send the photograph to me? Shouldn't she have sent it to someone who did know her?

"What are you going to do about it?" Penny asked as she handed the photograph back.

"Not a lot I can do with it," I said, putting it in my jacket pocket. "Not until I know who it is."

"And why she needs your help."

"Exactly."

Penny was smiling at me.

"What?" I asked.

"Nothing," she said, but the following morning she arrived with a photograph. Only this one was of her standing on a windswept promenade and it was black and white. The sun was shining but the wind made me suspect it was cold.

"A holiday in Margate," she said. "A few years ago."

Probably about five years ago, I guessed, but said, "Looks recent and... you're very pretty."

"It's for you," she said with a shy smile. "I don't like the idea of you having a photograph of another girl."

I grinned. "So you're my girl?" I asked.

"Let's take it one step at a time," she said.

★

Sleepy Cyprus presented no danger, unlike the streets of Palestine. I was relieved to be away from a war zone and part excited about being one of a two-man team. We were on a special mission with intriguing potential. But after almost two weeks here, I missed the boxing gym and I missed my old unit. I longed for evenings playing poker, the camaraderie and general banter of fellow officers.

Should I suggest to Wolfe that we move the office to be with the guys at 227?

He'd probably mock me or question whether I was the right man for the job. Intelligence work meant working alone at times. It's just that Palestine had been my first posting and was undoubtedly unique.

So I filled my non-working hours by getting as fit as I'd ever been—which I think must have been under Sammy's guidance in Manchester before I left for university.

Of course, a relationship with Penny would have provided a welcome distraction. However, since our evening after the cinema, she'd turned me down when I asked her out. Even after the photograph, she turned me down, blaming it on a *hair day*. I knew girls used that as a euphemism for other things so I accepted and started to wonder if our first date had been our last.

And then came Saturday night.

ELEVEN

I'd had another call from Wolfe, who still didn't need me. We had a brief conversation about the office. I moaned that we should have got one facing the sea so that we'd have cooler air blowing in. He'd laughed because we both knew we didn't have a choice. This was the assigned property and no amount of complaining would change things.

"At least there's the shade," he said. "You should count your blessings. I'd give anything to be near the sea and have a view of pine trees right now."

"Let's switch," I joked.

"You're bored?" He paused, and I wondered if he'd admonish me.

"I've a few things," I lied, then told him about the arrangement with the Hebrew translator at the Signals unit.

"Good man," he said. "I've some papers I need looking at. They're heading your way. Probably take a day or so—they aren't urgent, but if you could get a translation, that'd be marvellous. What else have you been up to, Ash?"

I gave a synopsis of my various meetings—without mentioning my run-in with Sergeant Major Ellis at 6GDU or Penny's sister—and started to talk about the murder investigation.

Wolfe interrupted me and I thought I'd probably provided too much information. "What have you got Penny working on?"

I took a breath. "Not much, to be honest. I'm not sure what—"

"Write up reports," he said. "Those meetings you talked about. Scribble them down and get her to type them up. Doesn't matter that they aren't investigations. It'll stop you becoming stale and her being idle. If the worst comes to the worst, get some white paint and ask her to paint coal."

"Yes, sir!" I said, and he chortled down the line.

"Look out for those papers, Ash, and keep out of mischief."

Penny stopped twiddling her pencil case around and looked at me expectantly as I replaced the receiver.

"He wants me to keep you busy and me out of mischief."

"But it's Saturday," she said, and flashed a cheeky smile.

I frowned.

"Saturday... Saturday night... if you're going to get up to any mischief it had better be tonight." She raised her eyebrows.

"I—"

"Lieutenant Ash Carter, I'm prompting you to ask me out."

*

We finished work early and Penny insisted she go home and change. When I picked her up, my eyes bulged. She looked fabulous in a white silk blouse and dark grey skirt with matching grey heels.

She'd asked me to wear my uniform and she returned my appreciative stare.

"You do look dashing in formalwear, Ash," she said.

"Dicky bows don't suit me though. So, it's a good job you didn't ask for black tie."

She stretched her legs getting into the Land Rover, and her knees flashed before she settled and covered them up.

"Right," she said enthusiastically. "You're an officer, so let's go to Maxims."

*

It turned out that Maxims was more than an hour's drive away in Limassol. We arrived at half-past seven and I found myself in an officers-only restaurant-cum-nightclub. Despite my uniform, I still needed to show my warrant card before we were allowed in. The concierge also insisted that I sign a register which he called the membership book.

"Have you been here before?" I asked as we sat at a private table, ate and listened to a band.

"Never."

"How d'you know about it then?"

"Every girl knows about Maxims, Ash. It's like a medal of honour. You know, bragging rights. Girl-talk, of course."

Although I didn't recognize any of the faces, I instantly felt at home. The hubbub of gentlemen officers enjoying one another's company. I didn't sense the same level of energy as Goldsmith's in Jerusalem—before it had been bombed—or the Blue Kettle Club in Ismailia, but I suspected Maxim's was *the* officers' nightclub in Cyprus.

The air rapidly filled with cigarette fumes, but I was used to it. When in a confined space with off-duty men, you expected to breathe in smoke.

Of the forty or so patrons, I counted only twelve women, all of whom were with partners. Wives and girlfriends, and all Brits by the look of it. No local girls, and Penny was the only non-white.

Most of the men weren't in uniform, but I didn't feel out of place and a few said hello. One large table had men only, who were from the Limassol barracks. They were noisy without being rowdy and I was again reminded of my old buddies from Palestine. Were they sitting around a table at some officers' club in Suez right now?

"Stop daydreaming," Penny said. "Take me onto the dance floor."

We danced a little before she suggested we go outside for some air.

"I'm sorry, I'm not a great dancer," I said as she leaned against the wall. It was fully dark now and we could see lights out at sea. A light breeze filled the air with the subtle scent of flowers.

"Never trust a man who can dance," she said. "That's what my grandmother taught me."

"Oh, why's that?"

"Because a man who worries too much about his own moves will be more concerned about himself than his partner."

It seemed plausible. Whether it was true didn't matter. It saved my face and I decided not to apologize next time I stepped on her toes.

She opened her handbag and removed the pencil case she often toyed with.

I must have looked surprised.

"I always carry it," she said as she opened it. "Best place to keep my smokes."

She took one out and now I realized why she played with her pencil case in the office.

"You smoke?" I said, hoping she didn't hear judgement in my voice.

"Only socially," she said. "And never more than one a day."

She lit it and held it out towards me.

"No thanks."

"I thought all soldiers smoked."

I shook my head.

She said, "You don't drink or smoke…"

"You don't drink either."

"True," she said, taking a long draw on the cigarette. "What's your reason?"

"Same as smoking," I said. "It's all about fitness."

She put a hand on my chest. "My grandmother never said there was anything wrong about a man who looks after his body."

"I'm glad."

"I noticed you exercising. Is it for anything in particular?"

I looked out towards the twinkling lights. "I used to be a boxer."

"That explains the punch last week. I thought you looked like you knew what you were doing. You said you could fight. I should have realized you were an actual boxer."

"Amateur."

She laughed. "You could hardly be a professional!"

True.

I realized her hand was still on my chest. She flicked the cigarette aside, gripped my tie and pulled me towards her. Our lips touched and I felt her warm breath on my tongue. For a moment I tasted her cigarette, but that was soon gone, and as the pressure of our lips increased I was lost in the passion of our kiss.

It had crossed my mind that she could have smoked inside; now I knew why she'd wanted me out here.

"You can't dance but you can kiss," she concluded, breaking away. "Let's go back in and enjoy more of the atmosphere before things get too hot out here."

Later in the evening she had been asking about Palestine—without prying into anything which might be secret—and said, "So you had a gun there."

"Yes."

"But not now?"

"Of course I have a gun. I just don't wear it because there's no need."

"It's a shame," she said. "I bet Ellis would have squirmed if he'd seen your weapon."

I said nothing.

"He should pay for what he did," she said.

"People like him usually do, sooner or later," I said. "In my experience." However, I knew this wasn't true. Maybe Ellis would commit another crime and get caught, but I thought it unlikely he'd pay for raping Penny's sister.

"I hope so," she said. "It would be a tragedy for him to get away with it."

Penny seemed melancholy for a while, and I wondered if she was thinking of her sister. I wasn't sure what to say, but it didn't last long and she was soon smiling again and asking me to dance.

*

Things were still going strong, but Penny suggested we leave at midnight since we had a long drive home.

"I could do that every Saturday," she said as I thundered along the curving coastline. "Such a scream!"

I didn't comment, but it hadn't been cheap. On the contrary, if we came regularly I'd need to restrict the visits to no more than twice a month.

At work, Penny wore her hair in short bunches. Tonight she had her hair loose, and when she was standing with her hands resting on top of the windscreen her hair streamed behind.

"I'm crazy!" she screamed into the wind, and I laughed.

"You should relax more," she said after dropping back into her seat. "Let your hair down once in a while."

"I—"

"Oh come on, Ash. You're always serious. You don't drink, you don't smoke…"

We'd had this conversation already, although previously it'd all been about me. So I said, "You don't drink either."

"That's because I've seen what alcohol can do." She paused. "My mother is an alcoholic. Doesn't even know what day it is."

I said nothing and listened to the thump and bump of the Land Rover for a while.

"Sorry," she said. "I've spoiled it, haven't I?"

I started to protest.

"I was having such a good time. I've had an amazing evening with an amazing man—attractive, intelligent and… all right he can't dance, but he clearly has a good body under that smart uniform."

"I've had fun too," I said. "The best time for a long time."

The conversation picked up again, and when we reached the outskirts of Larnaca she was laughing at my bad jokes.

"I'll drop you home," I said, turning right as I came into the town. Penny rented a one-bedroom apartment, south of the centre. My lodgings were way over on the other side.

"Come in for a nightcap," she said as I parked outside.

"But we don't drink."

"Do you drink cocoa? Of course you do. You're a boy scout. All boy scouts drink cocoa."

I agreed and we got out.

"It's not luxurious," she said as we entered her lodgings, "but I keep it clean and tidy."

We went into a tiny kitchen, so confined that when she stopped, I bumped into her. She didn't move away but rather leaned back into me.

"Cocoa, then?" she said. "Or something else?"

There was a glint in her eye and a tease in her voice. I leaned in and she put her arms around me. Her body pressed hard against mine. I'd thought about her lips for most of the journey home and now they found mine again.

From the kitchen, we moved into the lounge, where she had a sofa, a lamp table, and a low occasional table—one of those with multiple drawers like they have at apothecaries.

We stumbled onto the sofa and the kisses became fumbling and the fumbling turned into heavy petting.

My heart was going crazy.

And then she pulled away, gasping.

"What?" I said breathlessly.

"We have to stop." There wasn't much conviction in her voice.

"No, we don't." I reached for her, but she was off the sofa and straightening her skirt.

"It's too quick," she said, starting to gain composure. "Ash, it's too soon. It's been a fabulous evening and I don't want it to stop, but it must."

And before I could say anything else, she had opened the front door and ushered me out of her apartment.

TWELVE

I ran past Penny's home twice during the next day, hoping to catch sight of her. To help, I neglected to wear a shirt, so that she'd see my chest. A cheap trick I know, but I didn't see her and I guess she didn't see me.

The day dragged and I went into the office to occupy my time. It was Sunday, but in the army that doesn't necessarily imply a day of rest.

"You must be Maria," I said, bumping into a lady carrying a bucket and mop out of the building.

She dropped her gaze, awkward about eye contact, or in deference.

"I'm Lieutenant Carter. Thanks for taking the job." I paused. "You do speak English, don't you?"

"Yes, sir."

"And you're Greek?"

"I am, sir."

I smiled at her. "Well, it's good to have you onboard, Maria. If I need you to translate from Greek to English, would you do that?"

Now she looked up and bobbed her head. She had a face that suggested a hard life, and I figured she was in her forties. A peasant originally perhaps.

"A translator?" she said. "Translator or interpreter, sir?"

"I... er... both, I suppose. How about Arabic or Hebrew?"

"Just Greek and a little Turkish."

I nodded. Shame.

She said, "How much money will you pay?"

I converted from what we'd paid in Palestine and told her the rate.

"Good," she said, looking at me, and for the first time, I saw a twinkle in her eye. Peasant background or not, she was no dullard. "That's a better rate than Miss Cartwright quoted me. I accept your offer."

Her quick smile made me feel like I'd been duped, but never mind. It was War Office money and the rate seemed fair.

"Thanks," I said. "I'll let you know when you're needed."

She lowered her eyes and bobbed her head again, as though becoming the deferential servant once more.

I wondered which character she really was. Whichever, at least she was an excellent cleaner. The office sparkled and smelled of fresh lemons. I made a mental note that I'd better ensure my desk was bare before she came else I'd find my work polished to death or taken out with the rubbish.

Following Wolfe's suggestion, I wrote down notes from my various meetings. Concerning the murder case, I started a report as though I was the investigating officer. Again, I neglected to mention Penny's involvement due to its irrelevance. However, I wrote notes about visiting the murder site with DI Dickins and then the verbal version of the coroner's report.

When finished, I looked at it with disdain. Maybe I was in danger of losing my touch. Although something about the information niggled, I couldn't put my finger on it yet but knew it would come to me.

Perhaps it was the exclusion of Penny. I'd never omitted information before and it meant that my conversations with Sergeant Major Ellis and Major Johnson were partial.

What the heck? I had plenty of time. So I rewrote everything including Penny and included information about her accusation.

It felt much more satisfying when I bundled the paper together and left it on Penny's desk to type up.

★

I locked the office and strolled less than a mile to my lodgings. When I arrived I was pleasantly surprised to see Penny sitting outside.

She smiled but I saw uncertainty in her face.

"What is it, Penny?"

"I'd like to buy you dinner."

I shook my head. "No."

Her face could have broken the heart of a stone statue. "I've ruined it, haven't I?"

"What?"

"I'm sorry for leading you on. Please have dinner with me."

And then I felt like a klutz. "When I said no, I meant, no you can't pay."

She blinked, surprised.

"Penny, you've nothing to apologize for."

"Let me pay," she said, now smiling. "I insist—although it's local and inexpensive."

I acquiesced, and ten minutes later we were sitting in a tavern having ordered chicken and potatoes.

"I feel so bad about last night," she said as we waited for our food.

"Don't," I said. "I had a great time—amazing time. Certainly had more fun than I've had in a long while."

She beamed and reached forward to place her hand on top of mine.

"Me too!"

I said, "If anything, I should apologize to you."

She shook her head, as though I'd made the most ridiculous statement imaginable.

We were interrupted by the arrival of food, and I sensed an awkward silence for a few minutes. I started eating but she didn't touch hers. She was watching me.

"I didn't want you to get the wrong idea about me."

"Penny—" I started to say.

"You're a nice man, Ash."

Ah, there we go with the *nice* again.

"Let's not rush anything," she said. "It was my mistake last night. I normally wouldn't consider letting someone get to third base until at least six dates."

I smiled. "Which date is this?"

She raised her eyebrows. "Well, the first at the cinema wasn't really a date, was it? So if we count this evening, then we're on the second."

Later, we walked along the coast, hand in hand, and I said I hoped six dates didn't mean six weeks.

She'd laughed lightly and kissed me.

"No," she said after we ended the clinch. "Let's see each other a few times a week—if that's all right?"

Of course it was all right.

THIRTEEN

The following day crawled by. I gave Penny my notes and she asked that I didn't include her name.

"A girl has to protect her reputation," she said. Then: "Seriously though, maybe it's better that you don't mention the reason for the confrontation with Ellis."

I shook my head. "But if you want to report it—"

"As you can imagine, I've been thinking it over a lot," she said. "As you said, he'll get his comeuppance one day, but Sarah's day is past."

I wanted to argue, but it was her sister and I figured her decision. Maybe she'd change her mind again. After all, this exercise was just that—an exercise to keep us busy. We weren't about to make a legal case against Sergeant Major Ellis.

*

After work, we went up the coast beyond Famagusta. We found a secluded spot, listened to the rumble of the sea and watched the sun go down. She said she wanted to take me further and pointed to the mountains behind us.

"Too far tonight," she said, "but there are castles up in the mountains—Byzantine ruins. From up there you can see most of the island and the contrasts."

"Contrasts?"

"Bone-dry fields of clay and cool mountain forests. It's one of the things that I love about Cyprus. The diversity in such a small place. Wild rugged coast but also calm bays and beautiful beaches."

"Is that why you came back?" I asked, and then immediately regretted it. My question threatened to bring us back to the conversation we'd had before. However, I was lucky, because she either avoided it or didn't pick up on the implication.

She put an arm around me.

"I believe in fate," she said. "Fate told me my time here wasn't up... and now I've met you."

Penny snuggled into me and we counted stars before tracking back to Larnaca. She invited me into her apartment again and this time we really did have cocoa.

She sat cross-legged on the apothecary coffee table and we talked about our youth. I noticed she assiduously avoided any mention of her alcoholic mother, but her childhood was as fine as any who was a teenager through the terror of air raids and fear of gas attacks.

I avoided discussing my father and she didn't pick up on it. Instead, she was most fascinated by my amateur boxing career.

"You got a boxing blue from Cambridge?"

"I did."

Her eyes narrowed. "And you just gave up when you joined the army?"

"Not really. I kept boxing and last year entered the Middle East army boxing competition as the favourite."

She guessed I hadn't won. "What happened?"

"I retired."

"Hurt?"

I flashed back to the fateful fight with a man called Scott 'Slugger' Stevenson. He may have been the toughest opponent I'd ever fought. My fast hands versus his powerful blows. Who was the better fighter? We'd never know because he lost an eye. It had been a dumb accident, but I blamed myself, and despite being awarded the win, I retired in respect.

She was thoughtful for a while. "One thing I don't understand is, why go to Cambridge and then join the army?"

"The war," I said.

"You could have joined up before. As I understand it, you don't need a university degree to be an officer."

She was right of course. I knew of many young men who had taken the officer's exam, preferring to join up and fight for their country rather than go to university. It had been another sensitive conversation, that I didn't expect to get into, but I told her anyway.

"Although I come from a long line of military men, not least my father, I thought I wanted a different career."

She said nothing, waiting for more.

"My mother," I said after a breath, "she was born in Germany."

"So you were against the war?"

"I didn't want to fight the ordinary people. Fascists, yes, but most of the Germans weren't Nazi supporters." I said. "Even my mother agreed with the war. She was vehemently anti-fascist."

"Was?"

After another long breath, I said, "She took her own life. My father wasn't around. I was at university. It was after the Dresden bombings."

I didn't explain and she didn't ask me, but my mother had family in Dresden and my father had been instrumental in the fire-bombing strategy. I never had the chance to talk about it with my mother, so I was left with questions and guilt for leaving her alone.

Penny said, "You became an MP so you didn't have to kill innocent people."

And I didn't want to follow in my father's footsteps.

The conversation ended our evening on a down note, but after her goodbye kiss, I reminded myself that this had been date number three—officially.

FOURTEEN

I arrived at the office to find Penny with an attractive smile and glint in her eye.

There was a small envelope on my desk with my name on it. I started to open it when I realized Penny was holding a package.

"Just signed for it," she said. "It's from Captain Wolfe."

She handed over the package and I hastily tore it open. Inside was a sheaf of paper. I counted twelve pages, but they were all in Hebrew script so I couldn't interpret any of them. Without delay, I jumped in the Land Rover and headed over to the Royal Signals' base.

Penny called ahead so that Lieutenant Vaughan was expecting me.

He puffed out his cheeks as I handed him the package. "I've got a lot on. What am I looking for?"

"Any mention of the military or terrorist activity."

He nodded with resignation. "The usual intelligence stuff."

"Right."

"I'll be as fast as I can, but no promises."

I nodded and shook his hand. "Just call me if you find anything untoward."

Instead of heading straight back to the office, I detoured so that I passed 6GDU camp. I kept thinking about my conversation with Penny. I didn't believe in karma. I didn't expect Ellis to get his comeuppance. How many girls had he raped before Sarah? How many would he rape again?

Penny had said I should visit him wearing my gun. In truth, I don't think it would have made any difference. He knew I couldn't use it against him, just like he knew I couldn't hit him—especially not now it had been reported to Major Johnson. If anything happened to Ellis, they'd question me. It's what I would do. I'd be a prime suspect.

Better if I don't visit him, I thought as I stopped by the 6GDU sign. However, instinct took over, and the next thing I knew, I was driving across their field again, heading for the command tent.

Sergeant Major Ellis wasn't there, but I found him in one of the Nissen huts.

"You again," he said.

"You again, *sir!*" I said.

He grudgingly repeated it with sarcasm typical of a CSM. Then his eyes narrowed: "Is this about that girl again?"

"Of course it is. It won't go away, Ellis," I said. "You don't rape someone and expect it to be ignored."

He shook his head. "What did Major Johnson have to say?"

"He'll investigate," I lied.

Ellis shook his head. "Really? I don't think so... sir. And I think we're done here."

He nodded like he'd been dismissed and just walked away, leaving me feeling frustrated and impotent again.

*

That evening, Penny and I went to Famagusta and walked the ancient walls. Grass topped most of the stones and thin trees grew atop a broken tower in one corner. Penny told me how the medieval city had been damaged by earthquakes and wars and much of it hadn't been rebuilt.

Parts were in use but the vast majority of the modern development was outside the citadel walls.

I'd driven straight to her apartment after seeing Ellis but hadn't mentioned my visit. Penny had prepared a picnic and we now sat with our legs dangling over the edge as we ate cheese sandwiches washed down with lemonade.

We talked about our past again, and at one point she said, "We're stronger than we think. I used to tell Sarah that. Don't you agree? It sounds like you were taught that by your coach, Sammy."

"Mentally, you're right. Everyone knows the David and Goliath story. David won because he believed he could. There's no point going into a fight thinking you'll lose." I paused, playing with the straw in my lemonade. "But physically there's a different lesson."

"Oh? I assumed it was mental and physical."

"In boxing, I often recognized my opponent was much stronger than me."

She nodded. "David killed Goliath with a stone. I suppose if you have a weapon, it doesn't matter how strong your opponent is. A stone beats a fist, a bullet beats a stone."

I laughed. "I was talking about speed and agility, not guns!"

She laughed too. "I was kidding!" Then: "But how do you win with speed and agility?"

I handed her an apple from the picnic. "Sammy demonstrated this with a potato, but I suppose an apple works just as well. Use all your strength to force your straw into the apple."

As instructed, Penny pushed her straw against the apple skin until it buckled. "Can't be done," she said.

I took the apple, held my straw a couple of inches away and then jabbed. The straw penetrated the skin, and when I let go, it remained embedded.

"Impossible!" she said, taking the apple and repeating my demonstration. "Amazing!"

I could have bored her with a scientific explanation but knew better than to make a mistake like that.

"Speed and agility," she said thoughtfully. "I'll remember that."

★

I dropped her at her apartment and we kissed passionately on her doorstep until she finally pushed me away and dashed inside laughing.

I drove home grinning like a schoolboy.

My lodgings were in a block of four with a communal entrance. I'd not met the other occupants and the place immediately next to mine had been assigned to Bill Wolfe and was therefore empty.

As I unlocked my door I wondered if he'd ever come back.

And then I stopped and looked down.

The door had scuffed on paper as I'd pushed it ajar.

Another envelope. The same block capital writing on the front. Just my name.

Inside was another photograph, but black and white this time; a man and a woman at an event, I guessed. Not a formal photograph because there were people milling behind. However, the couple were both smiling for the camera. He wore a uniform that I didn't recognize. She was a beautiful young woman in a cocktail dress. She had curly, shoulder-length hair. And I had no doubt. This was the same woman as the one in the colour photograph I'd received.

I stared at it for a minute then flipped it over.

This time the words were: FIND ME!

I flipped it back and took a long breath. The woman was a stranger, but I knew the man. I knew him very well.

It was Major John Johnson.

FIFTEEN

"What are you going to do?" Penny asked me when I showed her the new photograph.

"I don't know," I said. "It's probably a prank."

"Have you met Mrs Johnson? I assume that's who she is."

"No, otherwise I'd have recognized her from the first photograph."

Penny looked out of the window for a while thinking, before she turned back to me. "Why would she need help? Why do you have to find her?"

I shook my head. No idea.

She took a breath as though making a decision. "Well, I think you should find her. After all, you are an investigator."

I said, "This is a bit different. She's the provost marshal's wife!"

"Meaning?"

"Meaning I can't just start asking questions about his wife and telling people she's asked for my help." As I said it, I was already changing my mind. There was someone I could approach with impunity.

"Ask Captain Wolfe what to do," Penny said.

I nodded. "That's a good idea, but in the meantime, I've a better one."

★

I found Jim Dexter in the Officers' Club at Alexander and I asked for a private word.

After I told him about the photographs he pondered the issue.

"How do you propose to investigate?" he asked me. Not *will you investigate*, but *how will you*.

I nodded. "First of all, I need to find out whether it's just a prank."

He pursed his lips, thinking. "I've been here as long as you," he said after a moment, "so I don't know the man, but my adjutant will. He's been based here for a few years. Come with me."

We left the Officers' Club and walked to the offices, where I was introduced to Staff Sergeant Wilks.

Dexter told the man that he wasn't to repeat anything we discussed and to be totally frank.

I asked, "What can you tell me about Mrs Johnson?"

"The major's wife?" Wilks said, looking surprised.

"Yes."

"Very attractive woman." He blinked. "Er... left the major at the end of last year. Ran off with another man, I hear."

I nodded. "Anything else?"

"She's very attractive—wavy dark red hair and nice eyes. And not English. She's French I think." From the dreamy look in his eyes I got the sense that Wilks had designs on the woman.

When he didn't say anything else, I asked, "Do you know the man she ran off with?"

"No, but..."

"But?" I prompted.

"Not specifically."

I nodded. "You're suggesting she had relations with various men?"

He took a breath. "Maybe."

Dexter frowned. "Come on, man, I told you to be frank!"

Wilks shrugged and squirmed. "Sir, I can't be sure. Mrs Johnson certainly caught men's eyes and wasn't afraid to respond. She was a flirt, sir… I mean in a nice way, not a loose woman as far as I know… but then she did leave the major, didn't she."

I said, "Did she flirt with anyone here?"

He shook his head. "Limassol. The clubs there. Especially Maxims."

"I know it."

"Too many horny single officers down there. Just be warned, Lieutenant. Have you got a girl?"

"I have."

"Then don't take her to Maxims. Don't advertise something you want to keep hold of."

Too late, I thought, but moved the conversation on.

"What is Mrs Johnson's first name?"

"Surena."

"She's a lot younger than the major."

"Yes."

"With a daughter," I said remembering the girl with a dog called Caesar.

"Verity is eight." He hesitated. "You're wondering how Major and Surena Johnson got together?"

I'd thought about it already. The big age difference. Her good looks, in a different league to the major. I said, "Did she get pregnant?"

Wilks nodded. "That's the story, although it's usually to trap a man rather than the other way around."

"But a mistake…"

Wilks bobbed his head. "That would be my guess. He's a lucky man."

"Was a lucky man. She left him."

"Right you are."

Dexter said, "Would the men play a prank on Major Johnson?"

"Which men, sir?"

"I don't know. Anyone, whether interested in Mrs Johnson or not?"

"Sir, Major Johnson is the provost marshal."

"Right."

Wilks shook his head. "Would anyone dare play a prank on him? I don't think so."

He had a point. I asked, "Does he have enemies?"

"Not that I know of."

"Who was Mrs Johnson's best friend?"

"I couldn't say. Possibly Captain Marsland-Askew's wife, they're of a similar age and she's friends with all the ladies."

He told me where to find the Marsland-Askews' home at *the village*.

I pulled out the photograph of Major and Mrs Johnson and slid it across the table. Leaving my hand on it meant that the staff sergeant couldn't pick it up and see the writing on the reverse.

Wilks said, "That's them."

I looked questioningly at Wilks.

"It was from before he transferred here."

I said, "That explains why he's not in a military police uniform, but—"

"US Army," Wilks said with a laugh.

"He was in the US Army?"

Again the laugh. "Of course not!"

I looked more closely at the insignia. First US Army.

"It's fake. Was this taken at a fancy dress party?"

"No, sir. Major Johnson was First US Army Group—the British one." And then I got it. There had been two armies deployed to distract the Germans from the invasion of Normandy.

"Fortitude," I said, providing the code name of the build-up of fake troops in Britain.

"Major Johnson was Lieutenant"—Wilks said it in an American accent—"Colonel Johnson of Fortitude South, part of the supposed invasion of Calais."

I didn't know whether any of this information would be useful, but if nothing else, I learned that Major Johnson had led an intriguing army career. He'd been in the Highland Infantry, been wounded and promoted to be a fake Lieutenant Colonel of the First US Group formed from the Eleventh Army. After the war, the unit had been disbanded and Johnson had come to Cyprus as provost marshal. His attractive young wife had stuck by him, possibly because of their daughter, Verity. But she seemed to be a flirt—although there was no evidence of other relationships so far—until she ran off with another man.

But none of that explained why she wanted help? And why me?

When Dexter and I were alone again he said, "I'm not sure where you go with this."

"Usually the way," I said. "Investigations are rarely as straightforward as you'd hope."

"But if it's not a prank."

"It's genuine and she wants help."

"What kind of help?"

I shook my head. "I wish I knew."

He waited a minute, as though expecting me to speak. When I said nothing, he nodded.

"You came to me for advice."

"Yes."

He nodded again. "You have to speak to Johnson. You can't investigate without checking with him first."

Subconsciously I think I wanted the CO to give his approval without me talking to Johnson. But Dexter was right. I couldn't avoid talking to Major Johnson himself.

SIXTEEN

"I hope this isn't about Mike Ellis again," Johnson said, shaking his head as I approached his desk. "I heard you went back to see him."

"Sir," I said, "I appreciate that this is a little awkward, but what can you tell me about this?" I slid the colour photograph of his wife across his desk.

His tanned forehead creased. "What the heck? How did you get this, Carter?"

"It was delivered to the SIB office."

Rather than study it, he put his hand over the photograph and moved it aside.

"What are you playing at?"

"Sir?" I said, confused by his reaction. His normal soft voice suddenly had an edge I hadn't expected.

"If this is about Ellis... If you're playing games..."

I raised my hands. "Honestly, Major. I know nothing about it or who sent it to me. That's why I'm here. Is that your wife in the picture?"

He gave me a hard stare with those eyes that still spoke of sadness, despite his toughness.

"This is no concern of yours."

"With respect, sir... did you write on the back of the picture?"

The glare softened. "No. Why?"

"Please turn the photograph over."

Johnson flipped the photo and stared at the writing.

"What... who?"

"I was hoping you would be able to answer that, Major."

"I can't. I don't understand."

I saw his jaw twitch with tension.

I said, "Is that your wife's handwriting?"

"I can't say."

The writing was in capitals, so his answer didn't surprise me.

"Would you tell me how she is? Does she need help, sir?"

Johnson didn't answer immediately because he stared off into space. I waited and heard the click of the clock on his wall and the fan overhead. Their sounds weren't in time.

Finally, he looked at me. "She left me."

I waited.

"Eight months ago, Surena left me for another man. There, are you happy now, Lieutenant?"

"I'm sorry to hear that, sir," I said, despite knowing this already.

Now he said nothing. He picked it up and looked at it. I noted a slight shake to his hands.

"Sir?" I prompted.

"I don't know why anyone would send you this."

"May I sit?" I indicated the chair opposite.

He thought for a moment before nodding.

I said, "Tell me about your wife."

Johnson cleared his throat. "Look, Lieutenant, I..."

"I can't ignore it, sir," I said. "It looks like your wife needs help."

"Then it's her lookout," he said after consideration.

"Sir?"

"She left me for another man, Carter. I'm hardly going to get excited because she asks for your help." He paused and tried to read me. I wondered if this explained why he had sad eyes. "Have you ever been married?"

"No, sir."

"Then you wouldn't understand. Surena probably left me for a younger, better-looking man. She made her choice and she has to live with it."

I took a breath. "If I'd been in your situation, perhaps I'd see it differently, sir, but I can't help being concerned for her safety."

He held my gaze for a long time. The clock and fan ticked asynchronously.

He said, "It's not a Branch matter. It doesn't concern you."

"You're right of course, it's nothing to do with SIB. However, I *am* involved. Someone sent me the photograph."

He took a long slow breath then cleared his throat. "Who do you think sent it?"

"Your wife."

"Why?"

"Isn't that obvious? She's in trouble."

He leaned forward, clenching his interlocked hands. "Then that's her lookout."

"I need—"

"You don't need to do anything, Lieutenant. That's an order." His calm voice told me he expected compliance. No question.

We locked eyes for a long time, neither of us speaking. I was wondering how to respond. Johnson wasn't in my chain of command despite his opinion to the contrary.

Finally, he looked away and slid the photograph off his desk and into a drawer. Then he surprised me by reaching forward and holding out his hand.

"Thank you," he said with sincerity. "Thank you, Ash."

★

On the drive back to the office I felt conflicted, but I kept reminding myself that Mrs Johnson wasn't a SIB issue; it was personal. Yes, I'd received the photograph, but I wasn't involved. And getting into a situation between a man and his wife—or ex-wife—especially a fellow military police officer, was wrong.

I was still worrying about it when I walked through the door and saw Penny holding the telephone out for me.

"Lieutenant Vaughan," she mouthed.

The news from 2 Wireless wasn't great. Vaughan's man had skim-read the documents and found nothing worth reporting—from an intelligence perspective.

"He'll go through the whole thing thoroughly, and we'll get it typed up as soon as we have the time," he said over the telephone, but I thought you'd want to know straight away."

"I appreciate it," I said. "But no need to type up the translation. We have an excellent secretary here." I smiled at Penny and she blew me a kiss in return.

★

I was frustrated and told Penny everything Johnson had told me, although I knew very little and still had no idea whether the message on the photograph was genuine or not.

Penny told me to stop fretting and relax for the evening. We left early and drove into the country and a village surrounded by scented pine trees.

We talked about anything but work, inconsequential things that provided a good distraction for the evening. Then, as the sun was setting, I drove back and we watched the sky change through a vast range of colours until the heavens sparkled with a million stars.

This evening, after we kissed on her doorstep, she invited me in for cocoa. She told me to wait on the sofa while she made it.

When she returned, she placed the two cups on a side table and took up her cross-legged pose on the apothecary coffee table.

She said, "You've got so much discipline—so much self-control. It's one of your qualities."

I thought about my visit to 6GDU and visiting Ellis again. It hadn't been planned and the impulse suggested anything but discipline.

"I have a confession," I said. "I didn't tell you but I confronted Ellis about Sarah again. So I'm not sure you're right."

"Did you shoot him?"

"Of course not."

"Hit him?"

"No. Would you rather I had?"

"Absolutely!" She smiled. "I'd love you to punch that bastard's lights out, but I know you can't do it. Not just like that. Not with witnesses anyway. But that's not the point. Yes, you visited him again and you were angry. But you controlled it."

"I suppose."

"And, by the way, I'm grateful. Yet again, you're my hero."

I wanted to protest but was distracted by her change of position. She uncrossed her legs, putting her knees out, feet together on the table.

"Shall I get the cocoa?" I asked, half rising.

"No, it'll be too hot. Just wait a minute."

She moved again. Her hands were behind her, supporting, and her feet separated. Her knees were up and she leaned back.

"Cocoa?" I said after a minute, without conviction.

Her skirt had ridden up so that I could see her inner thigh.

She shook her head, her eyes watching mine intently.

"You have nice legs," I ventured. "Lovely colour too."

She batted her eyes, leaned back further, and with a twitch of her legs, the skirt slipped. I could see white panties.

My heart threatened to push through my chest. My palms were damp. I couldn't take my eyes off those panties.

She laughed lightly.

So unfair! I wanted to shout at her, but my voice was lost somewhere in my constricted chest.

"I've been thinking," she said.

I still couldn't speak.

"We should count that first evening as a date."

My voice sounded funny when it finally came out. "That would still only make this date five."

She leaned back more and slid forward an inch.

"Did I tell you I'm no good at maths?" she said quietly. "Let's call this date six. Let's say it's time to stop being so restrained."

*

We made love on the table, which turned out to be an ideal height. Afterwards, we flopped onto the sofa and she opened her pencil case.

"Mind if I smoke?"

I pretended I didn't and let her lean against me, puffing on the cigarette. Her body fitted mine perfectly as she relaxed into me.

"Have you ever smoked, Ash?"

"Never."

"A cigarette after sex is the best. It just... well, it finishes it off so nicely."

She held up the cigarette. "Just try it."

"I'm fine thanks."

"There's that discipline—the self-control again," she said. "I'm glad you didn't hold back making love."

"It had been driving me crazy," I said. "I've wanted you so much. It's been hard since Saturday night."

She laughed at the unintended double-entendre. "Hopefully it'll be hard every time we go out now."

I wondered if she'd want me to stay, but she didn't ask. We finally had the cocoa and walked hand in hand away from town, through the cool night accompanied by singing cicadas. When we got back to her apartment, she kissed me, pointed me in the direction of my home, and whispered, "Tomorrow."

The cigarette smoke lingered on my clothes, but I could also smell her scent and didn't mind.

SEVENTEEN

I find that I exercise harder when I'm fretting about something, and in the morning, the photograph of Johnson and his wife still bothered me.

A five-mile run took me around the bay of Larnaca, almost as far as Dhekelia. There was a squall out to sea and I stood with my face to the sharp, wet wind for ten minutes before turning around and pounding the track back home.

Running usually clears my head, but today I was still troubled. Penny picked up on it straight away.

"I was brought up to do the right thing," I explained to her.

Never look the other way. Never walk away, my father had told me, and I could hear his voice in my head now. "If there is a right thing to do, then don't think, just act." Ironically, I despised my father for what he had done and yet his principles remained. Removing him from my life couldn't change my values, couldn't change the way I'd been brought up.

Penny interrupted my thoughts. "Ask Captain Wolfe."

"What?"

"I think you're troubled because Major Johnson is your senior. You don't feel you have the authority. Ask Captain Wolfe what he thinks."

I agreed, although I had no doubt Bill Wolfe would tell me to stand down. Penny had suggested this before and I'd avoided it. Wolfe would probably add it to the list of my weaknesses that had been exposed since being posted to Cyprus. However, I found that the decision to talk to Wolfe put the photograph to the back of my mind.

*

But the next telephone call wasn't from Bill Wolfe.

DI Dickins said, "Well, not only were you right about investigating our murder, but people did talk to us."

"Did you get a name for the victim?"

"His cousin recognized him." Dickins laughed, which for a moment I thought was inappropriate. But then he explained. "Everyone on this damn island is related! There are three hundred villages and when you finally get them talking, you find they claim to be cousins. Anyway, I just wanted to let you know you turned up trumps and we have a name."

"I hope it leads somewhere."

"We'll see," he said. "There are a lot of old unsolved murders that might be related." Then, before ending the call, he invited me to lunch the next time I was in Nicosia.

*

Bill Wolfe called early in the afternoon and by then I'd received the transcripts from 2 Wireless.

I had read and summarized the translations and provided the detail to Wolfe.

"Disappointing," he said, "but I'm not surprised. I'm moving to Tel Aviv, so I can be closer to the action."

When we'd been in Mandatory Palestine, our offices had been in Haifa. Showing my ignorance I asked him why Tel Aviv.

He didn't respond straight away and I wondered what he was thinking. Were there things he wasn't allowed to tell me?

Eventually, he said, "Tel Aviv is where they've set up their army HQ."

"OK?" I said uncertainly, wondering why we needed to be near the Israeli army headquarters.

"Open my desk drawer, Ash and read my *eyes-only* papers."

He told me where he'd hidden a key and I quickly retrieved the documents. There wasn't much. The papers explained the fragility of the region and the likely ongoing conflict between the Arabs and Jews since the former hadn't accepted the UN's Partition Plan. This had been written shortly before our departure and I knew that Transjordan and Egypt had already invaded the bordering territories. The main British concern was for the loss of control over the Suez Canal, but with military forces and defence agreements with both nations, the British Army wanted intelligence on everything and anything relating to the military build-up, strategies and potential actions.

It was a huge open-ended assignment. Too much for one man. Too much for a two-man team.

"I've read it," I said, my head full of questions, mainly about why this was being assigned to us, rather than government intelligence.

He said, "If you're wondering why the army wants us involved—"

"I am."

"—well, you should know that the army and government aren't the same thing. I have no doubt that our security service is here too, but the army always wants its own intelligence."

"When do I join you?"

"Not yet, Ash. Let me establish myself here first and gain trust. I'm posing as an ex-army military advisor, hoping to get access to sensitive information. Once I'm accepted I'll bring you in as an assistant." He gave me a new address and phone number and I relayed it to Penny.

We spoke some more and Wolfe started wrapping up the conversation, when I saw Penny waiting with an eyebrow raised.

"Bill," I began, "can I ask you something?"

"Of course. What is it?"

So I told him about the photograph I'd received, the note on the reverse, and Major Johnson's request that I didn't investigate.

He said, "You're bored."

"A little."

He didn't speak for a while and I waited, listening to the background hum of the wires. "Ash?"

"Yes?"

"How's the execution case? The one you offered your help with?"

I told him the little I knew and that it might be related to old cases.

"Intriguing," he said when I finished, and I knew he was trying to make it more interesting than it was.

I said nothing.

"Ash, there are unsolved murders. That's something to get your teeth into. Talk to that DI again. It sounds like he listened to you about canvassing the villages. He'll listen to you if you find anything in the other cases."

I said, "You're telling me to ignore the photographs."

"Yes, I fuckin' am! Johnson is right. This is not your problem, it's his. You gave him the photograph with the request for help. Unless you find real evidence that she's in trouble then you should stand down. And by the way, if you do find evidence, you either hand it over to him or your friend at the police."

I said nothing.

"Got it, Ash?"

I looked across at Penny, who was twiddling with her pencil case and frowning at me. I guessed she was mimicking my own expression.

"Penny will call DI Dickins as soon as we end this call, Bill," I said.

"Good. Use that brain of yours on the right case, Ash. And I'll call you in a few days."

EIGHTEEN

DI Dickins was busy when I arrived at the police HQ the following morning. I waited in the same comfortable room as before and he apologized profusely despite me having made no firm appointment.

"As I told you, our victim has a name," he said. "Tassos Michailidis, and he's from Lefka."

The town meant nothing to me.

"Is that anywhere near where he was shot?"

"No, over near the west coast. As I suspected, he is linked to illegal practices. It's a smuggler's paradise over there."

"You thought it was gang-related."

He raised a finger. "Quite. We were told that he had a run-in with another gang—one that we've been aware of for a few years. Come with me."

Dickins took me to his office where a buff folder lay on his desk. He opened it and slid out a photograph."

"Another victim?" I said.

"Gang execution. Similar to this Michailidis fellow except for one important thing." He pointed to the victim's forehead.

I could see the outline of three letters, just visible. I guessed they were less than half an inch high.

"Identified in the postmortem," Dickins said. "It's from an impact at or around the point of death."

"Branded?"

"The coroner thinks it's from a metal ring." He held up his good fist. "Punch the victim in the head and leave a mark. As you can see, it looks like X-I-S, but remember this is Cyprus. It's Chi-Iota-Sigma. Greek. The Greeks do love their acronyms." He chuckled. Then looked remorseful.

"What?"

"The team corrupted it to *kiss*. Kiss being easier to say than the Greek alternative. In fact, the mark was known as the kiss of death."

"There are more," I said.

He nodded. "This is the clearest, but there were a number of old cases shot in the head from close range, just like the man you found."

"Executed."

"Executed and punched in the head by a man wearing a ring," Dickins said. "The villager who identified Michailidis questioned whether it was the same gang. The Kiss gang we called them."

"And yet Michailidis doesn't have the mark," I said. "Does he?"

"No, he doesn't. We think you probably disturbed them. They scarpered when they heard your vehicle. Didn't have time to punch him. Or panicked and forgot."

I kept looking at the photo. "Or decided against it."

Dickins was watching me.

"How many have there been?"

"Fifteen execution-style. Sixteen including Michailidis."

"Sixteen."

Dickins hung his head. "I know what you're thinking. You're thinking we should be doing more to catch this gang."

I nodded.

"I agree it doesn't look good, but bear in mind this sixteen is over a period of four years and the last one was a year last September—before I got here. Anthem's covered them all. If you have the time, he can talk you through them."

I had the time.

DS Park came in and I sensed reluctance. Which was understandable since this was for my edification rather than any benefit to the investigation.

We drank tea and he talked. He described all the victims as Greek and showed me a map. Their bodies had been found in the Mesaoria Plain—the low land between the two mountain ranges of Cyprus—from outside Morphou in the west to Kondea in the east.

Dickins said, "From this, we think that the Kiss gang operate throughout the plains."

"You mentioned Michailidis was a small-time crook. What was he involved in?"

DS Park grunted. "Bootleg alcohol probably. I was in Lefka yesterday but failed to find anyone who would talk about Michailidis."

I said nothing.

"It's not unusual. The Cyps don't trust us. The best way to get them to talk is through interrogation. Problem we have here is we can't arrest the whole village."

I nodded. "Is bootleg and smuggled alcohol a big problem on the island?"

He shrugged. "Not that I'm aware of. Cyps are well-known drinkers. They do love their alcohol."

We talked about their other cases, and afterwards, Dickins took me to lunch. He apologized for not being able to take me to the English Club, since he wasn't a member yet. Instead, we went to the Ledra Palace Hotel, which was close to Wolseley Barracks. The Tyrolean Bar was as ugly and rowdy as a sergeant's mess, but the calm restaurant provided an easy atmosphere to chat.

Dickins told me again that he was only just into his second year of a three-year assignment. His predecessor had been shot by a suspect. DS Park had tried to save the man but the inspector died in his arms.

"Time goes more slowly here," he said, seemingly switching subjects. "Which is both good and bad. Good because it's less stressful than London and bad because I feel semi-retired. I'm actually glad you challenged me regarding the murder. It feels good to do some proper detective work."

I learned that he'd lost his hand to fire during the Blitz when a burning house collapsed on him. Later we spoke about family, and I figured that the house had been his. Both of his parents and his wife had been killed in the collapse. We sat in silence for a while and I wondered if he was thinking of that terrible time.

"What about you, Ash?"

"I'm sorry?"

"How did your family fare during the war?"

I used the delivery of our desserts as a delaying tactic as I considered what to tell him, before giving a very high-level summary of my parent's difficulties and my mother's suicide.

"That's tough," he said. "I'm sorry."

"Thanks, but it seems most people have a sad story these days."

He nodded with a mouthful of cream cake. "But I thank God that I have two healthy boys, both making their way in the City—London that is, not here!" He raised his glass of wine and I raised my water.

"To a better future," he toasted, and I agreed.

Then, over coffee, he asked why I was in Nicosia.

"Because I've been encouraged to find a distraction."

He frowned at me, a half-smile forming on his lips.

"I've an odd case," I said, deciding to explain.

"You have a case?"

"Do you know Major John Johnson?"

"The CO of 227 Provost Company at Alexander Barracks? Of course, I know the name but never met the man."

"It's about his wife. She's asked for help."

"With what?"

"That's just the point. I don't know." And so I told him about the note on the back of the photographs.

Dickins smiled kindly at me. "You really are bored."

"My OC said something similar."

"How are you going to help someone when you don't know where she is or what she wants?"

"I'll find her."

"What have you got to go on?"

I laughed. "Nothing. So if you hear anything—"

He nodded. "I'll ask around."

"Discreetly."

He tapped his nose. "Discretion, dear boy, is my middle name. Which is better than the famous Charles Dickens, whose middle name was Huffam."

We laughed together.

"And if you need a distraction, come back up on Monday and spend more time with Anthem talking about the old cases."

I thanked the inspector for lunch and his company, and asked if I might see the fifteen Kiss files. He said he'd get them together and let me have them next time I visited. We agreed on Monday. In return, he kindly promised to let me know of any further developments and find anything he could about Mrs Surena Johnson.

I could have left the city via the nearby Paphos Gate, but instead I strolled into the centre, got a cold drink and let random thoughts fill my head.

*

It was getting dark when I returned to the office. Penny had gone home but left me a message to see her later.

"How's your investigation going?" she asked me after a pasta dinner that she'd prepared.

"Equally slowly," I said as she sat on the apothecary coffee table and crossed her legs.

She must have seen enthusiasm in my face because she waggled a finger at me. "We should talk first. So, tell me about your day in Nicosia."

I gave her a rapid update.

When I finished she smiled. "So have you forgotten about the major's wife?"

"Yes," I lied.

"Good, because I was concerned you found her blue eyes and auburn hair too attractive."

I said, "Attractive, but not stunning like you."

She batted her eyes at me. "That sounds promising. It's Saturday tomorrow and I'd like to go to Maxims again."

I cleared my throat, thinking of the expense and what Dexter's staff sergeant had said. He'd warned me about the place when we'd discussed Mrs Johnson finding another man.

"We're not going back, because I don't want to lose you to a rival!"

She raised her eyebrows and then I realized her legs were moving too.

"Tell me more," she said. "So you don't want to lose me?"

I said, "I'd be a fool to let you go."

Her knees started to rise and so did my heart rate.

"You're gorgeous," I said. "Anyone would—"

Her knees dropped a fraction. "Anyone?"

"No, just me. I want you, Penny. You are mine."

I saw the light brown thighs and white knickers.

She leaned back. "I am yours," she said huskily, and a heart beat later I was all over her.

NINETEEN

The second time I arrived at Maxims, I was greeted by the concierge as though he'd known me his whole life. I was a member now and shown up two weeks consecutively. That probably suggested money. I could afford to be a regular visitor therefore I would be liberal with my cash. The concierge probably had instructions about buttering up the regular spenders.

I didn't mind his fussing. And I especially didn't mind that he told a waiter to give us a better table than the previous visit.

It all started well. The food was great, and when the music picked up, Penny and I hit the dance floor.

After a break, a young officer asked me if I'd mind if he danced with Penny. She seemed keen so I agreed. I'd had my eye on another table with men only, playing poker. None of them was from the Suffolks or 227 Provost Company, which suited my objective.

After a wave to Penny, so that she knew what I was doing, I introduced myself to the group and was invited to pull up a chair.

I played two hands before producing the photograph of the Johnsons. Three of them recognized the major and I learned that he hadn't been to the club in months.

One of them ventured: "I haven't seen his wife either."

"Because she left him," the man immediately on my left commented.

The rest nodded sagely as though they knew, and it transpired that they'd heard the story despite not recognizing Major Johnson's photograph.

"I'm looking for her," I explained.

That drew quizzical looks.

"Not because of the major." Why was I looking for Mrs Johnson? I expected the question. The problem had been playing on my mind. How do I look for the young lady without raising suspicions? So I lied. "I need to find her—to give her a message."

The man on my left took a puff of his cigar and winked at me. "She's attractive."

I glanced at the dance floor, where Penny was doing the jitterbug with a different officer, and shook my head. "I've got an attractive girl already."

"Dancing with another man," one of the group chuckled.

"Nevertheless," I said, smiling, "I'm still hoping someone knows where I can find Mrs Johnson."

After they'd all shaken their heads, I excused myself and moved to another table. I worked my way around the room and kept glancing at the dance floor. Penny attracted a lot of suitors, and I was happy that she wasn't favouring anyone. Only twice did I see her sitting at our table looking a little bored, but I was in the middle of conversations, and by the time I was free, she'd been coaxed onto the dance floor by some young officer.

Despite my efforts, no one had seen the Johnsons at Maxims for many months, and it seemed that he hadn't been here since his wife had left him.

When I returned to our table. I looked absentmindedly at the photograph. Major and Mrs Johnson were looking at the camera, but it was a fairly incidental photograph. Not formal because of the other people behind. I focused on the man immediately behind Mrs Johnson. He was closest and I had an odd sense that he had just turned out of shot. Then Penny interrupted my thoughts as she sat beside me.

"What have you been doing?" she asked.

"I played a few hands of poker. And chatting," I said, slipping the photograph away. "It's been a while since I've—"

"I was bored."

That surprised me. She'd seemed happy on the dance floor. I thought she didn't mind me being with the men.

"I kept checking you were all right," I said apologetically.

"Can we go?"

"Already?" I checked my watch. It wasn't even eleven o'clock.

"Take me home," she said.

She didn't say anything more until we were hurtling around the bay at about the same place where she'd stood up last time and shouted into the wind.

"I'm thinking that I should have stuck to my six dates rule," she said, her voice cold.

"Penny…"

"A girl wants attention, Ash. Attention from her boyfriend. I wanted you to dance with me, not random officers."

"Did any of them—? I didn't notice any problem."

She sighed. "They were all perfect gentlemen. That's not what I'm saying. Why don't men understand? Why can't they give just one girl their devotion?"

I wondered if this related to another relationship, wondered if a past boyfriend had been seeing someone else. Rather than question her, I decided it best to keep quiet.

We didn't speak again for a while, with the jolt and thump of the Land Rover's tyres filling the awkward silence between us.

"I didn't enjoy it. Not one bit," she grumbled eventually.

"I know," I responded, despite thinking that she'd seemed happy while twisting and twirling to the music.

"I saw you. I saw you showing people the photograph. You're looking for that woman, aren't you? And is that why you took me back to Maxims. It wasn't a date, it was a job. And that's what it felt like."

I could have pointed out that she'd been the one to request Maxims, but I didn't. I just apologized, although she didn't relax. She kept facing forward as the headlights bobbed and bounced us back to Larnaca.

I stopped outside her home.

"Can I come in for cocoa?"

"Not tonight," she said. "I need to think, and anyway, I've got a headache now."

She let me peck her on the cheek before scooting off into the apartment.

I leaned back in the seat, stared up at the star-speckled sky and blew out air. I'd mixed work and pleasure. A fatal combination. Not only that, but I'd failed to learn anything of use about Mrs Johnson and I'd upset the only person who meant anything to me.

However, I wasn't a novice at the game of love. I knew relationships had their ups and downs and I had every confidence that Penny would forgive me within twenty-four hours.

But I was wrong.

TWENTY

On Monday morning, Penny greeted me formally, like the work colleagues we were.

I'd decided that I wouldn't keep apologizing for my behaviour at Maxims. Instead, I told her I would be going to Nicosia to continue with the murder investigation. However, I pointedly added that I wouldn't be looking for Mrs Johnson today.

After getting the information about the old cases, I would travel around the country and see what I could discover. To this end, I thought I would need Maria's translation services and asked Penny to arrange for the lady to meet me at the office in the morning.

An hour later, I mounted the stairs to the first floor of the police HQ and went through the doors marked 'Criminal Investigation Division'. The main room, previously chaotic with activity, was now eerily quiet. My footfall sounded loud as I walked towards Dickins's office at the end.

When I passed a kitchen, a man appeared, holding a mug. He missed a step.

"Oh! You surprised me," DS Park said, a cigarette bobbing on his lips as he spoke.

"Just popped in to see the inspector."

"He's out." Park waved with his free hand. "In fact, you'll see everyone's out except for me—and I'll be off shortly. Can I get you tea?"

When I accepted his offer, he retreated into the kitchen and opened the valve on a hot water tank and filled a teapot.

"Where's the inspector?" I asked as he continued with his tea making.

"Morphou," he said, naming the large port to the northwest. "Trouble with suspected communists." He went on to provide me with some details and also about a burglary in Nicosia before asking me why I was visiting.

"Killing time, to be honest," I said, taking my mug of tea from him. "So I thought I'd take a look at the Kiss of Death files."

He looked at me inquisitively and blew out a thin line of cigarette smoke.

I said, "You never know, I might spot something."

"I won't take offence," Park said, stubbing out his cigarette. "However, I don't think you'll find something we missed."

He led me into a meeting room and told me to wait. Ten minutes later, he returned with a bundle of files.

"And a map with villages marked?" I asked.

He fetched me a map, wished me luck, and left me to my own devices.

I read through all fifteen files and noted the dates and where the bodies had been discovered. I took a break with a glass of water and leaned out of the window to get cooler air. I watched the traffic on the road outside the station before sitting down and going through the files again.

"Hot?" Park asked me.

It wasn't as bad as inland Palestine could get, but there seemed no air today. "Even with the windows open," I said, "it's stifling in here."

He laughed. "It's worse in winter. It's like the concrete sucks out any heat. You don't expect bone-chilling cold in Cyprus. I wish they'd invest in central heating."

"Why don't they?"

He laughed bitterly. "Disorganized and underfunded. You see, there's no motivation. Nothing has changed for almost a hundred years—except for a renaming of the police commission. That's what everyone grumbles about."

I was about to express my commiserations when the sergeant continued.

"You know, the government decamps to the Troodos Mountains between June and September because of the heat. Winter in Nicosia and summer in the cooler mountains. We on the other hand have to sweat it out here." He sighed. "What you doing for lunch?"

"Is that the time?" My watch said it was almost one in the afternoon.

"Come on," he said. "I know a good place for special beef stew, and I'm buying."

I'd had special beef in Palestine so I suspected the meat would be goat, and I was right. But it tasted good and the bread rolls provided with it were warm and fresh.

"Find anything in the files?" he asked, alternating between mouthfuls and puffs on his cigarette.

"No. What's your theory about the dates?" I'd noted that there had been a cluster of eight murders in July and August 1945 and then a few more later that year. Since then, the murders had been sporadic, and nothing for sixteen months before the execution I stumbled across.

"Coincides with the end of the war."

"Right, but that's not a theory."

"Well, many of us demobbed then. For example, I came here in June."

I nodded. "You think it's a group of ex-military men?"

"Quite a few Greeks deserted. Which, by the way, I find ironic since we fought alongside them." He tapped his left leg. "And I was wounded in the Battle of Greece—part of W Force."

He flicked away his cigarette stub then took a mouthful of food, and I suspected he'd lost his train of thought. I said, "You were explaining your theory."

"Oh yes, my theory. I think the deserters came here—probably originally from the mainland—and decided to play the Mafia game. They identified small-time gangs and eliminated the competition. They had a blitz early on and left a message—made their mark, as it were."

Literally, I thought. "Why stamp them with XIS?"

"So that others are warned? Like advertising that they did it." He put a fresh cigarette in his mouth and squinted at me through the smoke. "Oh, you mean *why those letters*! Well, it tells us they're Greek rather than Turks and maybe they associate with the unification with Greece. *Enosis* they call it. We looked into mainland, Mafia-type gangs but couldn't find any connection—no similar executions. No similar initials."

We ate some more and he asked me about my background and was interested in Palestine.

I said, "We could never relax like this. The whole time we had to be on the lookout for trouble."

Park breathed in the warm air. "Yep, it certainly is nice here. Better than Blighty. I know I moan about the office, but the winters aren't grey and drizzly and the money's good."

"Mind if I ask you about your name? Anthem's an unusual one."

"The family's to blame," he said. "The name goes way back. At first, as a kid, I found it embarrassing, but later I think it gave me backbone. I had to stand up for myself—be assertive."

"You're a smart chap," I said, and thought about what Dickins had told me about the previous inspector being killed. "When the DI vacancy came up, weren't you in the running?"

"Do you mean am I bitter that Charles got the job? No, sir! Anyway, I'm not officer class. I'm a working boy and happy with my lot. And the DI job has more pressure plus the political stuff. I'm no good at hobnobbing with the high and mighty."

We finished our food and strode back to the station.

I said, "We never finished off talking about theories."

He laughed. "We could talk all day about theories."

"But why a sixteen-month gap between the old murders and the recent one?" I asked.

I saw a thought cross his face but couldn't read it. He lit another cigarette then said, "Well, we never found the gang, but we have been successful regarding criminals. One theory is that we've made progress by... what's the word?"

"Attrition?"

"That'll do. We gradually whittled them down, not catching them for the murders but for other crimes. With the last one, two years ago..." He looked down as though contemplating the cigarette in his hand. "I'm sure you heard."

"About what?"

"Dickins's predecessor getting shot and killed."

"I hear you were there when he died."

Park took a shuddering breath. "You just don't expect it. Afterwards... well we'd have done something different. We'd have made sure the suspect was incapacitated."

"He grabbed a detective's sidearm, shot Chadwick and then turned the gun on himself before we could disarm him."

I looked at Park askance.

He said nothing.

"If he had a gun, why only shoot one policeman?" I asked. "Why not shoot others and get away?"

Park took a breath.

"What really happened, Sergeant?"

He stopped me by gripping my arm. "Can I trust you?"

"OK."

"No, I mean really trust you not to say anything to anyone. I'll deny it if you do. I didn't tell the truth because of the hassle—the reports, the likely inquiry."

I looked into his eyes and guessed. "He didn't turn the gun on himself, did he?"

"No."

"You shot the suspect."

He smiled. "I'll deny it if you say."

I patted his shoulder. "Your secret is safe with me, Anthem. And for the record, I'd have shot the bastard twice."

He laughed. "Good. In that case, I'll let you in on another theory. The execution you witnessed wasn't our Kiss gang. It was someone else and that's why there was no mark on his forehead. Maybe it was supposed to look like it. Maybe it's a new gang or someone stirring up old trouble."

TWENTY-ONE

I found a flower seller in Nicosia and bought a bunch of yellow chrysanthemums. I would have preferred roses, but my choice was limited.

When I returned to the office, Penny accepted the flowers gracefully but declined my invitation to dinner. Then she told me that Maria would arrive at ten o'clock in the morning after her cleaning work.

Maria arrived after ten, but I was already used to Cyprus-time being less formal than an Englishman might anticipate.

She said nothing as we drove to the village of Kondea, about four miles north-west of Famagusta. I explained that I would be visiting the towns and villages near where bodies had been discovered. Before I'd left the police HQ, I'd borrowed the photographs of the victims. Park hadn't been happy but had finally relented on the understanding I would return them within a week.

Eventually Maria spoke to me. "What do you hope to learn?"

"Anything that might shed light on the individuals and what happened."

I saw her purse her lips and nod slightly before she settled back into the seat.

Kondea turned out to be a run-down hamlet sheltering under the odd carob tree and populated by wild dogs and lizards. At least, I thought that until we rounded a bend and found a cluster of houses bordering a dusty square with a tavern and tiny church.

There must have been twenty people sitting in the shade drinking and chatting. I heard laughter and the thump of a hand on a table before silence descended. All eyes watched as I parked and then walked towards the largest group outside the tavern. Maria trotted behind at my shoulder.

"Good morning," I said to the first man. He had a shock of curly hair and a shaggy beard flecked with grey. In fact, all the men looked similar: nut brown worn faces with sleepy expressions.

I held up the photograph of the victim who'd been found close by. "Do you recognize this man?"

After no response, Maria spoke and I figured she'd repeated my question in Greek.

The man shook his head. I showed the photograph to the next and the next and they shook their heads. I turned my attention back to the first man.

"Does Kiss of Death mean anything to you?"

A shake of the head followed Maria's translation.

"What about *Chis*?" I said, trying to pronounce the Greek word. Maria said it properly and then the three individual letters. Again I was met with negative responses.

I asked everyone in the square and no one knew a thing. The whole time, I felt their eyes on me, scrutinizing, assessing, perhaps wary. What I didn't sense was any interest or intrigue. Why was this Englishman asking questions about a murder victim of almost four years ago?

In the next village, Prastio, I met with the same blank faces, shakes of the head and wary eyes. DS Park had been right; this was a waste of time.

As we drove south and then west to the next location, Maria took a loud breath.

"Yes?" I prompted. "You want to say something?"

"You are very British," she said. Then after a pause: "If you were a bit more... Cypriot, you would have better results."

She taught me how to say a few words and told me to follow her lead.

The hamlet of Arsos was almost identical to Kondea, although we saw people working in fields as we drove up and there were fewer at the local coffee house.

Eyes watched us park and walk to the tables in the shade of a tree. Maria ordered us coffee and greeted people. Smiles and conversation came back.

I said hello in Greek and thanked the lady who brought our small cups of black coffee.

A man spoke to us and Maria translated.

"It is good to hear an Englishman speak our language."

I nodded and smiled back as Maria replied.

"He wants to know where you are from," Maria told me.

"Manchester," I said.

"Ah, Manchester United!" the man said, and gave me a toothy grin and thumbs-up.

I took a few questions about the football team, although I suspected they knew more than I did. Then the questions became more general about England, the weather and our way of life. He had the clear impression that we all lived in mansions overlooking fields of green and gold.

After a short time of talking, people closed in and I saw interest in their dark eyes.

A man placed a glass of something in front of me which I first thought was water. At the last moment, I realized it was ouzo and pretended to drink.

"Now," Maria said to me after I'd talked nonsense about home life and my childhood, "ask your questions, but make them sound like a story."

And so I told them about the mysterious murders that had happened after the war—fifteen of them, all with the strange mark: XIS. This time, when I showed them photographs, there was muttering and excitement. They remembered the body found three or so years ago, but no one recognized the man's face.

I said, "But I thought everyone knows everyone!"

That brought chuckles which seemed to bounce around until they turned into guffaws.

I looked at Maria, and she said, "Yes it is a small island and many people are related and may call each other cousin, but that doesn't mean they actually know everyone."

After a pause she said, "You are doing very well, but it would be better if you accepted their hospitality."

"What do you mean?"

"The drink."

I explained that I didn't drink alcohol, and although Maria struggled with the concept, she came up with a plan.

"Accept the drinks, but pass them to me."

In the next village, I finally got someone to speak of *Enosis* and I could see that Maria agreed with them.

"We talk of union with Greece," she said, "but that doesn't mean we don't love the British. We enjoy being British—although it would be better if your people would learn our language. There are very few Cypriots who can speak English. And then there's the government. Has anyone ever seen someone from the government?"

She then spoke in Greek and I guessed she was repeating the question for the audience. The response was a resounding *óchi*.

I said, "So *Chis* is part of *Enosis*?"

Maria asked the direct question, and I saw the answer in their shaking heads before Maria translated.

This time when I was given alcohol, I accepted and managed to switch it to Maria, who had been given water. She knocked back the ouzo without hesitation.

Back in the Land Rover, she said, "Perhaps *Chis* is an earlier form of *Enosis*, but I've never heard of it and neither had they."

We stopped at three more villages and went through the same pantomime, and learned nothing. They remembered the body but didn't know who it was.

Eventually, we reached a hamlet called Marki. As we approached, Maria told me it was Turkish, and I recognized a Moorish style to the buildings, although I judged this to be one of the poorer villages we'd visited.

"Do the communities never coexist?" I asked.

"There are some places, but mostly they are separate. It's not a problem though. You see, most of these peasant villages are family clusters, so it is rare that they mix, although the Turks all speak Greek."

Marki was the village closest to where I'd found the body and I was keen to hear about the victim. Just like the other villages, we came to a centre with a coffee house. Ten men sat drinking, but unlike the Greeks, I sensed that silence and contemplation was the Turkish way. Although similar in appearance to the Greek peasants, these Turkish men wore caps and either baggy trousers or loose blouses.

They were wary and more reticent at first, but they were as keen as the Greeks to hear a story told by an outsider—especially a Briton who appeared friendly. Rather than ouzo, we were served brandy with thick black coffee.

We talked for a long time before I asked about who had recognized Tassos Michailidis. The head of the village, known as the *mukhtar*, had joined us and coordinated the conversations translated by Maria. When I asked about the victim, the *mukhtar* sent out young runners, who, Maria said, were looking for the witness.

However, after half an hour and more brandy, I discovered that no one admitted to telling the police. The police had come and asked them, but as far as the *mukhtar* knew, no one had identified him nor where he'd come from.

From Marki we circled around and asked in local villages in case the person identifying the body had come from elsewhere. We didn't find him.

Frustrated and disappointed, we continued west to the next location. Kato Moni was more than three times the size of most villages, and the green fields suggested better arable land and presumably greater farming success. Unlike other villages, this one also boasted two churches.

Although still in the plains, as we moved west, the Troodos Mountains got closer and closer. They now loomed, tall and grim to the south and south-west.

The sun was already beginning its descent, and while my head buzzed from gallons of coffee, my stomach craved food.

I headed for the local tavern, intending to eat more rather than question the people of the village. However, Maria soon got into a conversation and we were told to wait as a boy ran off.

Minutes later, he returned with an old man with a priestly beard and such bandy legs as to give him the gait of someone onboard a ship's deck. Eventually he made it to our table and shook my hand warmly.

He introduced himself as the *mukhtar*, and it appeared that Greek Cypriots also used the title for the head of the village. As usual he was keen to hear my stories, and very soon he was ordering wine, bread, cheese and olives. But not just for us; a large part of village seemed to be invited.

I learned that he had found the body years ago—although Maria later told me she thought he was exaggerating and saw it after someone else told him. I showed him the appropriate photograph and he confirmed it was the man.

"But I never saw him before."

"Or after!" Someone quipped, and both laughter and quaffing of wine followed.

They wanted to know the details of the other cases, and for the first time, someone asked me why I was investigating.

I explained that I wasn't the police—which Maria had already insisted—and that I was merely interested.

"You are a wise man," the *mukhtar* said.

I thanked him before he added:

"A fool throws a stone into the sea and a hundred wise men cannot pull it out."

Maria explained that it was an old Cypriot proverb.

After an hour of talking, I offered to pay for the food, but the *mukhtar* said, "A stranger never pays." Which was apparently another Cypriot saying.

As we left the village I asked Maria about the wise men proverb.

"He was telling you that, despite your intelligence, you will never solve the crime. Sometimes things happen. You are looking for an explanation and a pattern. Perhaps there isn't either."

I didn't bother arguing. Travelling through the Mesaoria, I learned that once relaxed and with their guards down, the Cypriots had a good-natured, sunny disposition. They liked their drink and they liked to talk. Although the Turkish Cypriots were more reserved and pensive, they also liked strangers who could tell them a story. However, I found the innocence and acceptance by these common folk something that I struggled to comprehend. I kept thinking about the proverb. We would never solve the murders.

I suspected their attitude would have been different if the victim had been a family member as opposed to an unknown stranger.

We travelled on and went through four more villages near where bodies had been found. The stories were similar. People either knew of the bodies or had seen them. However, the identities were unknown. It was also clear that no one believed this was anything to do with Cypriot separatists or any kind of rebellion against the Crown.

We had four more villages to visit when I asked, "Where are you from, Maria? Originally, I mean."

She looked at me as if I'd slapped her.

"I'm sorry," I said, thinking I'd offended her.

"You are so unlike your fellow Englishmen." She shook her head. "I am honoured that you have asked me. Well, my family come from a village to the north: Akanthou. It is beautiful with orange groves and flowers. Not at all like this harsh plain."

As if to demonstrate her feelings, she batted exaggeratedly at her dress, which, like my own clothes had become coated with red dust. It was at this point I guessed she was a little drunk.

"And yet you live in Larnaca?"

"For the work," she explained. "The British pay well, and since the war, you know I'm sure, property prices in Nicosia and Kyrenia especially have soared."

"What about the villages?"

"Most properties outside the capital don't have running water, so water rights are as important if not more important than the property. Indeed, you could say that without water rights, a property is useless. And water rights are as controlled as the Land Registry."

"So you can't afford the properties in the north?"

"That's what I'm saying."

"I understand."

"Do you?"

I stopped the jeep and turned around. It was time to go home. My translator was becoming inebriated and I was just learning the same thing at each village. Four more identical stories wouldn't help.

For a while, Maria waxed lyrical about the beautiful countryside in the north: the harbour at Kyrenia; the abbey above Bellapais; the beach at Amvrosios; the rugged coast further up, and the Byzantium castles.

When she stopped talking, Maria lounged in her seat with a smile on her face. The soporific sun was on our necks and I had started to think she'd fallen asleep when she suddenly spoke.

"All of the bodies were in the plain," she said as though with great wisdom. "Not one in the north. Not one in the south. Why is that?"

I'd been thinking the same since yesterday and had hoped we'd learn why today. The prevailing theory was that the gang was executing the people and leaving them as a message, but that looked increasingly unlikely.

I said, "Because the murderers aren't based in the plain. It's misdirection."

Maria raised a finger. "I think you are correct, Mr Holmes." And then she did fall asleep.

I reached the Nicosia road before turning south for Larnaca. Halfway, a Land Rover passed going fast towards the capital. The driver waved a hand in greeting and I caught a glimpse of a man with blond hair. It wasn't until we travelled in its dust cloud that I registered who it had been: Major Gee of the First Guards Brigade.

Perhaps the Cypriot silly sense of humour was rubbing off on me because I found it amusing that Gee had been in a car rather than on horseback.

After dropping Maria at her home, I was still smiling to myself when I got back to my digs. But the smile soon evaporated as I stared at my front door.

My rooms had been broken into.

TWENTY-TWO

The door lock required a simple key which was easy to pick. There was a scratch on the metal where there hadn't been before.

I tried the handle. The door was unlocked.

Before entering, I stepped over to Bill Wolfe's door and checked it. His was locked and undisturbed.

Returning to my door, I opened it carefully, wondering at the disarray I'd find. However, at first glance, the rooms didn't look disturbed.

But someone had been searching in here because items had been moved. A trick I'd learned in Palestine was to leave innocuous clues for myself. For example, I'd leave the bedside drawer open slightly—an exact distance. The drawer was now closed. Similarly, my suitcase sat on top of the wardrobe at a precise angle. It had been moved.

So someone had searched my room and put it back exactly as they'd found it—or so they thought.

I had a small amount of money hidden in a pocket of my suitcase. The money was still there.

The main hiding place was a false bottom of my wardrobe. In practice, a thief would find the money in the case and think that was it. However, the wardrobe space held the rest of my money, a couple of valuable personal items and my revolver. Everything was as I'd left them.

They hadn't found or taken any of my valuables. Did that mean it was an unfortunate opportunist or had the intruder been looking for something else?

★

Penny appeared more relaxed when I saw her at the office in the morning. I didn't mention my suspicions about a break-in. It was the sort of thing we worried about in Palestine and I didn't want Penny picking up on my anxieties. Real or otherwise.

After making me weak tea, she asked how my trip across country had been.

She laughed when I told her about Maria getting drunk and talking non-stop about her beloved home over the Kyrenia Mountains.

"We need to go," I said. "I want to see all those places—and I want to see them with you."

"Hmm, I don't know," Penny said, but I knew she was teasing me.

"Let's take a few days off," I said. "Let's go now."

"Really?" She looked at me askance, with a cute crooked smile, probably trying to assess whether I meant it.

"Yes!"

"This weekend," she said after consideration. "In fact, I'd like to take Thursday and Friday off to visit an old friend."

"Thursday?" I said. "You want time off tomorrow?" Of course it wasn't a problem, but I was surprised at her sudden decision.

"It's so quiet here, I... And I could buy a dress and new bathing suit."

I said, "It's fine, Penny."

★

I wrote up my notes, and after midday, handed them to Penny to type up. I included humorous descriptions of the people I'd met, like the village head with the bandy legs and wobbly walk. I mentioned questions about Manchester United and the mansions we lived in. I listed their unusual phrases and sayings. I even summarized Maria's comments about work in the south, property prices in the north and the concern over water rights.

As Penny typed, I could hear her quiet chuckles, and I was sure our relationship was on the mend.

Later, I rang DI Dickins and gave him an update.

"Where did you get the victim's name from?" I asked.

There was a pause, and I guessed he was checking his records. "It was the nearest village: Marki. You know that, Ash."

"I went there and no one knew the name. No one identified him."

"Ash," he said in the tone of a kindly uncle, "as I explained, the Cyps don't like talking, not least to authorities. They—"

"They were talking to me, Charles. Who got the name for you?"

"It will have been a 'Special'." I knew that referred to a Cypriot national policeman. They were considered second class, possibly not even real policemen, by the British. "The villagers will have spoken to him."

"All right," I said, "Then there will be a record of who he spoke to. Perhaps he got the wrong village. I noticed that sometimes there are smaller ones close by that don't appear to have names." I was being generous.

Dickins argued that the villagers probably had second thoughts about identifying him. From my experience, it seemed unlikely, and my gut told me that whoever the police Special was, he'd made up the victim's name.

*

Wolfe called before the end of the day and told me there were more documents on their way to be translated. Then he asked about my investigation into the gang-style execution.

I told him about the trip through the plains and that I'd learned the locals responded better to respect.

"Just a few words in Greek and they become your friend."

He laughed. "That's not the British way, Ash! Demand respect and beat them into submission if they don't comply. So, using your softly-softly approach, what did you learn?"

"Not a lot."

"They were still tight-lipped?"

"No, I think they honestly didn't know who those fellows were. Which is intriguing since it suggests that the bodies weren't left as a warning. And the police talk of a gang called *Chis*, or Kiss, but this meant nothing to the people I met—and, Bill, I met an awful lot."

"Don't give up, though," he said after a pause.

"I won't. There's an attitude here that some things can't be solved, they should just be accepted." I told him the Cypriot proverb about a fool and wise men.

"Sounds ridiculous," he scoffed.

"It's an ingrained attitude. So, no, I won't give up."

"Good." He paused again. "And nothing else to tell me?"

I suspected he was probing to see if I'd dropped the investigation into Mrs Johnson.

"Nothing."

"Good. As for me, do you remember Dave Rose?"

Dave Rose had been a friend working for the Palestine Police Force. The fourteen hundred or so officers were reassigned when we handed over control to the Israelis, with a large number of them going to Malaya. I understood that Rose had gone in that direction.

"He's still here," Wolfe said. "Joined the Israeli Police with a promotion."

"Why are you—?"

"—telling you this? Because if he recognizes me, we're buggered. My fuckin' operation—our fuckin' operation—will be over."

★

Penny let me take her out in the evening. We drove around the bay, past Dhekelia and on to a village by the sea. We walked along the beach holding hands and then watched waves splash into sea caves. Before finding a tavern for dinner, she showed me a white arch known as the love rock.

We talked a lot about our planned weekend away. I said I'd find accommodation in Kyrenia and promised we'd visit the castles in the mountains.

Eventually I said what had been bothering me since I'd agreed to her days off. Was her friend a girl?

"Your friend..." I said awkwardly. "What's her name?"

"Margie."

"Will I get to meet her?"

"Don't you trust me?"

"I... er..."

She laughed again. "Really, Ash, you should relax more. I'm more than happy to introduce you."

"When?"

"Maybe Margie will come back with me."

"Or I could drive you up there tomorrow morning."

She smiled. "That's kind but unnecessary. And anyway, I've already bought my bus ticket."

I started to protest and she held up a hand.

"Ash Carter!"

"Yes?"

"I've been giving this a lot of thought. You're frustrated with the execution... this Kiss case... and it may take weeks to make progress. I also know you're a good man and have been really bothered by those requests for help."

"Mrs Johnson," I said.

"Right. Like I say, I've given it a lot of thought and maybe I was being irrational. Maybe I was being a little jealous of her good looks."

"You needn't be."

She took a breath. "I think you should ask her friends what happened. Find out what happened eight months ago and who she ran off with."

TWENTY-THREE

I went door to door along the row of the married quarter's houses on Cambrai Crescent. I'd waited until mid-morning, to minimize the number of officers around. And just in case anyone might be suspicious of an SIB officer asking questions, I went in disguise. Nothing elaborate, just a plain brown suit and carrying a parcel. I also parked out of sight so that no one connected me to the Land Rover.

Each time a door was answered, I claimed that I was from the post office.

"I have a parcel for Mrs Surena Johnson," I said.

All the ladies who answered told me that Johnson lived in the end house. Of course, I knew that and explained the parcel needed to be signed for by Mrs Johnson and that we understood she had moved.

There was no answer at roughly half of the houses. I spoke to eight officers' wives and a Greek cleaner. The cleaner reminded me of Maria but appeared nervous and didn't want to be drawn into a conversation. The other ladies were happy to talk, although they had all been transferred here recently, so Mrs Johnson had left before they'd arrived.

The last door I knocked on was answered by another lady happy to have an interruption. I noted chintz curtains and I could see matching furniture behind her.

I was hot and frustrated, and she must have seen me look past her because she invited me in for lemonade.

"That'd be kind," I said, entering. "It's been a long morning. No one seems to know anything about the person I'm looking for."

"And who's that?"

She pointed to a seat and handed me lemonade.

"Mrs Surena Johnson. I need her signature for this parcel." I gave her my backstory and she accepted it without question.

"I know her," she said after a sip of her own drink. "But she's not been around for a long time. Can't Major Johnson help you?"

I smiled awkwardly. "That's where I started. The major told me he doesn't know where she is."

She looked at me and raised an eyebrow. "I don't want to blather but…"

I sat forward.

"She left eight months ago after an argument." She raised her eyebrow again.

I said, "Tell me more," as though interested in her gossip.

"There was a big bust-up and she stormed out. Not been seen since."

"So you don't know where she went?"

"No. But all very dramatic. Just up and leaving—and abandoning that poor child. I wouldn't like to leave my child with the major—not that I'm saying there's anything wrong with him, if you know what I mean?"

"Did you hear the argument?" I continued to be chatty, as though gossiping rather than investigating her disappearance.

"Unfortunately not, but Sophie did. Sophie lives next door to the major. She heard it all."

"Sophie's surname?"

"Cay. It's Sophie Cay."

★

Mrs Cay wasn't at home, and I decided to go back to the office for a break during the heat of midday. I returned in the afternoon and checked the other houses first, before trying the Cay's residence again.

This time, Sophie Cay answered. She was in her thirties with neat blonde hair and a cheeky sparkle in her blue eyes, like sunlight reflecting dew. She wore a light pink blouse with a black trim running down from each shoulder and square across her chest. The collar was tight with a black ribbon tied at the neck. Her skirt and heels were also black. I wondered if she always wore high heels around the house.

"I hear you're looking for me," she said, allowing her eyes to flash.

I matched her smile. "Yes, but I'm really looking for Mrs Johnson." I raised the parcel. "For a signature."

She nodded. "And yet I've seen you in uniform."

Busted!

"Ah," I said.

"What's your name?"

"Lieutenant Ash Carter."

Her smile broadened. "I knew it! Are you investigating Surena's disappearance, Lieutenant?"

"I need to find her."

"Why the subterfuge?"

"Because Major Johnson wouldn't be happy. I'd rather hoped to be discreet rather than underhand in any way."

She gave me tea and insisted that I talk about myself, telling her my real background before providing me with information.

Eventually, I prompted: "I understand you heard them arguing before she left—before she stormed out?"

"She didn't storm out."

"Oh?"

Mrs Cay took a sip of tea and looked like she was picturing the event. "She left in a taxi. I saw it arrive. She had the man load three suitcases and she just got in."

"The man?" I asked hopefully.

"I mean the taxi driver."

"Right. When was this?"

Mrs Cay confirmed the date eight months ago and checked her watch. "At about this time of day."

"What about her daughter?"

"At the school. Major Johnson was at Alexander."

"How did he react when he came home?"

She took a breath and looked serious for the first time. "He came over here and asked me if I'd seen anything. Apparently she'd left him a *Dear John* letter with no detail. He thought I'd know where she'd gone. He'd also asked Hazel and she'd told him nothing, so I said the same—although I didn't know anything."

"Hazel?"

"Hazel Marsland-Askew, lives at number fifteen with Captain Marsland-Askew."

Now I remembered. Colonel Dexter's adjutant had told me about Mrs Marsland-Askew.

"Do you think she knows anything—about where Mrs Johnson was going?"

Mrs Cay's eyes widened. "Who knows? Hazel normally knows everything and yet she's been very tight-lipped about it. And I'm glad."

"Glad?"

"Because, if Surena doesn't want to be found then it's best that no one says anything—if anyone knows."

I said, "Tell me about the argument."

"As I said, Lieutenant, Major Johnson wasn't there. Surena didn't storm out. She called a taxi and left. If anything, I'd say she looked excited."

"To be running off with another man."

Mrs Cay raised an eyebrow. "That's what I understand. Excited. Not after an argument."

I said, "To be clear then, there wasn't an argument?"

"Oh there were lots of arguments towards the end. I often heard him shout, although it's funny how his voice could sound different."

"People sound different when they're angry. In the army you learn to control your voice most of the time."

"Sometimes I think there's too much control," she said wistfully, and I wondered if she was thinking about her own husband, but she didn't elaborate.

We chatted some more and I finished another cup of tea. Before I went, I said, "She left for another man."

"Right." She smiled.

"Who?" I said. "Any names or ideas, Sophie?"

"No, but Hazel is your best person."

"I tried number fifteen this morning. No answer."

"She may be shopping in Nicosia, or you'll often find her at *the village* shops."

I left with a description of Mrs Marsland-Askew in case I spotted her around. I also asked that Mrs Cay said nothing about my visit.

"Mum's the word," she said, before showing me the twinkle in her eye. "And if you would like tea ever again, Lieutenant, feel free to drop by."

TWENTY-FOUR

I drove along the road and stopped at number fifteen Cambrai Crescent, where Captain and Mrs Marsland-Askew lived.

She wasn't in, but the Greek cleaner I'd seen at another house answered the door and confirmed that the captain's wife might be shopping in old Dhekelia village. Strangely, I got a different impression of the cleaner the second time. It was as though she'd had time to compose herself and wasn't nervous anymore.

She said, "Try the Ice Cream and Pastry Shop. The lady often goes there."

I drove past the shop she'd referred to but saw no one matching Mrs Marsland-Askew's description. I continued around the garrison and checked in at a large NAAFI in case she was there. Then I went back to the original line of shops and went into the Ice Cream and Pastry Shop, where I ordered a Coca-Cola.

Just as I wondered about giving up, Mrs Marsland-Askew entered, looked at me and smiled. She wore a checked dress with white collar and cuffs and broad red ribbon tie, red belt and red shoes. I thought about Mrs Cay and wondered if all of these army wives wore neck ribbons, belts and shoes that matched.

She deliberately swished her dress as she strode towards me, her red shoes clicking on the floor.

"You're the SIB chap," she said with a confident smile. "Sophie warned me."

"Warned you?"

"To be discreet." She tapped her nose. "I can do that. I was part of SOE during the war. One of the girls they parachuted into enemy territory. I know how to keep secrets, Lieutenant."

I nodded. "I received a couple of photographs of Mrs Johnson asking for help."

"Intriguing," she said, and then raised a finger as a waitress approached. She ordered tea and a scone for us both but said nothing for a while.

"Mrs Marsland—"

"—Call me Hazel." She touched her bow tie as though tightening it, but it was just for show.

"Hazel, what can you tell me about Surena Johnson?"

"What did the major tell you? I'm sure you've spoken to him."

"I have. He said that Surena left him eight months ago."

She nodded. "They weren't well suited."

"Because of the age difference, you mean?"

"Because he's so"—she dropped her voice—"controlling."

"Controlling?"

"Kept her on a short leash. In fact, he treated her like that dog of theirs. Maybe worse."

"But he got the dog for Verity, after Mrs Johnson left."

"Of course! I was just illustrating the point."

Our tea arrived and she served us both.

I said, "So you aren't surprised she left him?"

"Not in the slightest."

I said nothing.

"He was the jealous type, you see?" she said.

"She's an attractive woman."

Hazel Marsland-Askew nodded. "Surena certainly attracted a lot of attention. The major used to rant and rave. Once I saw the welts on her arms where he must have beaten her."

"Did she report him?"

"Surena was no angel. She liked the admiration men gave her. It must have made her feel good. After all, the major is about twenty years older. Yes, they would argue and fall out, but she also liked making up and the diamonds the major would buy her. So no, Lieutenant Carter, she didn't report him."

I nodded and waited for her to say more. Her eyes suggested she was just getting into the swing of things with more to divulge.

She screwed up her face as if there was a bad smell. "I don't know why she put up with the old goat for so long. What with the beating and arguing. And that batman of the major's—"

"Batman? You mean his chief clerk, Crawley?"

"Yes, him! Good-looking, stylish chap but he's always round there, fussing. Always fussing. I used to say to Digby Wallace—he's my husband, you know—that it was like there were three in that relationship. Personally, I wouldn't have stood for it."

And Surena didn't in the end, I thought. She had packed her bags and one afternoon caught a taxi.

"Can you think of a reason why she would need help?"

Mrs Marsland-Askew took a sip of tea, frowned and her eyes narrowed. "Why do you ask that?"

I showed her the photograph and note.

"You said *help*. This says *find me*. That's quite different, don't you think?" I heard a touch of sarcasm in her tone despite her smile.

"This is a second photograph. The first one asked for help."

"And where is that one?"

"Major Johnson took it from me."

"She's very pretty."

"Yes, but—"

"And you want to help her? That's nice." She raised her eyebrows and I saw a glint in her eyes. Was she hinting that I was interested because of Mrs Johnson's good looks?

I ignored the implication. "Why might she need help?" I asked again.

Mrs Marsland-Askew looked serious again. "Because of him."

"Her husband?"

"Yes. Isn't it obvious?"

I said nothing for a moment and finally nodded. The thought had struck me that Johnson had let his wife go too easily. So he'd tracked her down and now she needed protection from him.

"Where is she?" I asked.

"I don't know. And if I did, would it be wise to tell you? How do I know you aren't working for him? After all, you are an MP."

"I'm not working for him. I received the photograph asking for my help."

"Which isn't evidence. Not really. You could have written FIND ME. Major Johnson could have."

We finished our tea in silence. Neither of us had touched our scones.

"Are you paying?" she asked, after calling for the bill.

"I am."

She smiled and put both scones into her shopping basket.

"Thank you," she said. "If you can prove that you're working for Surena, by all means come back and buy me tea again."

★

I was getting into my Land Rover when the waitress appeared at the tea shop door. She beckoned to me.

"I'm sorry, sir, I couldn't help overhearing your conversation." She straightened her white pinafore nervously. "You mentioned Mrs Johnson."

"Yes, I'm looking for her."

"Mrs Marsland-Askew isn't the best person to speak to," she said awkwardly, like she was telling tales out of school.

"And you know who is?"

"Mrs Johnson has a closer friend. They used to come in here all the time together. She works in the hospital. If anyone knows anything it will be Isabelle Laurent."

TWENTY-FIVE

I found Sister Isabelle Laurent at BMH Nightingale. We stood in a quiet corridor and she confirmed that she often had tea with Mrs Johnson.

"Oh my God!" she said when I produced the photograph and showed her the FIND ME! note. "I've not seen her for such a long time. What do you think happened?"

She rapidly blinked warm brown eyes. Her shiny brown hair was pulled back and tied up beneath the nurse's hat. Overall I saw a friendly, open face, although possibly this was exaggerated by the hat ties that pushed her ears forward.

I said, "I don't know. I'm just starting to investigate."

"Do you think the message is from her?"

"That's my working assumption."

She nodded and asked me who I'd spoken to and what I'd learned. When I mentioned Hazel Marsland-Askew, Sister Laurent winced.

"Did Hazel tell you she was ex-SOE? She claims she was some kind of secret operative in the war. Treat what she says with a pinch of salt, Lieutenant. She's a chinwag, a gossip. Surena didn't have many friends, but she talked to me because of our French heritage, because of her nursing background, but mostly because Verity is my daughter's best friend."

She paused and looked at me. I was wondering how well Sister Laurent really knew Mrs Johnson. I'd heard people rubbish someone else in order to give more credence to their own testimony or opinion.

She looked back at me with innocence in her blinking eyes.

After a moment, I asked, "Why do you think Surena might need help?"

"I don't know. Perhaps you need to find her first. After all, that's what this photograph says."

"I will, but as her friend, surely you have an opinion?"

She thought about it for a minute, possibly wondering how to say what was on her mind, before shaking her head.

"All right," I said, "we'll come back to that, but how have things changed? Why send me the photographs now? Why not straight after she left?"

"I don't know. Perhaps the major is looking for her. Perhaps she wants Verity to join her. I don't know, Lieutenant. As I said, I think you need to find her and ask."

I thought about Mrs Johnson leaving without Verity. It must have been difficult to leave her daughter, especially with the tyrant that Johnson sounded like.

Then Sister Laurent surprised me: "Did you know that Verity isn't actually her daughter. She's her niece."

"I didn't know that." The new information gave me more confidence that the nurse was being honest about their friendship. Maybe I should disregard Mrs Marsland-Askew's opinions. Maybe Johnson didn't hurt his wife.

The nurse was nodding. "Doesn't make it easier for either of them though. Verity is still upset. Verity's mother was Surena's sister, killed in France. That's where the major met Surena. He was in the Lille hospital, and when he left for England he took Surena with him. Verity was just a baby, and I think Surena felt like she owed the major for saving them both. That's why she married him."

This new detail was more confirmation that I should believe Sister Laurent. To check what I'd previously been told, I asked, "Did the major ever beat Surena?"

"Not that I know of. She never complained."

She didn't report it.

"So you never saw any welt marks?" I asked, questioning the accusation made by Mrs Marsland-Askew.

"No."

I thought about the other things Mrs Marsland-Askew had told me. "Did Surena flirt with other men?"

"Absolutely, she did. Look, it's probably wrong of me to tell you, but the two of them... well, I think she liked it a bit. Maybe she'd go too far and they would argue, but he'd make it up to her afterwards."

I must have looked unsure because she continued.

"And the major liked the... what you might call a tease."

"A tease?"

"He liked the fact that other men wanted his wife. I think he actively encouraged it. I don't understand it myself, but I think he got excited by it."

That didn't tally with what Mrs Marsland-Askew had told me. She said they'd argued about her behaviour and he'd made up by giving her diamonds.

I asked, "Did Johnson give her diamonds as a way of apologizing?"

"He gave her diamonds. Gave her anything she wanted. I have no doubt he loved her. As you can see, she's a beautiful girl—elegant and somewhat sophisticated too."

"But she wasn't an angel?" I said, repeating what the other lady had told me.

She waited as two doctors walked past us in the corridor.

When we couldn't be heard again, she said, "She was a free spirit, Lieutenant. To be frank, the major didn't give her diamonds to apologize for being jealous. He gave her diamonds to keep her."

"You are her best friend," I said, "Where is she?"

"I don't know."

"Who was the man?"

A small smile played on her lips. "There were a few, but she didn't tell me who or where she was going."

I waited.

She said, "I find it odd that she's been gone for eight months and not been in touch with me or Verity. I'm concerned."

"What did she tell you, Isabelle?"

She breathed in and out, like she was considering the situation. "I don't want to betray her confidence."

"She's asked for my help. You're worried about her, so tell me what you know."

"Do you promise this won't get back to Major Johnson?"

"Not from me."

I met her eyes, hoping she'd read my honesty, but she shook her head.

"Tell me something," I said eventually.

"All right," she said, "I don't know much, just that she met her new man at Maxims. She said it was true love and kept him a secret from her husband. All I know is his name is Alex."

*

Penny called me before I left the office for the evening.

"Missing me?" she asked.

"Of course!"

"I'm having fun. How's your day been?"

So I told her about my meeting with the three ladies and what I'd learned. Johnson was either beating his wife or he wasn't. He lavished her with gifts including diamonds, either to keep her or by way of apology for losing his temper. Or perhaps both. However, Mrs Johnson wasn't innocent. She liked to flirt with other men and finally fell in love with someone called Alex and ran away with him.

"Ash, it seems to me that Mrs Johnson is afraid of her husband. He sounds controlling and domineering. It's no wonder she left him."

"But it doesn't explain why she needs help now, eight months later."

"Unless she's afraid he'll do something. Ash, you need to be very careful. If Johnson finds out…"

"I know. I've promised her nurse friend that I wouldn't divulge anything to Johnson."

We spoke some more and I was talking about our weekend away when, mid-sentence, the pips started. She said the money had run out.

I immediately asked the operator to place a return call and the line was answered. The General Post Office in Nicosia. I described Penny, but the operator there couldn't see anyone matching her description.

I was becoming accustomed to Penny's company. It's one thing to miss someone but the feeling is heightened when a call suddenly ends. It was like a hole had appeared and swallowed her up.

TWENTY-SIX

I pushed open the door to Maxims and stood for a moment in the reception area. There were toilets to my right and a concierge desk and cloakroom to my left. I smelled stale smoke and a cocktail of cooked food and beer. The whine of a vacuum cleaner broke the silence.

I strode through the double doors into the main hall. Pubs and bars always strike me as sad places when empty, but Maxims didn't have the usual grime of such establishments. Granted there was the smell that had immediately assaulted me, but an army of young Greek men was busily cleaning the place, and in the daylight, I saw clean linen and curtains.

As I approached, the man with the vacuum cleaner looked up and stopped the dreadful noise.

"Who's in charge?" I asked.

"Mr Simons. You'll find him in the office."

He pointed and I walked in the direction indicated, through a door marked 'Private' and along a corridor.

I saw a tall, thin man come out of an office, glance in my direction and then disappear through a door on the other side.

When I reached the door I saw it was an exit to the rear delivery area. Opposite was the manager's office.

"Mr Simons?" I said leaning in.

"What? Yes, who are you?"

As I introduced myself, my back brain registered that he was white whereas all of the staff were locals.

Simons had a ruddy complexion and quick eyes. At first, I thought he looked nervous but then decided it was because he was overweight and the warmth of the day found its way into this small office.

"You're not in uniform," he said, eyeing me.

"I'm not obliged to wear it and these are cooler clothes," I replied. "Do you need to wear that jacket and tie?"

He glanced at his blue suit and shrugged. "Keeping up appearances," he said smiling for the first time. "Now, Lieutenant—Carter did you say?—how can I be of service?"

I pulled out the photograph of Mrs Johnson with the major folded back. "Do you know this lady?"

His eyes narrowed as he studied the photograph. "Good-looking woman."

"Yes."

"Couldn't fail to recognize her, although I've not seen her for a long time. That's Mrs Johnson. Distinctive hair."

"Right," I said. "I'm looking for her."

"Are you now?" He studied me, then, "Why?"

I let the question hang in the air.

"I'd like to take a look at your membership list."

He smiled kindly. "You won't find her in there, Lieutenant. Just the gentlemen members." He paused. "Major Johnson is in there of course but I presume you don't need his details."

I said, "Could I see it please?"

After a hesitation, he said, "Of course. We'll need to go to the concierge desk."

Simons took me back along the corridor and into the hall. I felt all eyes upon us although the staff continued to look busy. At the desk, Simons fished out a key, opened a drawer and pulled out a register I recognized. My details were in there.

"Who are you looking for?" he asked as he opened the page. Then: "Oh, I see you joined us a week last Saturday. Glad to have you as a member, Lieutenant."

"Alex," I said. "I'm looking for a member called Alex."

Simons flicked a glance at me and then back to the ledger. "How far back do I go?"

"Let's say within the last twelve months."

"As far as I'm aware, there's only one Alex in here then."

"His details, please?"

The manager turned the pages and then pointed. "There you go. Sub-Lieutenant Alexander Lazzell."

I noted the address. "And you're sure there are no other Alex or Alexanders?"

Simons slid the ledger towards me so that I could handle it. "He's the only one for at least two years."

I flicked through and confirmed that there were men named Alexander, but who hadn't been for more than two years, presumably redeployed.

I thanked the manager and he offered me his hand. It was pudgy and moist and I wiped my palm on my trousers as I left.

Outside again, I spotted the tall man I'd seen earlier in the corridor. He was sitting in the cab of a dusty blue-grey truck.

The way he turned his head away gave me the distinct impression that he had been watching me. I deliberately detoured around his vehicle to reach my Land Rover. I'd already noted that he was white and had the brush haircut of a squaddie. But his relaxed posture told me this was no soldier. I knew he was tall and thin from earlier in the corridor. Close up, I saw he had unusual features and scarring, as though his cheekbones had collapsed. I'd seen something similar before, after a road traffic accident. A face scarred around motorcycle goggles.

He looked straight at me again.

"Motorbike accident?" I asked.

He looked confused, then shook his head when I drew a line across my face.

"What? No." I couldn't place his accent. Maybe south of England, maybe London. Uneducated and higher-pitched than I'd expected for his height.

"Do you need help?"

He forced a laugh. "What? No! I was just daydreaming."

Then the scarred man fired up the engine and reversed his truck away.

★

Sub-Lieutenant Lazzell was based at HMS Mercury, the Royal Navy shore base. The address said Limassol, but it was around the bay, beyond the old town and harbour.

Army bases are typically regimented—mostly straight lines and functional. After I drove through the security gates and along Main Drive, I could see that Mercury was deliberately designed with curves and variety.

At the first junction, a small village-style church was on my right. On my left, there was an administration block and a sign with twenty or so locations noted. Most were pointing straight ahead. I was looking for Nelson Block and continued past *heads* and workshops before a spur took me towards Nelson.

This was the officer's block, and a desk clerk offered me water and a chair in a meeting room while he located Lazzell.

I waited thirty minutes before emerging from the room and asking whether Lazzell was on his way.

"Sorry, Lieutenant," the clerk said. "He's currently in Mountbatten."

According to the sign outside, Mountbatten Block was for junior rates, with a dining hall, laundry and Warrant Officers' mess. But there was also the Mercury Club, and that's where I found Lazzell.

We made eye contact but he carried on with his meeting, and after five minutes I decided to intervene.

"If I may have a word, sir?" I said.

"Are you the chap from Branch who wants a chat?"

I held out my hand. "Lieutenant Carter."

He sighed. "Right. Fine. You can have five minutes, Lieutenant."

Lazzell took me to a table out of earshot of others before speaking again. "So what's this about, Lieutenant? I trust it's important."

"It's about Mrs Johnson."

His jaw tensed. "I've nothing to say."

I raised my voice slightly. "I'm investigating Mrs Johnson's disappearance and I've been given your name."

He glared at me. "Right. Fine. Let's take a walk."

We were soon outside and heading for an area marked Broadwalk.

"Who sent you?" he asked finally.

I showed him the photograph. "She was last seen eight months ago—before she got in a taxi and met someone. Was that you?"

"No."

"I was given your name."

"By whom?"

"Captain, tell me about your connection with Mrs Johnson. And don't deny it because there clearly is one."

We walked a few paces and I heard his breathing. Then he said, "As you can see, she's gorgeous. What you can't see is that she liked to flirt."

"And she flirted with you?"

"Right. But we ended it before she stopped going to the club."

"And that was eight months ago?"

"More like a year. But listen here, old chap, it wasn't just me. She was flirting with lots of men."

"Why did you stop? You said you stopped before she disappeared." I twisted his words but he didn't correct me, although I saw concern in his eyes.

"Because I got a note from Johnson. He warned me off. He bloody well threatened me!"

TWENTY-SEVEN

I waited for him to say more, but he said nothing and stared at the nearby parade ground.

I said, "I need you to start from the beginning, Alex. Tell me everything."

He breathed heavily before speaking. "Surena was quite the flirt. I'd heard rumours that she was a bit of a goer. The major didn't dance and seemed happy to watch his wife enjoy herself on the dance floor. Men would cut in, so she'd dance with quite a few. But she made me feel special. It was the occasional contact and look in her eyes."

His words made me think of the mistake I'd made last Saturday letting Penny dance with lots of men while I worked the room asking questions. I dismissed the distracting thoughts.

"So you knew she was flirting with you."

"Yes. And then later, we went outside for air and we kissed. I felt she was teasing me and she broke it off before it got too serious. That happened the second time."

"Tell me about the second time."

"Well it started the same way, but with more flirting. Then, when we were outside, the kissing turned to…" He paused and looked out across a parade ground. "It's really hard for a chap to talk about it—you know, in the cold light of day."

"Try. Imagine you're bragging to your mates."

He stared off into the distance. "It's not just that. You're SIB. You're a detective. And based on your photograph, I surmise that Mrs Johnson is missing."

"Did you have anything to do with her disappearance?" I said, playing along with his assumption.

"I don't think so." He paused and looked at me earnestly. "But maybe unintentionally."

"Explain."

He took a breath. "There was a lot of heavy petting—you know, really heavy stuff. She drove me crazy but we were both out of control."

Being out of control with a girl, I could relate to that. As he said it, I couldn't help thinking of Penny again.

He took another breath. "She undid my fly and got out my John Thomas. We messed around for a while until she broke it off suddenly and said she had to get back inside."

"And that was it?"

"Until the following Saturday. At first, I thought she was ignoring me. I thought she regretted going so far the week before and wondered whether her husband had put a stop to her antics." He paused for a long time.

"But…" I prompted.

"She danced with everyone except me. She was her usual flirty self, but my advances were rejected. That was until towards the end of the evening. We didn't dance. She looked at me in the way girls do, and made sure I watched her walk to the exit. Then she stopped and held up a cigarette, looking at me as if asking for a light even though I was across the room. So I followed, and once outside, she grabbed me and we started at it again. Slowly at first, but then the heavy stuff." He took a breath, preparing himself. I waited.

He said, "She blew my whistle."

"Blew your—"

"Come on, Lieutenant. You know. She went down on her knees for me."

"OK," I said.

"But that wasn't the shocking thing. While she was doing it, I saw someone in the shadows watching. I think it was her husband. My immediate thought was that he would be mad, but when we went back inside, he acted as though nothing had happened."

"He didn't seem angry with her?"

"No. I even wondered if he'd been enjoying it. Maybe he liked seeing that as much as seeing his wife on the dance floor with other men. So I was looking forward to a repeat performance the following week. But they didn't turn up."

"And that was the last time you saw her?" I said, intrigued by this story.

"No, they started coming again, but I'd been warned off by then. Johnson sent me the note threatening me. Telling me to avoid Surena and never talk about it—or else."

I asked if he'd kept the note, but he hadn't. Although he said the major wasn't foolish enough to sign it.

When I left Lazzell, I said I would be in touch, although I doubted he'd tell me anything else.

On the drive back to Larnaca, I thought about what he'd told me. I believed him. I'd also asked for the names of other officers who she'd had relations with but he claimed he didn't know who they were. I didn't believe that. However, I figured they'd been warned off too and Lazzell didn't want to identify them as potential suspects.

What he'd told me left me feeling unbalanced. On the one hand, Johnson was perhaps titillated by his wife's flirtatious behaviour, and possibly even enjoyed watching her sexual activity with other men. He hadn't shown any anger at the club, and yet he later threatened her potential lover.

Lazzell had pointed out that he lived in single quarters. He thought that ruled him out. But it didn't. The story of

Mrs Johnson leaving with a man made me assume that he was not in the military or just leaving Cyprus. But the note said HELP ME! What if they hadn't left? What if he'd tricked her? It struck me that there was a real possibility that he was still living the single life and keeping her somewhere against her will.

Either this was about someone holding her or Johnson hunting his wife.

Whichever, I resolved to confront the husband. However, it was Friday and I had something much more important to do.

TWENTY-EIGHT

Two hours later, I was outside Penny's apartment in my best clothes. The arrangement was for me to pick her up on Saturday morning and then drive to Kyrenia. But I couldn't wait and wanted to show enthusiasm for her return plus some spontaneity. Red roses I'd bought in Limassol added to the romantic gesture, I hoped.

But what I hadn't bargained for was Penny being out.

I entered her apartment and looked around for signs that she'd been there. Surely she was back from Nicosia by now?

However, I saw no evidence. Her kettle was cold and it didn't look like someone had been in and gone out. There were none of the usual signs, like a jacket tossed over a chair or clothes on the bed. The sinks in her kitchen and bathroom were also dry.

Checking made me feel like I was prying, but I started to worry. Darkness was closing in fast.

I was about to leave when I saw her running up her path.

Flinging open the door and stepping outside, I almost gave her a heart attack.

"Ash!"

"Is everything all right?" I asked, both concerned and relieved.

"Yes, oh yes!" she panted, taking the roses from me. "Thank you for these. They're beautiful. Sorry that I'm so late. I missed the bus, had to catch the last one."

I hugged her hard, and after hugging me back, she pushed away.

"I thought I was seeing you tomorrow."

"Grab your things, baby," I said in my best romantic voice. "We're going tonight."

For a moment I thought she would turn me down, but then her face softened.

"Lovely. Let me clean up and we'll be on our way." She went inside and I followed.

"Buy anything nice?" I asked, nodding at the bag in her hand.

"Just odds and sods." She tossed the bag onto the sofa but it slid onto the floor. I went to pick it up.

"Would you unzip me?"

She had her back to me and I undid the top clasp and pulled down the blouse's zip. Perspiration speckled her back.

She didn't walk away until I kissed her neck. Then she took a pace and turned around.

"I've missed you," I said, reaching for her and hoping for another kiss.

She smiled and pushed me away. "Wait, I won't be long. Just get out of these slacks and put on a nice dress."

*

I thundered north and went from the little green hills outside Larnaca, through the long harsh plain to the capital, then into cooling air below the Kyrenia Mountains. A full moon followed us and eventually lit pine trees that towered like ghostly grey sentinels.

Then we were over the top and descending on a steep, winding road with the flickering lights of the town welcoming us like a siren's call.

The hotel overlooked the castle and harbour. I awoke to the clink of fishermen's boats and the arms of my lover. But it wasn't until I opened the curtains that I fully understood the beauty of Kyrenia: an old port with an azure sea, a long spit of sand and flowers everywhere. Colourful flowers growing by the roads, in beds and in window boxes. This was another country, not the subsistence life of the Mesaoria Plain or the regimented British Army world of the south, but natural and lush and relaxing.

After breakfast, we toured the twisting lanes of the town before climbing a track lined with pink and purple cyclamen. Here we found the town of Bellapais and enjoyed lunch at a tavern boasting the Tree of Idleness. Apparently, to sit in its shade would result in the inability to do any work in the future. This didn't stop a cluster of old men enjoying their coffee and game of chess under the tree.

I greeted them in the Greek that Maria had taught me and it brought smiles and waves. Our attempt at conversation ended there until an English speaker joined our table and told us the town's history and that we should visit the abbey.

Accompanied by the murmur of pigeons, we followed the cobble path to the abbey on a high bluff. Far below we could see motor cars on the roads that snaked through the valley of palm trees and a splash of colour from the carpet of flowers. To the south, we could see over the mountain to the plain, with Nicosia shimmering in the heat like a mirage.

We chatted about nothing and about everything, although Penny insisted that we leave work behind. Based on my experience with her exactly a week ago, I decided she was right.

Later we drove west and saw ladies at spinning wheels and men with camel trains. We passed beautiful houses surrounded by lemon trees and fishing shacks along the beaches.

Outside Lapithos, I had to brake suddenly as a water truck came through the gates in front of me. The property had a high chain fence rather than the more typical wall. Inside, I could see a large orchard and a castle-like turret poking up above the trees. I looked for a name, but there was just a stone marker with a red flower beside the road.

Then we were in the beach resort of Lapithos with its mix of a quaint old town and bohemian shacks on rocky outcrops. We swam, ate lunch and contemplated the ocean.

Back in Kyrenia, we toured the castle, spent time in coffee houses and boutiques, ate dinner in a tavern, and returned to our hotel to make love.

On Sunday morning, I drove east along the coast, through orange groves and fields of yellow fennel. We saw the coast of Turkey like an illusion across the sea, rising, falling and disappearing as we rode the twisting hills.

I had planned that we return on Sunday night, but we wanted to see the Byzantine castles, and by the time we reached Kantara Castle it was too dark to see it properly. It was after ten and would take at least three hours to get home. So I drove down to the coast and found a place with lights on advertising available rooms.

I couldn't imagine the landlady got much business and figured her inflated price was part compensation and part recognition of our need.

However, in the morning, the sun rose over a spectacular view of rocks and the sea. And the breakfast filled me to bursting.

We drove back to Kantara Castle, where a kestrel circled over the towering white ruins. Eating a picnic, we made nonsense plans about staying here forever and forgetting work. Perhaps the shade of the tree in Bellapais had affected me.

But I hadn't told Wolfe I would be taking a long weekend break and he had said that more translation work was on its way.

So, reluctantly, I drove over the mountains and along the Nicosia road, back to the real world.

The heat of the day was gone by the time I entered Larnaca. I said I'd drop Penny at her home, then check the office for messages and post before seeing her later.

However, as we pulled into her street, I immediately noticed vehicles outside her apartment: a military police van and Land Rovers.

I parked and got out. "Wait a second, Penny," I said.

"Lieutenant Carter?" an officer said, approaching me. It took a moment to realize he'd come out of her front door. I didn't recognize him, but he was a first lieutenant. He signalled, and four more uniformed MPs closed in behind him.

I said, "Did Major Johnson send you?"

The man looked at me, then past me at my vehicle.

"What's going on, Lieutenant? Is this about Mrs Johnson?" I said, starting to think that the major was pulling a stunt.

The lieutenant shook his head. "It's about Sergeant Major Ellis, sir."

"Sergeant Major Ellis?" I turned. I could barely see Penny in my passenger seat, but I threw her a smile anyway. "Good."

"Good, sir?"

"The complaint I made against him..." The lieutenant's brow furrowed. I began to doubt what was going on.

He said, "Sir, is that Miss Penny Cartwright in your vehicle?"

"Yes."

The four MPs moved quickly from behind the officer and closed in on my Land Rover.

"Wait a minute!" I said. "What the hell is going on?"

"Sir," the lieutenant said, "We're arresting Miss Cartwright for the murder of CSM Michael Ellis."

PART TWO

"Does a raven not peck out the eye of a raven?"
- Cypriot Proverb

MURRAY BAILEY

TWENTY-NINE

"This is bloody ridiculous!" I snapped at Johnson in his office.

"Lieutenant Carter, I'm giving you the courtesy of my time this morning. Don't test my patience, young man."

I didn't give two hoots for the major's patience, but I did want information, so I decided to take a breath and calm down.

I said, "My apologies, sir. Please tell me what happened."

"Miss Cartwright lured CSM Ellis from the Kings Head pub at nineteen fifteen on Friday night. She took him to an alley and stabbed him through the left eye. He's currently in the morgue but there is little doubt that the blade pierced his brain and killed him."

"It can't have been Penny."

"And so speaks her lover." He raised his eyebrows at me. He knew about our relationship. So what? That didn't make her any less innocent.

I said, "She couldn't have met Ellis in Larnaca, because she was with me."

"At nineteen fifteen?"

I hesitated. I could lie, but that wasn't in my nature. "Shortly afterwards."

"What time precisely?"

"I didn't check my watch at the moment she arrived home but I would guess about nineteen forty-five. But that's close enough."

Major Johnson pulled a disbelieving face. "Close enough?"

"Because at nineteen fifteen she was on the Nicosia bus. She then ran home and was with me."

Johnson's mouth opened and closed. "You have evidence she was on the bus?"

"No, but—"

"Of course you don't. We have witnesses who saw her outside the Kings Head. And we know she had a motive: you told me yourself that she accused Ellis of raping Miss Cartwright's sister."

"Ah, you accept the rape allegation now?"

He smiled thinly. "You had no evidence of the rape and you have no evidence of her being on the Nicosia bus. I thought you Branch men were good at detective work. It appears I was mistaken."

I breathed in and breathed out. No point in getting angry. "I'd like to see her if I may, sir."

Penny was in the military prison that they called 'the Glasshouse'. It was a reference to the prison in Aldershot which had been damaged in riots two years previously. This wasn't made of glass but it was just as hot and airless.

Penny was in the same clothes she'd worn for our weekend away and sitting on a bench, staring at a wall. She'd spent a night in here and her make-up was smeared through crying. When I put my arms around her she sobbed into my shoulder.

I said, "This is nonsense, Penny. I'll get you out."

"They're saying I murdered Sergeant Major Ellis," she said after composing herself. "I hated him, but I didn't kill anyone, Ash."

I said, "Do you own a stiletto blade?"

She shook her head. "Why would I—? Of course not!"

"Exactly. They say Ellis was stabbed through the eye with a stiletto blade."

"Like assassins use?"

"Exactly, like an assassin would use."

She shook her head again. "This is a nightmare."

"You'll be fine," I said. "We just need to prove you were on the Nicosia bus at seven thirty."

"How?"

"The bus ticket. Do you still have it?"

"Why would I keep—? Wait! I think it's in my slacks. I remember putting it in my pocket after the conductor punched it."

"Great. I'll get it."

She smiled weakly. "I must look a state."

"I'll make sure they let you clean up."

"Why am I here, Ash?"

I wondered whether sleep deprivation had affected her memory. "Because they think you killed Ellis."

"No, I mean why here? Why a military prison? I work for you, but I'm not in the military. I'm a civilian. Why aren't I in a police station?"

"Because it's a military matter."

She put her head in her hands. "This is crazy."

"Yes. I'll get you out, Penny. I will."

"How can they think it was me?"

"Witnesses. They claim there were three witnesses."

"Do you know who they are?"

I'd obtained the names from Johnson on the way to the jail. "Two of them are army. Warrant Officer Samuel Crane and"—I paused—"Sergeant Gary Payne."

She looked at me with disbelief.

"Yes, him," I said.

"The man you punched. The man from 6GDU?"

I nodded.

"How can he be trusted? One of Mike Ellis's cronies! That hardly seems fair."

I nodded again and hugged her. She was right, and Payne's bias should work in our favour.

★

Payne was waiting for me at the base when I arrived the following day. I would be able to interview him providing he had a colleague present. We didn't exchange pleasantries as we met and walked into a Nissen hut. I smiled at the second man as we sat on opposite sides of a table. He looked familiar and I think he was one of the others from the cinema three weeks ago.

I said, "Tell me about last Friday night. What do you know about how Mike Ellis died?"

Payne didn't immediately respond, and he exchanged glances with the other man.

I said, "I'm not trying to catch you out, Payne. I just want the truth. I want to know what happened."

Payne said, "Well, it's not really about Friday night. Not really."

"What do you mean?"

"I mean, I thought I'd seen the girl before. When I saw her talking to Mike on the Friday before at the Kings Head. It wasn't until his murder that I realized it was the same girl who had been with you."

"You realized later?"

"Well, I didn't see her whole face, just side-on like. I put two and two together."

He must have read the disbelief on my face.

"It was her, I tell you. I swear."

"To be clear. When you say *later*, when was that?"

"On Saturday after we knew he'd been murdered."

From Payne's statement, I was surprised he could be considered a witness. The case was already looking as flimsy as tissue paper.

He said, "I put two and two together because she made a date with him for Friday night."

"Let's be clear, Sergeant. Did you see her on Friday."

"No, but—"

"And you can't be certain it was her on the previous Friday."

"Well—"

"You didn't see her whole face."

"Yes, but—"

"Thank you for your time, Sergeant."

I left 6GDU much happier than when I'd arrived. My next visit was to Warrant Officer Crane at Alexander Barracks.

He was accompanied by another sergeant and both men saluted as I entered.

"At ease," I said. "This is just a chat."

Crane seemed to relax.

I began with: "How did you know Sergeant Major Ellis?"

"I'd seen him around—mostly in the Kings Head in Larnaca. He went there most Fridays."

"How long have you been in Cyprus, Sergeant?"

"A month, sir."

I'd already figured he'd transferred from Palestine, so he possibly hadn't had time to form a close friendship with the victim.

I said, "Tell me about Friday night. What did you know on Friday about how Sergeant Major Ellis died?"

"Nothing."

"I'm sorry?"

"Sir, I didn't know how Ellis died—not until I heard later."

I nodded. "All right. What did you witness?"

"Well, Dick and I"—he nodded towards the other sergeant—"were at the pub. It was very busy and we were outside having a ciggy. Sergeant Major Ellis was inside."

"What time was this?"

"We arrived at eighteen forty. Ellis arrived ten minutes later."

"Approximately," the other man said.

Crane inclined his head. "Approximately. I didn't actually check my watch."

I said, "Continue."

"Some time after nineteen hundred hours—I guess about quarter past—Ellis came out and passed us and walked to the end of the building. He approached a woman and the two of them went down the alley on the right."

The alley he referred to led to the road behind the pub. Ellis had been found beyond the next road between two buildings.

I was thinking about the timing. The less time between the bus arriving and Penny getting home, the better.

"You said you guess quarter past. Could it have been later?"

Crane shrugged. I suppose so. But not much.

That made me smile. I could work with the uncertainty.

"Had you seen the woman before?" I asked.

"I noticed her standing outside the pub. I clocked her because I thought she would go in or was waiting for someone."

"Sergeant White," I said, addressing the other man, "You were there."

"Yes, sir."

"What did you see?"

"I'm not a witness, sir."

I kept my voice casual. "It's all right, I'm just asking informally what you saw."

"I remember a girl in the shadows, sir. White raised his eyes so I knew she was a looker."

"Did you see her face?"

"No, sir, that's why I'm not a witness. I did see Sergeant Major Ellis come out and walk past, but again, I didn't see where he went."

"That was just me," Crane confirmed.

I said, "And how did you know it was Penny Cartwright?"

"I didn't. It was after twenty forty-five when the MPs showed up and started questioning everyone. I told them what I saw and it seems I'm the only one who saw Ellis meet the girl."

"Penny Cartwright has been arrested. Again, how did you know who she was?"

"I was shown a photograph on Saturday. It was her all right."

"But you just saw her for a fleeting moment as she walked past."

"Like I said, she was a looker. I remembered her face."

"How dark was it?"

"There was a full moon, but she was in the shadows."

"So you didn't get a good look at her face."

He shook his head. "Sorry, sir, but I'm sure it was her."

I had to agree that Penny was attractive enough to catch men's eyes. However, the evidence was still circumstantial. It hadn't been Penny who had met Ellis. And based on what I'd heard, whomever Ellis met didn't necessarily kill him.

I thanked the men for their time and went off to find the third witness.

THIRTY

I wondered how they'd identified Penny so quickly. Payne thought it was my girlfriend. He said he'd seen her before and he had. He remembered her from the confrontation at the cinema. Not from the meeting at the pub. And Crane just saw her face in the shadows. Crane had been shown a photograph on Saturday and confirmed her identity.

The first two witnesses left me feeling like there was no case against Penny, but that all changed when I spoke to the third witness: Mr Gunn.

"I saw her run," he said. The man was an accountant who had been working late. He'd seen a man and girl go down the side of the building.

"For sex," he said disapprovingly. He had small dark eyes and darker hair that needed a wash and cut. The room smelled of old paper and dust. "Happens all the time. They come out of the pub with a prostitute and find somewhere dark to do the deed."

We were in his office and I looked through dusty windows at the street below.

"Show me," I said, "Show me where you saw them."

He closed the heavy ledger in front of him and pushed back his chair. "I've already explained it to your chaps," he grumbled but led me down the old wooden staircase and out into the daylight.

We walked west for a hundred yards then he pointed between two buildings. I noted that the Kings Head was on the main road to my left. Outside in the bright sunshine, it was hard to imagine that the alley would be dark.

"From there," he said, pointing across the road, "down into here."

"What time was this?"

"I er... I left work at seven thirty, so..."

"You were just leaving work?"

"Yes, getting on my bicycle."

I thought, a hundred yards in the dark, then said, "Where do you live?"

He gave me a street name.

"Which direction is that in—approximately?"

He pointed east.

I scrutinized him, but he didn't seem to realize there was a discrepancy. I filed that information away for later and returned to his story. "So you saw them go into the alley. Did you see her face?"

"No."

I breathed with relief. "OK. Tell me what happened next."

"She ran out again after a couple of minutes. Too quick... I... I suspected something."

"Did you actually see her come back out of the alley?"

"Yes."

"Then what?"

"Well at first I thought she was fleeing from the man, but when he didn't immediately appear, I looked down where they'd gone. And I saw him lying on the floor."

"Did you check on him?"

"No. Well, I took a few paces in, just to be sure."

"Then what did you do?"

"I followed her on my bicycle. Kept my distance. I followed her all the way to her house."

"You saw her go in?"

"Yes. Well, not straight away. She met a man on the doorstep and they went inside together. So I saw the house and told the police." He gave me the address and I blanched. It was Penny's address all right, and the man he'd seen had been me.

"But that's about a mile," I said. "You're claiming she ran for a mile?"

"She did."

I scrutinized him again and shook my head. "Mr Gunn, I think you aren't telling me the whole truth."

He swallowed.

"You were preparing to cycle home, east, when you saw them go into the alley."

"Er... yes."

"After about two minutes she came out again. You took a long time getting your bicycle ready. Or were you cycling and looking the other way?"

Gunn said nothing.

I hadn't noticed a bicycle either inside or outside the office. I said, "Where's your bicycle?"

"I didn't bring it today."

"Ah," I said, as though that told me a great deal. He looked at me, his small eyes appearing worried.

I pointed back towards the office. "A hundred yards away. You didn't really see anything, did you? Or did you just see someone run out of the alley?"

Gunn bit his lip.

I smiled. This wasn't a reliable witness.

He looked at the ground. "I was hoping... man to man, can I tell you the truth?"

"You better had!"

"I... I wasn't a hundred yards away. I was... I was hanging around."

"Hanging around?"

"I did see them come from the alley beside the pub, cross the road and go down this space."

I said nothing.

He swallowed and blinked. "I come here most Fridays and Saturdays."

And then I got it. "You're a Peeping Tom!"

He nodded sheepishly, but said, "I don't like that term."

Damn! The inconsistency in his story was to cover his embarrassment. He wasn't leaving work, he was just waiting for couples to leave the pub and find a secluded spot.

I let him worry for a moment then said, "It doesn't matter why you were there or what you were doing. What matters is what you saw."

"Yes."

"Did you see the young lady run from the alley?"

"I did."

"Did you follow her to her house, as you described?"

"Yes. The man gave her flowers."

So he had seen us. He saw me give Penny the roses.

"Are you absolutely sure it was the same girl?"

He looked thoughtful. "Well, yes, it must have been."

"Must have been?" Hope beat rapidly in my chest. "Must have been?"

"Because of the timing. Only…"

"Only?"

"Only she seemed to be different."

"How different, Mr Gunn?"

"It was dark of course, so I can't be sure, but the hair…"

I waited for him to explain.

"I thought she looked different. She had a headscarf at first and later she didn't but that's not it. I think maybe it was the hair. A different style possibly to what I thought before."

Now it was my turn to swallow. "Mr Gunn, what did you think before?"

"I thought it was curly. Remember, it was night-time, but I got the impression it had a touch of red perhaps."

THIRTY-ONE

I found Sergeant Crane supervising a class on explosives. He wasn't speaking, and approached when I caught his attention.

"I told you everything I know, Lieutenant," he said when we were outside the classroom.

"Tell me about the girl you saw. And don't think of the photograph you were shown. Think back to Friday night and describe her."

He closed his eyes for a while before speaking. "Well, as I said, very attractive. She had a tan, slim with fine features." He closed his eyes again. "Early twenties, I'd say." He shook his head. "Boy, it's hard to describe someone and explain why you found them attractive."

"What else do you remember?"

"She had a loose-fitting coat or jacket—I could see she was slim under it. I think she was wearing a dress and she had a bag. Couldn't tell you what the colours were. The coat was dark, maybe black. The bag was possibly light brown. I wasn't really paying attention to the outfit."

I took a breath. Penny had turned up wearing a dark blue cotton jacket over her blouse and I'd have described her bag as tan-coloured. However, I was sure these were common. The real information was the dress. Penny hadn't been wearing a dress, she'd had slacks on. I was a hundred percent sure of that. And there was the other inconsistency mentioned by Mr Gunn.

I hadn't wanted to prompt him, but since he wasn't forthcoming, I said, "Tell me about her hair."

"Her hair?"

"Could you see her hair? What colour was it?"

He smiled. "Oh, of course, didn't I already say? She had reddish-brown hair. I could see it under the scarf."

"You're sure?"

"Yes."

"Style?"

"I don't know style names and it was under a scarf, but it was wavy if that helps?"

Crane had confirmed the headscarf as well as the hair colour. "Thank you," I said, my voice full of relief. "It helps a lot. Will you add that to your witness statement?"

"Of course!" I could see him struggling with the information. "Sir, the picture I saw—Miss Cartwright—it looked like her, but of course I couldn't tell if it was an old photograph. Girls change their styles all the time."

I stared outside.

"Sir?" he asked. "Are we finished, sir?"

I looked back at him. "You only saw the girl briefly."

"Yes, but she was memorable."

I pulled a photograph from my pocket and I flashed it at him like it was a warrant card.

"I didn't quite see," he said.

I flashed it again. Slower this time.

"A pretty young woman?" he suggested. "Dark curly hair?"

Now I showed him the photograph properly. The second one I'd received. The folded one with Major Johnson hidden.

"Could that be her?" I asked. "How about I add that she has reddish-brown hair?"

His face told me everything. Doubt.

THIRTY-TWO

I stormed past the chief clerk outside Major Johnson's office. The man blustered after me as I burst through the door. The major looked up, alarmed, before a glower transformed his face.

"What the hell, Lieutenant?"

"That's my question to you!"

"Sir?" Crawley said over my shoulder.

The major considered him for a few beats before waving the clerk away. I heard the door click shut.

Johnson said, "This had better be reasonable, Carter. Don't think I won't put you on a charge for insubordination."

"Release Penny Cartwright."

"Is that it?" He stood and the temperature in the room went up a notch. "Is that why you've come barging in here—just to demand her release?"

"You have nothing."

"We have plenty."

I tried to control my temper by taking a breath. "I spoke to the witnesses. All you have is circumstantial evidence."

He clenched his teeth, probably deciding whether or not to debate this with me now. Then I saw his eyes narrow. "She had motive. She had the opportunity and she was seen fleeing the scene of the crime. What more do you bloody need?"

"That wasn't her fleeing the scene. Mr Gunn—by the way, he's a voyeur, a pervert if you prefer—saw a woman go into that alley and come out. That wasn't the same woman he followed home. That wasn't Penny."

He shook his head, showing disbelief. "Then who was it?"

"Someone similar. Someone pretty, but with distinctive hair colour and wearing a scarf."

"Rubbish. The witnesses—"

"The witnesses didn't mention the hair colour. When they were shown the black-and-white photograph of Penny, they couldn't know the difference between dark auburn and black."

I pulled the creased photograph from my pocket and tossed it towards Johnson. It fluttered to the floor and he bent to pick it up then stared at it.

"What's this?"

I couldn't tell whether he was annoyed or confused. Maybe both.

"I was sent another photograph of your wife. I showed this picture to the witnesses and—"

"What?" The anger came more to the fore again, as did his Scottish accent. He'd unfolded the picture to reveal him in the US Army uniform beside his wife. "Why have you got this, Carter? I distinctly remember telling you to back away. She is not your concern."

"Maybe she is, sir," I said, hoping to calm him down.

He remained angry. "She is not!"

"Her hair colour—" I said, "it matches what the witnesses saw."

Johnson laughed, although it was more of a growl. "You're trying to tell me that it was my wife and not your little girlfriend who killed Ellis? Are you an idiot, Carter? Your girlfriend is in enough trouble without trying to point your finger at me. It's preposterous!"

"Is it? Is it, sir? How many young women do you know that have auburn or dark red hair?"

*

When I left the major's office, Crawley waved me into another office and closed the door.

He had concern in his normally bright eyes. "I'm sorry to hear about your girl. But it's not the major's fault."

"I wish I could believe that, Chief."

"I heard you were looking for his wife even though he asked you not to."

"What do you know about them?"

He raised an eyebrow. "What do you mean?"

I noticed that he'd deflected the question, but I guessed he would be unlikely to cast aspersions on his boss without being prompted, so I said, "I've heard various stories. Someone told me that he used to beat his wife."

"No, I can't believe that. In fact, I can tell you categorically that he didn't beat her. I'm certain."

"But she was a flirt. She saw other men?"

"Well... she was attractive, Lieutenant. I don't know what to say."

I shook my head. Crawley was close to the major. Mrs Marsland-Askew described him as the third party in the relationship. He would know.

"Yes or no, Chief? Did she see other men?"

He cleared his throat. "Yes."

"And the major threatened his rivals."

Crawley studied my eyes. "Who told you that?"

"Yes or no?"

He shook his head. "Look, Lieutenant, I want to help but I don't want to get into trouble. How about you tell me what you've learned and I fill in some gaps?"

"I haven't learned much. I know she was unhappy, left Johnson a *Dear John* note that she was leaving for another man, caught a taxi and hasn't been seen or heard from since—until I got the photographs that is."

"Do you know where she went?"

I looked at him, hard. "Do you?"

"After she left, I did a bit of checking," he said with a nod. "I found the taxi firm. She went to the harbour in Limassol. The driver couldn't confirm that she got on a ship, but he said she met a man."

"A description?"

"The chap couldn't remember. All I got was: white, average height, and not wearing a uniform."

"That narrows it down," I said sarcastically.

"And that day, eighteen boats were going to as many destinations."

I had to admit it wasn't promising.

He said, "Can I see the photograph?"

I showed him the reverse of the one I still had.

He shook his head. "Find me?"

"This is the second photograph I received. The first said *Help me!* What do you make of them?"

He pouted, turned the photograph over thoughtfully and then back.

"Who sent them?"

"I don't know."

"A prank. That would be my guess."

I didn't bother saying that I'd considered it and thought it unlikely that one of his men would think it funny to do such a thing to the provost marshal.

I shook my head. "Does Johnson have enemies?"

"The major?" He blinked and then surprised me with a smile. "No, Lieutenant, I don't mean someone playing a prank on the major. I mean someone is pulling your chain. You're the new boy after all. And—"

"Carry on, Chief."

"And the SIB can act like they're superior to the rest of us. Maybe someone is knocking you down a peg."

I nodded. It was a possibility and it made me regard Crawley with respect. He was undoubtedly smart and, although unlikely, I would do well to have this man on my side.

"Interesting," I said. "Anything else you can tell me, Chief?"

"Yes. Whatever is going on with your girl and the murder of Mike Ellis, it has nothing to do with Mrs Johnson."

THIRTY-THREE

I waited for an appointment with Lieutenant Colonel Dexter, and I used the time to make a phone call to DI Dickins in Nicosia. There was a long delay and, when he came on the line, he could only speak briefly. He started by telling me he had no more information on the execution case.

"We can't find the Special who gave us the supposed victim's name," he said. "I'm embarrassed."

Rather than get into a discussion about it, I just said, "I've a problem here, Charles."

"Your other investigation—the lady who wants help?"

"Yes and no. Maybe. I know you've not got time now, but my friend has been arrested, charged with the murder of a soldier."

"I'll help him if I can, Ash. But military matters—"

"It's a girl and she's a civilian, so I want her transferred to a civilian prison."

He said nothing for a moment before asking for Penny's details and saying, "Don't worry, Ash. I'll make sure she gets a comfortable cell."

It felt like I could breathe for the first time in hours.

Dexter's clerk gave me a cup of tea and I thought through what I'd say to the CO.

When I told him the situation, Dexter listened carefully, chin in hand.

"He's provost marshal," he said when I'd finished. "You can't go up against him, Ash."

"But *you* could."

"Based on what? That the woman *might* not have been Penny Cartwright and *could* have been Mrs Johnson because of her hair?"

"Yes! Johnson is compromised. He can't run this case."

Dexter smiled at me kindly like I was his errant nephew. "It's not enough. I'm sure Miss Cartwright's lawyer will focus on the continuity and discrepancy, but you have no case against Mrs Johnson."

"I have a theory," I said. I'd been thinking about it constantly since I'd learned about the hair. An attractive, young woman. It was too much of a coincidence. Surely.

"Mrs Johnson asked for my help."

"The notes you received on the photographs?"

"Precisely. Why would she need help?" I paused for effect. "Because she was being forced to do something."

"And was that to kill Sergeant Major Ellis?" Disbelief shone in Dexter's eyes.

"Jim," I said, "she was either being forced to kill Ellis for someone else or Ellis was the problem."

"Right?"

"Ellis is a rapist. Maybe she wanted protection against him. Maybe she needed help because of him, and when I didn't help, she took matters into her own hands."

"You know there's a problem with your argument. Suggesting that Mrs Johnson's motive was revenge against Ellis, with no proof, just fuels the fires; it's the prosecution's case against Miss Cartwright. And they have plenty of evidence."

"Circumstantial at best." I paced the room while Dexter watched me.

"You know the problem, Ash."

I stopped pacing and nodded. "There's more evidence pointing at Penny than Mrs Johnson."

"Much more. *And* this hair colour thing has arisen after the witnesses gave their statements." He leaned on his desk. "I want to help, Ash, but—"

"Get her moved. I want her out of the Glasshouse and into the Nicosia Central Prison." The case would be prosecuted in a civil court and I argued that Penny was in danger.

"Danger from whom?"

"She's accused of killing an MP. She's being held in a military jail. Who knows who—"

"Major Johnson won't like it."

I nodded, and for the first time that day, I smiled.

"All right. Get her legal representative to put in a request to me and I'll approve it. I presume you'll speak to your contacts at the police."

"Already have," I said.

He nodded and looked at me with empathy. "You know what you have to do now, don't you?"

"Yes," I said. "I need to find Mrs Johnson."

THIRTY-FOUR

She'd spent a second night in the Glasshouse, but Penny looked better, probably more accepting of the situation or maybe just resigned.

I'd spoken to her legal advisor and explained the process for getting Penny transferred to Nicosia. It was early morning and he said he'd join me at the Glasshouse as soon as he could. When I told Penny about Nicosia, she let out a long breath, like she'd been holding it in all night.

I said, "It won't be the Ritz, Penny, but it'll be better than here."

"I'll be able to relax. The way the guards look at me here…"

I hugged her hard and said reassuring things. Despite telling Dexter that Penny might be in danger, I didn't believe it for a minute. The guards might despise her for possibly killing an MP, and she'd get no favours, but she'd be fine. They wouldn't harm her.

However, privacy and respect were another matter entirely, and a jail with a female block was more appropriate. She'd get that in Nicosia. I also thought she might even get favourable treatment since Dickins would be looking out for her.

"Their case is full of holes," I told Penny. "I spoke to the witnesses and it really all hinges on a man who thinks he saw you leave the crime scene and followed you home."

"Who?"

"A Peeping Tom. He was hanging around hoping to watch couples do the deed. But there's a continuity issue. He saw a man and young woman go into the alley, and he saw her come out. Then there was a break while he checked on the body before he went after the girl."

"And he saw me?"

"Yes. He saw you running—"

"Because I was late for you."

That wasn't quite right. We'd gone north on Friday night, but our plan had been to go north on Saturday morning. However, she was tired and the mind plays tricks when it's tired.

I said, "He followed you home, told the police and from then on you were the suspect. Then there's another issue. The investigating MP may have led on another witness, prompting him by showing your photograph. He has described you, but we don't know how much of that is genuine memory and how much prompted by being shown your photograph.

"He also described you as wearing a dress—and we both know you were wearing slacks."

"Yes, I was casual because of the grubby bus ride."

I nodded. "And both witnesses saw a headscarf which you didn't have. More importantly, they said the girl had reddish-brown hair. Wavy hair."

She rolled her eyes with relief. "Oh, Ash, this is great news." Then she focused on me and I could see the thought cross her mind.

"There's something else, isn't there?" she said.

"The description could match Mrs Johnson."

"My God!" Penny gripped my arm. "She has auburn hair. I remember. And we could be mistaken for one another—in the dark, don't you think?"

"That's exactly what I think."

"The Peeping Tom saw her go into the alley. Saw her come out. Followed but lost her and then saw me. Followed me and I seem the guilty one!"

She gripped my other arm and the shake in her body transmitted through my bones. "Oh thank God! So, do you think it was her?"

I shrugged but nodded. "I need to find her."

"What was her motive?"

"It doesn't matter," I said, not wanting to mention Penny's sister's rape. "She asked for help, and I don't believe in coincidences."

"Good," she said. "Please tell my legal representative that you're going to find Mrs Johnson, that you think it was her."

I said, "What did he say to you?"

"He said his focus was on the bus ride and timings. The ticket and timing would prove it couldn't have been me."

"I found the ticket in your pocket. We could track down the bus conductor and hope that he remembers you. He'd be another witness for your case."

She nodded. "That's what he said."

I didn't comment, but the man hadn't asked me about the ticket. The legal representative was from A-Branch. Army.

I said, "I'll get you another lawyer. A civilian. And I'll talk to the bus company. There's a colander full of holes in the prosecution's case."

She smiled hopefully.

"Anyone else on the bus?" I asked. "Did you speak to anyone?"

"Yes, but how do we find them?"

I thought for a moment. "What time did the bus arrive in Larnaca?"

"It was due at seven, but it was late. It must have been after seven twenty when it arrived. That's why I had to run. My legal representative said that Ellis met the girl around seven fifteen. It couldn't have been me, you know that, right?"

I nodded but was thinking about what she'd said. She was misremembering the arrangement again, but then perhaps she'd planned to see me anyway.

Rather than challenge her on the point, I said, "Perfect! He's right, that'll help your case. I'll go to the bus depot and confirm the time. And we can ask your friend... Margie, wasn't it?"

"Yes, Margie."

"We can ask her to confirm the time you caught the bus."

"As a witness?"

"Yes. We show you got on that bus and its arrival time in Larnaca and that you couldn't have been outside the Kings Head pub when they said you were. It was just an unfortunate coincidence that the pervert saw you run home when he did."

She nodded but didn't look convinced. "Won't my friend be considered biased?"

"Possibly, but..."

She took a slow breath. "I'd rather not involve Margie if I don't have to."

"Because?"

She shook her head. "Margie... won't be a good witness. The judge will see anxiety and think it's all lies. And then I'll be convicted for certain."

Tears welled in her eyes, and I held her for a minute, trying to provide comfort while thinking about what I'd do.

If Mrs Johnson was the killer, then finding her would solve our problem. Even if she didn't confess, it might be that the witnesses would recognize her or at least confirm the doubt.

Penny's A-Branch legal advisor arrived and tried to reassure Penny by saying, "Under military law there's a long way to go before charges of murder are brought.

They'll delay with a holding charge." He nodded at me. "You know how this works, Lieutenant. There will be the investigation, they'll take witness statements, they'll examine evidence before questioning the accused. Only when they have a cast-iron case will it go to court."

I shook my head. "This is a civil case and they're moving fast. Johnson wants a quick resolution."

The legal advisor smiled. "It may seem that way, but I know how this works. The holding charge is one of theft. They allege that the victim had five pounds stolen."

I didn't bother arguing; as he spoke he just reinforced my opinion. I'd wait until I'd found an independent lawyer and then dump this man as fast as a hare disappears at the sound of gunshot.

He said, "The other news is that they've found the headscarf. It was on the next road along."

I shrugged. It didn't matter, the scarf wasn't important. "The hair is what matters," I said. "It wasn't Penny."

"Right," he said. "Leave that to me. In the meantime, you could talk to the bus company and confirm the times, Lieutenant."

The man was trying to get me out of the way by making me busy. I ignored his patronizing tone. "I will."

"And, Miss Cartwright, we should get the statement from your friend. If the bus conductor doesn't remember you—"

"No," Penny said.

"But we may have to," her current advisor pressed.

Penny looked at me. "Ash, find the person who really killed Sergeant Major Ellis."

I nodded.

The legal advisor looked at me. "So what will you do first, Lieutenant?"

I thought, find your replacement, but instead nodded encouragement to Penny.

"I'm going back to speak to a man in Limassol."

THIRTY-FIVE

Alex Lazzell was in Nelson Block and the clerk said he could get a message to him. I shook my head and said it wasn't important. Whether the clerk thought that was a bit strange, I don't know, but he just nodded and put his head back down focusing on his papers.

I found shade outside Nelson Block and waited.

Officers came and went and two hours passed before Lazzell appeared. He looked relaxed and distracted as he chatted with a colleague.

I followed.

They walked north and I slunk behind a building when they stopped, still deep in conversation. Then they parted. The other officer continued north towards what was signposted as the Drill Shed. Lazzell turned left into Crescent Road. On the right of the curve were housing blocks.

He kept walking; I kept following.

About three-quarters of the way along, he followed the path to one of the blocks and I darted for cover again. I hugged the wall in case he glanced my way, but Lazzell never looked.

He went up to a door, inserted a key, turned it and then pushed.

I started running.

He was all the way in by the time I barrelled through the closing door. I hit him like a rugby player, my left collarbone blasting into his midriff. His feet came off the ground and I kept going, driving into the apartment until he thudded into the wall opposite.

His face was full of shock, his breath gone, his body a crumpled heap.

"Get up!" I snapped.

He gasped and coughed. "What the hell?"

"Get up, Lazzell!"

The naval lieutenant coughed and used the wall to ease himself up. A defensive hand came out.

"Don't hit me."

"Where is she?" I barked, my voice edged with menace.

He blinked. "What?"

"Surena Johnson. Where is she?"

"I don't know. For Christ's sake, man. I told you I don't know."

"I don't believe you!"

"But—"

"I know she ran away with a man called Alex." I pointed to him. "And that's you. I also know that she caught a taxi to Limassol." I'll grant you that Crawley had told me it was Limassol harbour, but the taxi driver hadn't seen her get on a boat.

He said, "Can I sit down?"

I motioned him to a chair.

When he said nothing, I prompted: "Come on, Lazzell. Where is she?"

He looked at me with moist eyes. Was he going to cry?

"I honestly don't know. I stopped seeing her—and it was only twice. I told you, Johnson scared me off. He said he'd kill me if I carried on with her."

I shook my head. He sounded convincing, but this could be an elaborate act.

He said, "Look around my house. You'll soon see she's not here."

"Don't move!" I said and quickly checked the three rooms. I didn't expect to find a woman but I thought I might find evidence that one had been here. Clothes or make-up perhaps. I found nothing.

"Fine," I said. "So you've got her somewhere else. You have another place. You're holding her against her will or forced her to kill someone for you."

He sighed and rubbed his eyes, pulled himself together then said, "Do you know how crazy you sound?"

Did I sound crazy? Maybe I did. I was desperate and desperate men did irrational things. I took a long breath, sat opposite Lazzell, and looked him in the eye.

"I need to know where she is. I need to find Mrs Johnson because… because my girl is in danger."

He frowned at me. "Is Major Johnson threatening her—your girl?"

I wondered about explaining but thought better of it. Instead, I said simply, "In a way. The point is, I need your help."

He smiled weakly, probably because of the irony; I'd attacked him, accused him, and now I was asking for his help.

Still with a hard edge to my voice, I said, "Convince me that it wasn't you."

"Well, I wasn't her last."

"Who was that?"

"Another officer."

"Who was that?" I asked again.

He said nothing for a beat before saying, "Would that get you off my case?"

"Yes." I wasn't a hundred percent sure, but if it moved the investigation forward, I was willing to be less than honest with the truth.

"Then I'll introduce you to Sam Lewis."

Thirty minutes later we were in the Officers' Club, sitting opposite Midshipman Lewis. He'd been eating and now looked too unwell to take another forkful.

"Tell him about Mrs Johnson," Lazzell said.

Lewis licked his lips, looked from Lazzell to me and back to Lazzell again.

"Tell him!"

"We aren't to talk."

"Because of a threat?" I asked. "Did Major Johnson threaten you too?"

"I received a letter." He looked at Lazzell again. "Alex?"

"Tell him."

"We aren't to talk about it. Johnson said he'd kill me if I carried on with her."

I shook my head. "It's ridiculous. He wouldn't dare. You should have reported him."

Now Lazzell spoke to me: "As I said, he didn't sign it. It was easier to stop seeing her. Plenty of other fish in the sea. Sure she was a good-looking girl, but it was never serious."

"Just fun," Lewis added.

"So we stopped going to Maxims," Lazzell said. "Easier that way."

Lewis looked uneasy. "Well, er... I've been a few times since."

I said, "When was the last time you saw Mrs Johnson?"

"The last time I was with her was in July last year. But I saw her a couple of times at Maxims after I'd been warned off." He nodded, thinking. "Yes, the last time she was at Maxims was about eight months ago."

I nodded. "That's when she disappeared."

"You didn't say why you think it's one of us—someone in the Royal Navy," Lewis asked.

I hadn't said it but I liked his assumption. It fit with what Crawley had said about meeting at Limassol harbour. However, rather than answer directly, I pointedly looked at the lieutenant.

"I was told she left with Alex."

Lazzell blew out air. "And I told you, it wasn't with me. Maybe it was the person who said it was me! Have you wondered about their motives?"

Lewis was looking thoughtful.

"What?" I asked.

"There are a lot of people called Alex."

"But only one who was a member of Maxims around that time."

Again the thoughtful expression. "What about Alex who works there?"

I blinked with surprise. "Alex—?"

"Well Alexis, I think he's really called. You know, he's one of the wog waiters."

★

Maxims was preparing for the evening. It was a Wednesday night and would be less busy with diners. There would be music but no dancing.

Mr Simons was shouting instructions in the main hall when I arrived. On top of being irritated, he appeared flustered and gave me a fake smile when I caught his eye.

"How can I help again, Lieutenant Carter?" he called from about twenty feet away. "As you can see, I only have a few minutes. We open shortly."

I noticed the staff hesitate and throw glances my way.

"Alex—" I said.

"Yes, Alex Lazzell."

"I understand you have an employee called Alex or Alexis." Again I noticed the staff looking at me.

"Used to," Simons said. "Left a while back."

"Eight months ago?"

He looked thoughtful. "Yes, I suppose it was. I could check"—he flapped his arms—"if you wouldn't mind waiting until we open."

I raised a hand, pulled up a seat and waited. Fifteen minutes later he beckoned me to join him and we left the hall, went down the corridor and into his office.

"Yes," he said after thumbing through files in a drawer. "Alex left eight months ago. Bugger just walked out."

"Surname?"

"Velopoulos. Alexis Velopoulos."

"Didn't resign?"

"No, just didn't turn up one day. You know how these wogs can be. Hard work just isn't in their nature. Give them a way out and they'll take it in a flash."

He gave me the date and it tallied with the date I'd been told Mrs Johnson had caught the taxi to Limassol.

"You didn't tell me why you're looking for him."

"I'm actually looking for Mrs Surena Johnson."

"Major Johnson's wife—a very handsome woman." His eyebrows rose as he spoke. "And you are looking for her because?"

"Because I need to," I said curtly, ending the conversation. "Please ask your staff about Alexis. I need to know where he is."

Simons pouted but nodded. "Not now, but after work. I'll ask them tonight and if you call tomorrow evening—before seven—I'll happily furnish you with any further information."

The darkness had rushed in while I'd been inside. I banged my steering wheel with satisfaction as I got into the Land Rover. I was making some headway and my spirits picked up on the drive back to Larnaca.

As I pulled out of the car park, I spotted a motorcyclist sitting on a stationary bike. I drove away from the club and then, in my rear-view mirror, I saw him move into the road and follow. Had I seen a motorcycle when I'd left HMS Mercury? Instinct said yes, although I couldn't remember where exactly.

I pressed my foot to the floor and increased the distance between me and the following bike. I watched its headlight bobbing behind me. We were on a main road, the only road between Limassol and Larnaca. Was I being paranoid? Was this just a coincidence?

On the bend where the road left the bay and went inland, I spun the wheel and skidded into a sheltered dip. With lights off, I turned around so that I was facing the road.

A glow appeared as the motorcycle came around the corner. I switched on my headlights and the biker went past. He looked towards the sudden burst of light. And I saw the flash of a face.

A face I'd seen before.

The tall man with the scarring around his eyes.

THIRTY-SIX

I shot out onto the road and gave chase, but the scarred man's bike was faster than my Land Rover. He also switched off his lights, so I soon lost him in the darkness.

As I drove onwards, I scanned the roadside in case he'd crashed or hidden, but I didn't see him.

When I reached the town, I drove the streets looking for a motorcycle. I saw two Royal Enfields, green and clearly military. I took a good look at them but was sure I was looking for a black motorcycle and a different design—possibly a BSA. I didn't find one.

★

My priority for the next day was to follow up on the ticket and bus ride, but I had time before visiting the bus company in Nicosia. Maria wasn't at home in the morning and I was told by a neighbour that she wouldn't be available until after ten o'clock. I used the time to call DI Dickins.

He told me that Penny had already been transferred to the women's wing of the Central Prison.

"I'll make sure she's all right, Ash. Will you visit?"

I told him I was travelling up today to question the bus company as part of the investigation. I'd visit Penny afterwards.

"I'll let them know you're coming," he said.

"I have another favour, Charles."

"Fire away."

And so I told him that the army had allocated an army lawyer as Penny's defence council. "Ordinarily, I think it would be fine," I said. "But the man isn't top-drawer. I'm hoping you know someone you trust. Someone who asks the right questions and won't be intimidated by the likes of Major Johnson."

Without hesitation, he gave me a name and said he'd arrange it. Then he added: "And I'll let them know the other news."

I heard something in his voice. It was like a comedian about to deliver his punchline. "What other news?"

"I received a note about Sergeant Ellis."

That was intriguing. Why would someone send Dickins a note about the murdered soldier? Surely the military police were the obvious recipients. I waited.

He said, "The note—well it was a telephone message—says that Ellis was taking bribes."

"Taking bribes?"

"They're the words used, Ash. And before you ask: it was a man who left the message and he didn't leave a name."

"Who else knows about this, Charles?" I asked, disappointed.

"As far as I know, it's just me and the operator who took the message."

"All right, tell Penny's defence lawyer, but no one else for now, if you don't mind. This could be big, Charles."

*

Cypriot buses were a regular sight on the roads and were cream with a green stripe. At least, they had been cream, but due to the dust and irregular cleaning, the colour was more grey-pink. They had seating for twenty passengers, although I'd regularly see people standing inside or even sitting on the large tailgate.

The Cyprus Transport Company, or KEM as they were more commonly known, was based between Ledra Street and Liberty Avenue towards the centre of the walled city.

I let Maria do the talking when we went into the office, and she explained that I was checking on a passenger who had travelled from Nicosia to Larnaca on Friday evening.

The sweaty clerk wearing a blue suit and off-white shirt asked to see the ticket.

I handed it over, and he turned it over and over as though twisting it would reveal hidden secrets. Finally, he gave it back and spoke to Maria.

She translated: "He says that it is a return ticket."

"Yes," I said.

She shook her head. "He cannot tell you when it was used. It was for one journey from Larnaca to Nicosia and then back. There are no dates."

"All right," I said undeterred. "Can he tell us whether the bus due to arrive in Larnaca on Friday evening at seven was late by about twenty minutes?"

The two exchanged words. Back and forth for longer than I anticipated for a simple question. However, at no time did the official check anything.

Finally, Maria said, "No. The only occasions when they record delays is if there is an incident like a squabble between passengers or a puncture."

"And was there anything on Friday?"

"No," she said.

"Please ask him to check."

Maria asked, but the man didn't do anything except look disinterested and answer her back.

Maria said, "He doesn't need to check because he knows there have been no incidents for over a week."

"Please ask him if we can speak to the conductor."

Now the official checked a document and told us to wait. We sat and waited. After a stuffy half an hour I asked Maria to find out how long the bus conductor would be.

"His next bus is due in later," she said after disturbing the clerk again. "Probably half an hour."

I took a breath of the warm air. "Tell him to send this chap out to see us as soon as he arrives," I said, barely containing my frustration at the official's relaxed attitude; after all, he didn't seem busy.

There was a café outside that appeared to be owned by the bus company and was used more as a waiting room than a coffee house.

The staff were equally unfriendly, and when two Coca-Colas came they were as warm as the air inside the café.

I watched the minute hand of a large clock slowly move through half a circle. Maria ordered sandwiches and drank coffee, which she said was only a little warmer than the Coca-Cola. I drank tepid water.

The minute hand had almost completed its circuit when a solid-looking man in the tan-coloured suit of a bus company worker came in.

He introduced himself as the conductor on the bus that had left Nicosia on Friday at five fifteen. Maria told me the man was Armenian, and I judged from her turned-up nose that she didn't think much of him.

I asked, "Was the bus delayed?"

"I can't remember," he told Maria. "We don't worry too much about the time unless there is an incident."

Maria added that she understood what he was saying. I did too, judging by her own relaxed attitude to the time.

I said, "What time do you think the bus arrived in Larnaca on Friday evening?"

"I couldn't say. I didn't check."

I produced Penny's photograph and showed the conductor.

"Do you recognize this lady?"

"Maybe," he said. "The bus was very full. The bus is always very full."

I breathed in and out. "Were there any non-locals on the bus that evening?"

"Maybe," he said. "But she isn't white British, no?"

"No," I said, and he gave a *there-you-go* kind of shrug before Maria translated.

"What does that mean?" I asked, and Maria repeated the question.

"It means: how was I to remember?"

Again I breathed so that my exasperation wasn't too evident. "She's very attractive. You would recognize her if you'd seen her before, I think."

"Yes," he said.

"Yes, what?"

"Yes, sir," he said. "I think I've seen her before."

I leaned forward. First my hopes were dashed and now he was saying he'd seen her. "Yes?" I prompted.

"I think I recognize her," he said through Maria. "Only I can't tell you when I last saw her. I can't say she was on the Friday late bus."

*

Maria waited in the shade of a tree while I went into the prison. As Dickins had promised, they were expecting me, and the sign-in process was quick. A minute later I was being escorted along a depressing grey-painted corridor to the women's section. It smelled of disinfectant and overcooked pasta.

Penny beamed at me as she entered the interview room where I'd been waiting.

"I've already met the new lawyer," she said after we hugged. The smell of carbolic soap on her skin and the brightness of her eyes told me she was doing better than at the Glasshouse.

I gave her an update, giving her more detail of my trip to Limassol than necessary. I kept the bad news shorter, the lack of evidence from the bus company, but quickly added that Maria and I would question people arriving in Larnaca by bus tomorrow.

"Hopefully someone on the bus will remember you."

"Frustrating that the conductor thought I'd been on an earlier bus. We don't need the prosecution finding that piece of information!"

"Not an earlier bus," I explained. "He just said he'd seen you on the bus before. Anyway, I'm hoping that the conductor will think about it. People misremember things all the time. Just like the witness who thought it was you outside the Kings Head that night. Hopefully, the driver will change his story and—"

"Does he want money? Is that it, Ash? You know how some of these people can be—maybe Armenians are less trustworthy than Greeks. Maybe he wants payment to be able to remember."

I winced. I thought I'd do anything to get Penny off, but I wasn't ready to pay a witness. Maybe I'd change my mind as the court case loomed. However, the mention of money prompted me.

"There's a suggestion that Ellis was taking bribes."

"Bribes? What for?"

"I've no idea and we have no more information, but someone wanted the police to know. So that's at least one positive new development. That would give us a motive."

"And more doubt about me?"

"It's something to address with your defence lawyer. We should make sure he follows the motive angle as well."

After that, we talked of our weekend in Kyrenia, the orange grove valleys and the mountain castles. We made plans about doing it again as soon as she was free.

We hugged long and hard and I felt reassured as I left her there in that foreboding grey block behind barbed wire.

★

On the way home, Maria was quiet for a long time, picked at imaginary dirt under her fingernails. Eventually, she said, "I should apologize."

"For what, Maria?"

"For getting drunk on the job last week." She was referring to the day we spent talking to people in the villages.

"You did drink rather a lot," I said, laughing.

"I hope I didn't say anything I shouldn't have."

"No, in fact, I'd forgotten all about it. And you did me a big favour. My head was buzzing with caffeine. Goodness knows how I would have coped with ouzo and brandy!" *Except for throwing up*, I said to myself.

She smiled. "We didn't have a good day today."

No, we hadn't. We'd identified that the ticket wasn't proof of the bus Penny had caught and we'd discovered there was no evidence of the time she'd arrived back in Larnaca. Even if she had been on the bus, then if it arrived on time, the prosecution would argue Penny could have still met Ellis outside the Kings Head.

I said, "Are you free tomorrow evening?"

She looked surprised, perhaps horrified. "Mr Carter…"

Her misunderstanding made me smile. "Maria, I want to know if you're available so we can meet the late bus. You can question the passengers for me. Perhaps one of them was on the bus last Friday and will recognize Penny's photograph. Hopefully, they can also confirm the delayed arrival time.

"Ah." She looked relieved. "Yes, that wouldn't be a problem."

I drove on and we had reached the hills outside Larnaca before she spoke again.

Her voice was quiet. "This would never have happened if not for me."

"Pardon? Are you still worrying about getting drunk, Maria?"

"I have a confession, Mr Carter."

And then she told me a story that made my mouth drop open.

*

Maria hadn't just happened to become our cleaner, she'd been told to take the job. And the reason: to find out whether Lieutenant Ash Carter, the detective, was independent of 227 Company.

Maria had left the first photograph at the office. Because I hadn't appeared to be looking for Mrs Johnson, she then posted the second at my home.

I stopped the Land Rover.

"Who sent you?" I said, part in disbelief and yet relieved that the mystery had been solved.

"My cousin. You met her."

"Who's your cousin?"

"She cleans for the Johnsons. She cleans for many of the families at Dhekelia Village. You spoke to her twice."

I thought back to when I was doing house-to-house visits, posing as a postal worker. The cleaner who had directed me to the Ice Cream and Pastry Shop. I'd found Mrs Marsland-Askew and then the waitress had directed me to a closer friend Sister Laurent.

"Did your cousin write the notes?"

"No, sir."

"Then who did?"

"The girl—Verity Johnson. She wanted to know where her mother is. She wanted it investigated."

I sat and stared into the distant heat haze. Did this news change everything? Mrs Johnson wasn't asking for my help. Which probably meant that Mrs Johnson wasn't in trouble.

"Wait a minute," I said, swivelling towards my passenger, my heart rate picking up a notch. "You're

English is near perfect and you used the past tense. You said Verity *wanted* to know where she was. Does that mean she's found her?"

"No, sir. At least I don't think so."

"Then what?"

"Verity Johnson has also disappeared."

THIRTY-SEVEN

As I drove up to Johnson's home, I saw DS Park walk down his path. The detective stopped and watched me get out of my Land Rover.

He lit a cigarette and nodded a greeting.

"You know about his daughter?" I said, approaching.

"Yes." His eyes scrutinized mine as he blew out a line of smoke. "How did you find out?"

"My cleaner."

"Your cleaner?"

"Long story," I said, not wanting to get into it. "My cleaner was told by the Johnsons' cleaner."

"Ah," he said. "That explains it. Are you here to talk about that?"

I shook my head. "Something else."

"You're being cagey, Lieutenant."

"Have you spoken to Dickins today?"

"Yes?" he said with doubt, so I decided he didn't know about the bribery allegation. After a silence, he continued: "Sorry about that name a Special got from the Greek village. We've not been able to find out who reported it."

"Curious," I said.

He nodded then raised his eyebrows. "But I hear you have other priorities now. I'm sorry to hear about your girlfriend. Innocent, I'm sure."

"Thanks," I said, then pointed to the Johnson's house: "So, any news about Verity?"

The detective's face registered my redirect by narrowing his eyes, but he didn't challenge me. Instead, after a few seconds, he said, "No. It looks like she's run away. That's why the major wants our involvement."

Now it was my turn to narrow my eyes in thought. I'd heard of missing army kids before. In those cases, the MPs had taken charge, interviewing and searching.

"I'm sure the major has his reasons—will explain," DS Park grunted. "Well, I better get back to Nicosia. Have a good day, Lieutenant."

I watched him walk towards an unmarked police car and pull away and then walked up the path to Johnson's front door.

"I'm sorry to hear your news," I said when the major answered my knock.

He looked shaken and pale, and didn't speak until we were in his office. Then he took a long breath.

"What did you hear?"

"That your daughter, Verity, has… run away," I said, using the term DS Park had just used. It sounded less worrisome than disappeared, and I wondered whether Maria had got the interpretation wrong.

He nodded.

When he didn't immediately say anything, I asked, "Why the police, if you don't mind me asking, sir?"

"The police?"

"I just spoke to DS Park. He said they were involved."

"Right," he said, finally sitting down. I took the chair opposite. "Civilian matter."

"Sir?"

He looked out of the window to his left and then back at me. "She's run away to her mother."

"Mrs Johnson?" I said, as my heart picked up a beat. "You know where she is?"

"No, but I know Verity wanted to be with her... I suppose her mother was in touch." He took another slow breath and I could see how shaken he was by this. I sensed he was afraid, but now I thought his fear was of losing the girl he thought of as his daughter to the woman who'd abandoned them.

He continued: "It makes sense to let the police run with this rather than deal with it as a military matter. They can look for Surena... which will lead to Verity."

I wondered what to say, and as a delaying tactic asked, "Couldn't you do both, sir? It's usual—"

"Usual?" he snapped, suddenly switching from melancholy to anger. "Don't lecture me on what I should and shouldn't do, Lieutenant!"

"No, sir," I said, and at that point decided I would tell him. "It was Verity."

"What was?" he asked, now looking startled as well as annoyed.

"Verity sent me those photographs. She wanted me to find her mother."

"She sent... how do you know?"

"My cleaner," I explained. "Your cleaner passed the photographs to mine, who delivered them. Verity must have identified me as a detective when I first visited you here. She was outside when I left. Maybe she overheard us talking."

He nodded slowly.

I said, "I'm still looking for Mrs Johnson."

"No, let's leave this to the civilian police, Lieutenant."

"To find your daughter, yes," I said. "But I believe your wife holds the key to Ellis's death." If I could talk to her, at least I could eliminate her from enquiries if innocent or gain a better understanding of the killer's motive.

I could see that he wasn't having any of it.

"You think it will clear your girlfriend?"

"She's innocent, sir. This whole thing has been a misunderstanding." It has to be, I thought.

"You're naïve, Lieutenant. A good man, I'm sure, but you aren't wise."

Now it was my turn to look out of the window. I breathed in and out and counted to ten thinking of the Cypriot proverb. *A fool throws a stone into the sea and a hundred wise men cannot pull it out.* Maybe if I wasn't wise, it would help me.

"There's more," I said, looking back at him. "The reason I came to see you today... it's because there's a suggestion that Ellis was taking bribes or being paid off."

He shook his head. "Who suggested that?"

"I'm not at liberty to divulge my source."

He shook his head again and I hoped Johnson thought the informant had contacted me rather than Dickins.

"It's a good, reliable source," I lied.

"I'm dealing with my daughter's disappearance"—ah, he said it. Disappearance rather than runaway— "and you come talking about Ellis supposedly taking bribes."

"It's important."

"Not to me," he said.

So what? I thought. Justice doesn't depend on whether it was top of the provost marshal's agenda.

*

"Where the hell have you been?" Wolfe asked when he called the office. I'd forgotten to check with the operator and he said he'd tried three times.

"I sent the last parcel almost a week ago. I hope you have a translation for me, Ash."

The envelope was lying unopened on Penny's desk and I apologized profusely.

"Not good enough, Carter," he said, and I registered that he'd switched to my surname. I'd disappointed him again.

"I know, Bill," I began, "but Penny's been arrested for a murder she didn't do and I'm desperate to get her out." And so I told him the detail, told him that the OC of 6DGU was a sergeant major whom Penny said had raped her sister. I told him that I'd recently confronted Ellis and also reported it to Major Johnson. Then last Friday Ellis met a woman outside the Kings Head pub and they walked to an alley. A voyeur, expecting to watch them have sexual relations, instead found Ellis dead moments after she left the alley.

"Where was Penny at the time? Was there an alibi?" Wolfe asked. Not *did she do it*, but an assumption of innocence. *Good man.*

"She'd been on the Nicosia bus. It was late, arrived after the woman had already met Ellis. Penny ran home and passed nearby. The voyeur was looking for the woman, saw Penny and thought it was her. He followed and it all went horribly wrong from there. The investigating MP got a photograph of Penny and witnesses confirmed it was her."

Wolfe tutted. "Bloody incompetent! Is Major Johnson handling this?"

"One of his lieutenants. Without investigative experience, I'm sure."

Wolfe said, "I'd come back and help if I could. Tell me more."

"It seems Penny may have looked a little like the woman, but once the witnesses had seen her photograph it fixed their impressions."

"But she couldn't have done it because of the bus, right? You confirmed the timings?"

"So far I've been unable to get the evidence that she was on the bus, but I'm planning to ask passengers getting off the same bus tomorrow night."

"Hoping there will be some regular passengers who remember her?"

"Yes. But my main strategy is to show that someone else could have done it."

There was silence on the line and I imagined him thinking. Then he said, "Who?"

"Major Johnson's wife."

"Shit, Ash. You haven't been fuckin' investigating her all along, have you?"

I avoided answering his question. Instead, I responded with: "You'd be amazed at how similar they look."

"Jesus, Ash! This isn't about you and Major Johnson, is it? You've not got into some kind of fuckin' pissing match with the provost marshal, have you?"

I said, "There can't be many young women as good-looking as Penny and Mrs Johnson, and she's missing."

"And asked for your help?"

I didn't bother explaining what I'd learned about the photographs—that her niece had sent them via our cleaners.

"There must be hundreds of"—he hesitated, perhaps choosing the right word—"tanned good-looking girls, Ash."

"But not with auburn hair," I said assuredly. "Bill, I grant you it's a stretch, but from the description, it's more likely to be Mrs Johnson than Penny. And the major's behaviour…"

"Explain."

So I told him what I'd learned and how Johnson may have been jealous and even violent—although the source may have been unreliable. However, I'd learned of Johnson's threatening letters to his wife's suitors.

We talked some more and I think I convinced him that Mrs Johnson's disappearance was suspicious and that the major may be looking for her. I also told him about the bribery information.

"Then you have to get Ellis's post office account records. His transactions should tell a tale." He paused.

"But before that, I urgently need those documents translating. Look, Ash, I'm as concerned about Penny as much as you are and we are duty-bound to help her, but we've also got a job to do. Understood?"

I said that I did and wondered if Wolfe would be less understanding than he was if he'd known about our relationship. He'd said, "I'm concerned about Penny as much as you are."

No, Bill, I don't think so.

*

At ten past seven on Friday evening, Maria and I met the bus from Nicosia and questioned everyone who got off. Out of the fifteen passengers, only three had been on the same bus last week and not one of them recognized Penny's photograph.

THIRTY-EIGHT

Streaks of orange and purple lit the horizon as I finished an evening run. Frustrated with the case, I'd run further than usual—all the way through a village called Pyla, where there were Roman tombs on the hills. I'd seen an army sign for a detention camp. After a switchback that crossed a river, I'd come to another War Office sign and seen the perimeter of the camp. Behind fences topped with barbed wire, there were a handful of Nissen huts and a vast field of tents.

But these weren't prisoners of war or criminals, these were the unfortunate Jews who had been picked up in the Med.

In the twelve months before we handed over Palestine, a hundred thousand Jews had tried to enter the country illegally, most through Port Haifa where we'd been stationed. They had been persecuted by the Nazis and now the British were stopping them from finding the Promised Land.

I'd heard many thousand had been held on Cyprus but assumed they'd been released. From the thousand dejected faces, young and old, I could see this hadn't happened. At least not completely.

I kept going until I reached a wooded section that dropped into a valley, and from there I looped back around, deliberately avoiding the depressing detention camp.

I'd set off running to clear my head, to then think about Penny's case. Initially, I found lots of nonsense in my head rather than solutions. And after seeing the depressing camps, and the horror that the British had treated the Jews little better than the Nazis, I found my thoughts turning to Israel and our mission there. Was bureaucracy or something more sinister at play with the Jews stuck in limbo on Cyprus? Were we all just pawns in a game played by politicians? Did the individual not matter?

Was Penny a pawn?

Out of breath and with my head still spinning, I opened the front door to my apartment. In the corner of my eye, I glimpsed movement. Starting to turn my head, I realized a figure was rushing towards me. Dressed all in black, including his face, his intention was clear.

Instinctively, my feet shifted and my hands came up in defence.

What I hadn't anticipated was the impact from behind. Another man cannoned into my back.

The force jolted me towards the first man. I threw a punch but was off balance and going down. However, I didn't hit the ground because the man in front pinned me in a bear hug. The man behind locked an arm around my neck.

One second I was falling forward. The next I was being dragged backwards, my legs peddling in reverse. We went through my front door and the man behind jerked. I slipped, and they pummelled me to the ground.

My uncontrolled impact against the floor was accompanied by knees on my chest, driving the wind out of me.

I tried to squirm and managed to roll onto my front. I had planned to push up, explode at them, gain the upper hand. But they'd let me roll. Before I could begin my press, the weight came down on me again, only this time I figured it was both men on top. A yell forced its way from my throat, partly due to the impact and partly in frustration.

With knees between my shoulder blades, they pulled my arms, like they were tearing off chicken legs. Twine went around my wrists. I tensed, hoping to create some slack, but they were wise to the move as they tightened. A blow made my head bounce off the stone floor and I must have eased the tension, because the twine tightened, cutting into flesh.

My legs had been thrashing uselessly, but now they too were pinned and tied together.

"Hood," I heard one grunt, and after another blow to the back, my view of the floor was blotted out. A bag was pulled roughly down and twine went round my neck. For a head-pounding second, I thought it was over. I couldn't swallow. My carotid artery was compressed. I couldn't breathe.

One of them said something, maybe to me, maybe to the other, but immediately the garrotte slackened enough for me to suck in warm air. I was flipped over as easily as a sausage in a frying pan. The pressure of knees was on my chest again and, as I exhaled, a gag cinched tight around the bag. Again I thrashed and choked, but this time there was no relief. The gag stayed and I sucked air around it.

My head was still pounding. My brain was racing like crazy trying to make sense of what was happening. The restricted warm air through the gag, combined with the surge of adrenaline, made me want to vomit. I wanted them to talk. I wanted to know what was going on, but they said nothing.

The one who was still on my chest got off and the weight eased. I forced myself to breathe more slowly and through my nose. Stay calm and think, I told myself. However, the time for thinking was over. I knew that the best time to escape was close to the point of capture. Now that I was trussed up and unable to speak, I had no more opportunities.

I couldn't hear them, but I knew the two men were still there. They weren't searching my home, they were waiting. Were they waiting for someone else?

Who were these men?

I began to count so that I'd have a sense of the time, and it was three hours before anything happened. By this time, I'd calmed myself, breathing slowly with my eyes closed.

Without warning, I was pulled to my feet, and a hand raised my arms behind my back urging me forward. My tied legs meant that I could only shuffle.

"Move!" one barked. My arms were raised and I started hopping, afraid that I'd face-plant if I didn't go faster.

I heard my front door open and then we were outside.

"I can't see the steps!" I screamed through the gag, but it was already too late. I was falling forward down the short flight. A last-second twist took the impact on my left shoulder but jarred my head.

Perhaps this had been their intention because I was picked up and carried between them.

I tried to struggle. I could flex my knees and waggle my head. We were outside and someone might see us. I wasn't a roll of carpet, for Christ's sake. *Someone notice!*

Then I realized why they'd waited. Darkness. No one would see. No one would be coming to my aid.

I heard a clunk and then my head crashed into metal. I was folded and dropped side-on and hit more metal. With a push, I was in.

As I guessed where I was, the car boot slammed shut. Once again, I couldn't breathe. Thick, warm air smelled of petrol.

The vehicle bounced on its suspension as my kidnappers got in and started the engine. The car set off and I tried to quell the rising claustrophobia. Think. Calm your heart and head, I willed myself.

They hadn't carried me far. I figured the car must have been parked on a side road, probably hidden. Had it been facing east or west? I tried to picture Larnaca, and when we turned right, I figured we'd been going east.

We turned again and bumped along an unmetalled road. I bounced between the floor and roof of the boot, and after more turns, I'd lost any idea of distance or direction.

Nausea returned, and I thought I'd pass out. Maybe I did, because I lost all sense of time, and it wasn't until the car hit smooth road again that I could breathe more easily.

We turned, went straight and then stopped. I waited for the boot to open, but after a few seconds, the car moved again. However, it didn't go far and we soon stopped again.

The engine went off. I heard the car doors open and close. But then nothing.

Were they leaving me here to die? I remembered the smell of petrol. Was this the end? Were they going to set fire to the car and burn me alive?

Despite knowing that I couldn't break the bonds on my wrists or legs, I squirmed. Instinct. When you know you're about to die, you can't go quietly. My legs were cramped but I found enough purchase to push up. My head banged against the boot. It hurt and was only a dull sound, but it gave me focus. I did it again and again.

Without warning, the boot jerked open. Hands grabbed me under the armpits and dragged me over and out of the boot. I crumpled to the ground and felt grit bite into my exposed flesh.

Hands grabbed me again and I was bustled forward until I bumped into a wall. I heard a chuckle.

Dazed, I was moving again as the hands twisted me round the obstacle and forward for what seemed like a hundred rapid mouse-steps. Then I was falling, face into the dirt. And it was dirt. I could smell it through the cloth hood.

"On the bench," I think a voice barked, because the sound was muffled by my hood. I was dragged roughly like a rag doll. I wanted to fight, I wanted to show them I wasn't a doll, but my movements only caused mirth. I also received a blow to the head.

"Shut up, you shit slime!" someone said close in my ear. I guess it was a figure of speech since he must have known I couldn't talk.

Another slam to the side of my head and I was down and sitting. On a bench. My fingers felt wood and I wondered if I could use it to wear down the twine binding my hands. Maybe. If they left me alone for a very long time.

The room didn't seem cavernous. I could sense the men close. I could smell their body odour. I could smell the alcohol they'd been drinking. My ears strained and I judged there were four or five of them. I could hear their feet and breathing.

I forced myself to relax and observe. They weren't going to kill me. They hadn't gone to all this effort to get me here if they were going to kill me. I tried to make sense of their whispers. I heard my name and I heard them say *The Man* a lot. I got the sense it wasn't me. I got the sense that it was who they were waiting for.

Distant footsteps caused the others to stop fidgeting. A door opened and someone came in.

"This him?" I heard a muffled voice say, and I figured this was *The Man*.

I think someone said, "It's Carter." I pictured the speaker as the first man I'd heard in my home, although they sounded similar. Coarse and distant voices.

I breathed in and out. Calm.

A gun barrel jammed into my temple.

"Then what are you waiting for?" a voice said. "Shoot the fucker!"

THIRTY-NINE

I heard the hammer click back.

Accept my fate or fight?

I jammed my feet down on the ground, jolted upright and twisted. Aiming my head at where I pictured the man with the gun, I butted with all my strength.

I'd imagined headbutting a face but felt something softer, maybe a shoulder meeting my forehead. The man yelped, and I dived towards his voice, again butting. This time pain jarred my forehead and neck but I made good contact.

We went down, and for a second it felt good. I was on top and in control. But I wasn't. Not really. That sweet moment of victory was over. Hands grabbed me and my arms were wrenched. Blows rained into my ribs and legs and the beating only ended when I was picked up and flung back onto the bench.

They weren't making the same mistake twice. Now, my hands and legs were lashed to the bench and I was pinned and exposed.

Bam! A roundhouse smacked into my face. My jaw clicked out and back and I tasted blood. I wanted to spit it out but could only choke it down in small swallows.

The barrel jabbed against my temple again and I pushed against it. Defiant despite being powerless.

The hammer clicked.

"You fuckin'—" I figured the man with the gun said.

Other voices, and I heard someone say, "Better not, he's SIB." Another said, "Let's just do this now," and I heard: "So much easier."

"Do it!" someone else barked. Was that the man in charge?

There was silence except for lots of breathing. Mine and theirs. The gun barrel didn't move.

I found myself counting and almost willing the bullet to leave the gun. I knew I'd never hear the shot. A bullet to the temple and I'd be dead before the sound registered.

I reached a count of thirty-five when the barrel was taken away.

There was laughter and talking again. Finally, I caught a growl from the man close by. "Next time it'll be for real." I figured this was the man with the gun. I wanted to see his face. Had I broken his nose with my headbutt? I hoped so.

Feet began to move. Were they leaving? The door shut and the silence pressed in.

My ears strained. My breathing and heart echoed in my head. Was I alone?

Minutes passed and I realized I could hear breathing close by, maybe inches from my face.

I straightened and nodded. Not sure what I was saying, maybe just acknowledging his presence.

"This was a warning," a voice mumbled. He was close, and I now wondered whether it wasn't just the hood muffling the sound. I suspected the men were masking their own voices, probably with a neckerchief or similar around the mouth.

A warning for what specifically? I tried to grunt "What?" and hoped he'd remove the gag. He didn't.

"Keep your nose out of business that isn't yours," he said.

I grunted the question again.

There was no response for a moment, and I figured he was thinking it through, deciding what to say.

Finally, he said, "Stop investigating. The executions and Mrs Johnson. Don't involve the MPs. You do anything else and you will feel the kiss of death."

An hour later, I was thrown out of the car, still trussed up, still wearing a hood. It stuck to my face with sweat and probably blood.

The cicadas were loud in my ears and I could smell earth. It was still night-time. In the distance, I heard a dog howl.

I was thirsty and in pain. They hadn't shot me, but if I was in the middle of nowhere, I wondered if I'd last very long like this—especially if I was exposed in hundred-degree sunshine. Or food for a starving dog.

I rolled painfully and felt sharp stones against my skin. Eventually, my fingers touched a rock with a jagged edge and I began to rub the wrist bindings against it.

After an interminable period, I paused for breath.

Dante surely had a Circle of Hell like this.

My head swam, and I wondered whether I'd faded in and out of consciousness.

I thought I heard a car and tried to stand, but I stumbled and immediately fell. Then it took me a while to find the sharp stone again, or more likely it was a different stone.

I began the back and forth movement, sawing through the cords—hoping I was sawing through the cords. Darkness, heat, laboured breathing. The world started spinning again.

The next thing I knew, light was filtering through my hood. My mouth and lips were sore and dry. I smacked them together. It wasn't until the hood lifted that I realized the gag had been removed.

Someone was talking to me. A reassuring voice. A man.

I heard him say, "Painful?" and "Water?" and "Hospital?" before I blacked out again.

*

The next time I awoke, I was indeed in a hospital bed. "Nightingale," a nurse said when I asked after she'd handed me a cup of water. So I was in the British Medical Hospital next to Alexander Barracks.

I drank the liquid before realizing it wasn't just water. A bitter taste suggested some kind of painkiller.

A senior nurse—a ward sister I guessed based on her dark blue uniform—came over.

"How do you feel?"

"Marvellous," I joked.

"The man who brought you here thought you might be a soldier."

I had been in my running gear. I had no ID, no warrant card on me.

My jaw hurt from being punched, and it clicked as I moved it. My mouth felt like it had a brick in place of a tongue. I sipped more water.

"Lieutenant Ash Carter," I said.

"Lieutenant…?" she prompted.

I tried again. "Ash… Carter."

She smiled, wrote it down and then held her pen waiting for more.

After another drink, I told her I was 3rd Company, Special Investigations Branch. That made her frown, presumably because she hadn't come across us before. Hardly surprising since it was just me and Captain Wolfe, and he was in Israel.

"What… can you tell me?" I asked.

"You have two cracked ribs, abrasions all over your body—though nothing a bit of iodine won't fix. And it looks like your jaw is a bit sore."

I nodded.

"Are you hungry?"

I nodded.

"I'd organize a fish and chips dinner with the works for you, but I doubt you could eat it. So I'll get some lovely raspberry jelly instead." She winked and then waited a beat. "Are you ready to make a report, or shall I call the MPs later?"

"Later," I said. "Much later."

I had no intention of filing a report, not yet anyway.

After my jelly, which was more delicious and appreciated than expected, I slept then woke up with a start. I'd been reliving my ordeal, bound with a hood. Thinking each laboured breath could be my last.

I lay, eyes closed, with a thousand thoughts swirling through my head. I needed to prove Penny was innocent. I needed to find Mike Ellis's real killer. Was that Mrs Johnson? I'd made no progress it seemed, except for pissing off the Kiss gang. I had no doubt it had been them who'd kidnapped me.

Mrs Johnson must be connected in some way to the gang. But if I started poking around again they'd kill me. I had no idea who they were, so what the hell was I going to do?

When I opened my eyes a nurse was sitting by my bed, watching.

Sister Isabelle Laurent. Mrs Johnson's friend.

She checked my pulse and touched my forehead.

"I hear you were found bound and gagged not far from the road to Famagusta. You don't look too good."

"I've had better days."

She lowered her voice to a whisper. "You have been looking for Surena, haven't you? Is this something to do with your investigation?"

"It must be."

"Who are they, who did this, Lieutenant?"

I didn't just read concern for me in her eyes, I read desperation.

I shook my head. "What's wrong?"

"Have you heard about Verity?"

"She's run away."

"She's not run away, Lieutenant." Sister Laurent took a long breath composing herself. "She's been kidnapped."

FORTY

The first nurse who had attended me returned and Sister Laurent sidled away. I had registered the bandage around my chest and the nurse checked it was secure before tending to my abrasions. The iodine stung and, like a mantra, each time I flinched, she told me it was doing good.

She removed a plaster over my left knee and I saw a two-inch gash. Thankfully, she used ointment rather than the iodine before taking my hands. Both wrists were bandaged, and she removed them to reveal some ugly-looking cuts along with welts caused by the bindings. I figured I'd been sawing at my skin more than the rope.

When the bandages were replaced, I was offered more painkiller but waved it away. She took a look at my mouth and jaw.

"No permanent damage there," she said.

I opened my mouth wider than I'd done so far since waking up in the hospital and my jaw graunched.

"I wouldn't do that," she said with raised eyebrows.

"How long?" I asked with a smaller mouth.

"Before you can move your jaw comfortably? It'll take a while. A few days, maybe a month."

I wasn't worried about the jaw. I'd seen displacements after boxing matches. I'd had one myself, although not as severe as this one, and I knew it'd recover. Although I also knew it could take longer than a month to stop the clunking.

"How long before I can go?" I asked.

"Ah." She checked my notes. "You should rest for a day and we'll check how the ribs are doing—to make sure there's no internal damage."

I was distracted by a uniformed MP hovering by the ward's entrance. After I was pointed out, he strode to my bed and the nurse took her leave.

The MP had a clipboard and an earnest expression on his face. He was a corporal from 227 Provost but I don't think I'd seen him before.

He went through the name, rank and number routine and then progressed to asking me what had happened.

I said, "I don't remember."

He said, "Try, sir."

I shook my head.

Don't involve the MPs.

He said. "You were found on the road to Famagusta."

"Or on the road *from* Famagusta. And before you ask, I don't remember how I got there."

"Sir, can you tell me who did it?"

"No. Nor do I know why."

I batted away a few more questions and he finally nodded, satisfied that he'd filled in his form. And I was satisfied that I'd told him nothing.

My abductors had been specific about only a few things, and for now I would comply. If you're told not to do something, then there's no point in doing it, unless you have a good reason. Unless you have a plan. I'd learned that the hard way at school: upset the form master and receive a caning for my trouble. Better to bide my time. Assess, evaluate and then act.

Sister Laurent returned.

Her first words were: "What did the MP want?"

"Just a report—which I won't give." Then, quieter, I said, "What did the major say?"

"When?"

"When you told him about Verity being kidnapped? I thought back to when I'd discussed it with the major. He hadn't seemed alarmed. Knowing she'd been kidnapped was far worse than thinking she'd run away."

She looked uncomfortable for a second. "He said nothing. He said nothing because I didn't tell him."

I looked at her askance.

"He doesn't like me," she whispered. "And to be frank, I'm a little scared of him. When Surena first left, I went looking for her and asking questions. He didn't like it and told me to stay away."

A doctor walked past and Sister Laurent pretended to check my bandages. Then she asked me the same question she'd asked before.

"Who did this to you?"

"I don't know."

"But it's linked, because you were looking for Surena and now they've taken Verity. Do you know what I think? I think Major Johnson is involved somehow."

"Where are my clothes?"

"From this morning? Burned I should think, except for those." She pointed to my once-white plimsolls.

All I had on was a pair of underpants.

"Could you get me something to wear? I'm leaving."

"But…"

"And we can talk in private."

She pursed her lips, thinking, and then sighed. "All right."

Fifteen minutes later, and after a great deal of fuss from the ward sister, who didn't want to sign me out, I was in a corridor of the hospital facing Sister Laurent.

"How do I look?" I asked, knowing that the brown trousers she'd given me were too large and their short length seemed enhanced by my dirty plimsolls.

"Like you should be in a hospital bed," she said.

"Do you know anything about a soldier called Mike Ellis?"

"No. Is he involved too?"

I shook my head. I didn't know. I was about to ask whether she knew anything about a bribe but remembered Dickins saying it had been a man who had left the message for him.

Instead, I told the sister about Limassol and that Alex might have been Alexis.

She looked relieved that I'd made some progress. "And where is Alexis now?"

"I don't know, but finding him is high on my list of priorities. My working theory is that he's involved with a gang. Did you ever hear Surena talk about a gang?"

"I don't know anything specific, just that she'd heard about trouble at Maxims. You've been there, you said?"

"Trouble as in gang-trouble, you mean?"

"I can't be sure what Surena meant."

I thought for a moment, wondering about the connection. "Have you heard of Kiss—the gang?"

"Of course. Everyone who's been here for a few years knows about the Kiss of Death. Although I don't recall anything in the papers for a while. A long time now. Do you think it was them? Do you think Surena is somehow..." Her voice trailed off and I wondered what she was imagining.

"Could Alexis be connected?"

"To that gang?" She paled. "Oh, I hope not! Isn't it more likely to be the major?"

My theory was also that Verity had been picked up by the gang because of Mrs Johnson, either as a reward or leverage. However, I kept this to myself.

Instead, I ventured: "I'd like to talk to your daughter."

Sister Laurent's reaction surprised me. "No! No, you can't." Her voice hadn't been hushed and she dropped it to a whisper again. "Sorry, but Betty has been traumatized by seeing her friend taken. I can tell you that all she saw was Verity being pulled into a small black car by a man. Poor Betty hasn't dared leave the house since."

"I'm sorry," I said, disappointed that there wasn't more information. "If Verity or Surena get in touch, will you let me know?" I wrote down the office phone number and handed it to her.

"Of course," she said. Then: "What are you going to do now?"

"Now," I said, "I'm going home. I'm going to lie down and sleep in my own bed."

★

When I got home, I locked the door and jammed a chair under the handle. It wouldn't stop anyone, but at least I'd hear them coming in. With my gun in my hand, I tried to sleep.

I'd taken another dose of painkillers, but when they wore off, my whole body felt like raw meat. My head was also full of images. I'd seen trauma in other people before but never experienced it. I thought I was tough, but a visceral fear ached as much as the cracked ribs.

It wasn't until I spoke to Captain Wolfe on Sunday that I better understood my reaction.

FORTY-ONE

"Fuckin' hell, you could have been Tom Flynned!" Wolfe's voice exploded down the telephone line. I'd spent the morning in bed recovering. I was back in the office and reviewing the translations of his latest batch of documents when Wolfe called.

Thomas Flynn had been a reporter at the *Palestine Post*, a British newspaper in Palestine. He'd been abducted and the SIB had joined the police in tracking down the criminals.

An ultra right-wing group known as the Stern Gang demanded a retraction and apology in the paper for Flynn's release, but after the paper complied, the gang went silent. Flynn's body was found a week later. I hadn't been involved in the discovery, but I knew the state of his body and the horrific torture he likely endured affected all those who had. Bill Wolfe included.

"Did you think they were going to kill you, Ash?"

"Yes."

"My God! You shouldn't be back at fuckin' work," he said.

"The work helps."

I took the opportunity to run through what we'd learned from the papers: the location of their military camps and approximate number of men. There was also discussion of something they referred to as *The Institute*, which sounded like a codename for covert action. Wolfe had told me of concerns for the region, especially the potential destabilization of Britain's strategic Suez Canal operation in Egypt. The Jews had fought Britain until independence and now Israel was at war with the Arabs, principally the occupying forces of Transjordan and Egypt. The Canal Zone could be targeted by either side or both, and Britain would not only lose its foothold in the region but find itself in the middle of a war again. However, there was no talk of this in the translated documents.

"Good," Wolfe said when I finished telling him the highlights. "That all fits with what I'm learning on the ground. As soon as I'm off the telephone, please call HQ and update them."

"Will do."

He said, "So let's get back to this fuckin' mess you've caused."

I feigned a chuckle.

"How are you sleeping, Ash?"

"Not at all."

"They picked you up at the apartment. You won't be safe there."

"I have my gun."

Now it was his turn to laugh. "No. You need to move into the officers' quarters at Alexander Barracks."

I'd thought about that but didn't like the optics. The Kiss gang had said not to involve the MPs, but moving into the barracks might look like I was involving the 227. Discussing it with Wolfe made me realize I had another option.

"I'll go somewhere else," I said.

"And I think you do need to tell Johnson. Even if his wife is involved—"

"Then he's compromised, Bill!" I said interrupting. "Would you tell him? Would you involve the provost marshal?"

He sighed. "After you were warned not to? I guess you're right."

I said, "I need to keep well away from them—for now. I'll involve the army if and when I know more and have a plan. And then it will be Colonel Dexter rather than Johnson."

"You're going to carry on investigating?" His tone was incredulous.

"Of course! For Penny's sake. She's innocent, Bill."

"If I could come back…"

"I'll be fine."

I listened to telephone background noise for a minute before he spoke again. "I've been thinking. Do you know Major Martin Gee, up at Wolseley?"

"I met him briefly. First Guards Brigade."

"That's right. I never met the man." He paused, and I looked at the phone as though it could tell me why Wolfe had mentioned Gee.

Then he explained. "Penny used to work for him. If you won't seek help from anyone else, then at least mention it to him. You should have someone on your side."

"I'll think about it," I said.

"Good. Now, we're done, so make that fuckin' call to Branch HQ and tell them what we've learned about the military bases in Israel."

I placed a call to the SIB office in London and had to wait ten minutes before I was put through to a subaltern who said nothing as I gave him the report I'd discussed with Wolfe. I felt like saying, "Finally we're making progress!" but kept to the facts and figured he was taking notes.

I finished and heard nothing for a few seconds. Then in a disinterested voice, he said, "Anything else, Lieutenant?"

"That's it for now."

"Get it typed up and flown over," he said and ended the call.

I replaced the receiver and looked at it for a long while. That was the army for you. I could have declared that the coal had been painted white and then repainted black and I would have heard about the same level of interest. It made me wonder whether we were doing anything important or just some top brass's good idea. *Let's divert two men for special duties and see what happens.*

I also wondered whether military intelligence was as much about doing *something* as any resulting benefit. I had no doubt that I'd never know whether our information was of use or not. There would be no pat on the back or other recognition unless it served a purpose. And that purpose was often political or for public relations.

Almost three years in this job and I was already becoming cynical.

That thought made me decide to stop distracting myself with meaningless work and focus on the most important thing: proving Penny was innocent.

FORTY-TWO

After two-finger typing my report, I visited Army GHQ on the harbour road and dropped it off. It would go in the overnight bag to London and I wondered if it would be read by anyone.

Giving it no further consideration, I spun the tyres and then slammed on the brakes. A vagabond staggered in front of my Land Rover and held out his hands, begging.

But he was no beggar.

"Pretend," he hissed at me. He was Greek and young. I wondered if I'd met him before. "I have information," he said under his breath.

I dug into my pocket and pulled out some coins.

"Mustn't be seen," the man said. "You're looking for Alexis. His parents own a shop in Nicosia."

I handed him the coins. "Who are you?"

"Yanis," he whispered, then immediately ducked away, running behind my vehicle.

"Wait!" I shouted, and might have given chase if not for my injuries. I sat still for a moment and tried to remember where I'd seen his face before. And then I had it. He'd been the young man with the vacuum cleaner in Maxims.

*

I wanted to go straight to Nicosia and look for Alexis's parents, but it was Sunday and I was still in pain. After another night with a chair at the door and a gun in my hand, I drove north.

Before beginning my search, I parked at the police HQ and went in search of Dickins. Again he wasn't in, but I saw DS Park.

"I heard!" he said, staring at me.

"What did you hear?"

He smiled. "Lieutenant, you will learn in Cyprus that only one thing travels faster than a forest fire, and that's gossip. We heard that you'd been beaten up. And your face…"

I nodded. "I think it was the gang."

"Kiss? You're lucky to be alive."

"It was a warning," I said. "I'm not to investigate—although they specifically mentioned MPs and Mrs Johnson."

"Interesting." He frowned, pondering on what I'd said.

"Does the name *The Man* mean anything to you?"

"Isn't that an expression for the boss, sometimes used about government officials? You know, workers against *the man*?"

"I think the Kiss gang call their boss *The Man*."

Park looked at me like a doctor considering how to tell a patient bad news, but he didn't. After a moment he said, "Why do you say that?"

"When I was being held, I heard them talk about *The Man*."

"Interesting. It's not a name we've come across before."

"What about Verity Johnson?" I asked. "Is there any news?"

"None. Do you think she's linked to this?"

I took a breath. "You probably don't know, but I've been told that she didn't run away. She was kidnapped."

His eyes opened wide. "What? That doesn't—" He stopped himself and shook his head.

I explained that she was seen being bundled into a small black car. There was no other information.

"Major Johnson didn't tell me," he said after I couldn't say more.

"He doesn't know."

"Curiouser and curiouser," he said. "Who told you?"

I said I couldn't divulge my source, before switching the subject. I asked if he knew the name Velopoulos.

"No why?"

I decided to keep my reasons to myself. I also kept quiet about the young man called Yanis and what he'd told me.

However, I did say: "Maxims in Limassol—could you check it out?"

"I've heard of Maxims. It's exclusively for officers." His voice showed distaste and his neck twitched. "Sorry, Lieutenant. You know how the Other Ranks find it... er... difficult to respect officers. Old habits and attitudes die hard."

I nodded. I certainly did know how ordinary soldiers thought most officers were a waste of space.

Park forced a smile. "Of course, you're an exception."

"Thanks, Anthem," I said half in disbelief. "So Maxims... Mrs Johnson disappeared with a man from there—"

"This Velopoulos chap?"

Boy, he was smart. "Yes," I said, "and I was followed by a man I saw there." I described the man on the motorcycle, the one with the scarring around his eyes.

Park didn't know him, but said he'd ask around. He also said he'd update the inspector for me and would let me know unofficially if they found anything more about the missing girl.

He said, "I see you're wearing a gun now."

Since Saturday the gun hadn't left my side. "If the gang come for me again, I won't hesitate."

He nodded his understanding.

After shaking his hand I set off to find Alexis Velopoulos's parent's shop.

★

I started at the top of Ledra Street and worked my way down. Most of the shopkeepers spoke English, although they shook their heads when I asked for people called Velopoulos.

I passed the bus depot and got to a major junction with Paphos Street. To the right appeared less Greek and more Turkish or Armenian, I judged from when I'd visited the cathedral. Ahead was similar, but veering to the left was a military hostel in the centre of a circus. And beyond there, I saw a cluster of shops. That was where I finally hit success and was told to look for a linen shop on Hermes Street.

Retracing my steps, I found Hermes and walked as far as an open market before spotting the linen shop.

I entered and was greeted by an elderly Greek gentleman.

"How can I help sir?" he asked in an educated English accent.

"I'm looking for Alexis," I said.

His face remained impassive, although I detected concern in his eyes. After all, I was wearing my revolver.

"Alexis Velopoulos," I said. "I understand that he's from here. And that his family owns the shop."

"I don't think I can help you, sir," he said.

I shook my head at his mistake. If he didn't know the name, he would have simply said he couldn't help. Thinking implied knowledge.

I saw a woman at the rear watching surreptitiously, peering around a clothes rack.

Directing my voice towards her, I said, "I'm a friend… I'm looking for a friend."

The woman stepped from behind the rack.

The man shook his head. "I don't believe you are Alexis's friend."

I pulled the photograph of Mrs Johnson from my pocket and kept my explanation simple. "I'm Surena's friend."

The woman stepped closer. I could see intrigue in her eyes, although the man remained suspicious.

I said, "We haven't heard from Surena since she went away eight months ago."

The woman said, "Can I see your identity papers, Mr—"

"Ash Carter," I said, and held out my warrant card.

The man cleared his throat. "You're an MP, working for Major Johnson."

"No, I'm a detective—Special Investigations Branch. I don't work for the major."

The woman stepped forward again, and now I sidestepped the old man and faced her.

"Are you Alexis's mother?"

She nodded, and I saw sadness in her eyes.

I said, "I know he used to work at Maxims in Limassol. His friend Yanis told me to find you."

I saw recognition in the old woman's eyes.

"Do you know where Alexis is?" I asked.

"I... We haven't heard from him since..."

"Since he eloped with Surena?"

She nodded and blinked tears from her eyes.

"Where did they go?" I asked.

The man said, "Even if we knew, we wouldn't tell you."

"Her friends are worried. Surena's niece is worried"—I threw that one in for good measure—"I think *you* are worried."

The woman said, "It's not like him. He's such a good boy."

Not so good that he doesn't run off with another man's wife, I thought.

I said, "But you knew he was leaving?"

"Yes."

"Where did he say they would go?"

"The mainland," the man said. "We have family in Athens. They would start there before moving on."

"But they didn't arrive," the woman added.

"They probably found something else," the man said, nodding encouragement towards his wife.

"Yes," she said unconvincingly, and I sensed they'd had this conversation many times.

I said, "When was the last time you saw him?"

The man gave me a date eight months ago, just before Mrs Johnson left.

She said, "So Alexis isn't good at keeping us informed. It's only been eight months since we've heard news from him."

I had a difficult but burning question and I couldn't find a way of asking it without sounding awkward. I decided to just say what I'd been wondering.

"Did Alexis ever mention a gang?" I asked.

The man cocked his head like he hadn't heard me properly.

"Specifically the *Chis* gang?" I said XIS the Greek way, rather than Kiss.

After a sharp intake of breath, the woman said, "You aren't suggesting...?"

"I'm not suggesting anything. I'm just looking into a connection between... between Surena Johnson and a gang."

"I think you should leave," the man said, bristling and stepping between me and his wife. "Alexis would never be involved with bad behaviour. He is a good boy. I think you are trying to trick us—"

I raised my hands. "No tricks. I just heard that—"

The woman stepped sideways so that we could look eye to eye, although she must have been a foot shorter than me. "Yes," she said.

Her husband looked at her and shook his head, but she kept her eyes on mine, assessing me, hopefully seeing my honesty.

"They didn't say 'gang', but Surena told us about trouble. She said she knew some things."

"What?" I asked.

"We don't know," the man said, and the woman agreed.

I left them with a promise that I'd let them know if I discovered anything and the man wrote down my telephone number in case they heard from their son.

My next visit would be to Major Gee. As I walked back to my Land Rover, I thought about what I'd learned.

Alexis's folks appeared decent and I got the sense that he was as well. I'd expected some confirmation that he was part of a criminal gang, but I hadn't got it. That had thrown me. However, I'd been told that Mrs Johnson was concerned about trouble. I'd also learned that Alexis hadn't been in touch for eight months.

It meant something; I just wasn't sure what yet.

FORTY-THREE

"Penny Cartwright used to work for you," I said after taking a seat in Major Gee's office and explaining why my face looked a mess.

"Not really," he said, with that permanent smile of his. "She was in the typing pool here."

For the second time in an hour, my head swam with confusing thoughts. Had Penny lied to us?

"Ah, I see the misunderstanding," Gee said, smiling even more than normal. "I wrote a letter of recommendation for her. She was a diligent worker—a good typist. Shame about her sister, but Penny is made of stronger stuff. I knew she'd come back to Cyprus, only hoped she'd return here. So she's working for you now, eh, Carter?"

His voice seemed strange, like he knew something I didn't. And there was that damned smiling mouth of his. Then again, I was tired and hot and frustrated, so maybe my radar was off.

I said, "Did you hear?"

"Hear?"

"What's happened to her?"

He sat back with a mixture of surprise and concern in his eyes. "No. Tell me, man. What's happened?"

So I gave him an overview of Sergeant Mike Ellis's murder and Penny's arrest.

As I spoke, the colour drained from Gee's face.

"My God!"

I said, "It's got to be a simple case of mistaken identity. Penny caught the seventeen fifteen bus in Nicosia. It was scheduled to arrive at the Larnaca bus depot at nineteen hundred hours but was delayed. She ran home from there and was seen by a man who'd just observed Mike Ellis's likely killer leave the scene of the crime."

Gee frowned. "I don't understand."

"There was a period when the witness lost the likely killer. The next person he saw was Penny."

"And running made her look guilty?"

"Absolutely!"

He rubbed his chin, thinking. "So you need to show she was on the bus. Did she keep the ticket?"

"Yes, but it was a *return* and impossible to know when it was used."

"Surely that's enough. She was on the bus, she couldn't have done it."

I shook my head. "I've been to the bus company and they couldn't even confirm the time the bus arrived in Larnaca. I also spoke to the conductor and showed him a photograph of Penny. He's no good as a witness."

"Did he say she wasn't on the bus?"

"No, no, not that. He just said that he might recognize her but couldn't remember her being on that particular bus. But it had been a week ago and he doubted he'd remember anyone on the bus except for a handful of regulars."

He nodded. "Did you get their names and interview them?"

"No names. I met the bus with a Greek speaker and no one remembered her."

"Friday," he said absently, then nodded again. "Sounds like a reasonable plan."

I figured he'd been distracted and not listening. I didn't have a plan. I'd already questioned the passengers.

I said, "This happened a week ago. Penny had been in Nicosia on Thursday and came back on the last Friday bus. I've already questioned passengers."

His eyes came into focus. His smile remained. "Right. Got it."

"Maybe I should meet the bus again this Friday. It would also help to find her friend—the one she was visiting."

His right eye closed in a squint, and I wondered if he was questioning the sense of it.

"I know," I said. "Penny won't tell me anything. She doesn't want to involve her friend."

Now he nodded. "Thursday and Friday, you say? What's her friend's name? Maybe I know her from when Penny worked here."

"Margie. That's all I know. Her friend is Margie."

Gee said nothing.

"Do you know the name?"

He cleared his throat and looked uncomfortable.

"Sir?" I prompted.

"Margie," he said slowly. "That'll be me."

FORTY-FOUR

"Margie?" I said, feeling my mouth dry up and my jaw click. "*You* are Margie?"

"It was her pet name for me. Martin Gee... Mar-gie. You see?"

He winced, and I wasn't sure whether it was because of the choice of effeminate name or guilt.

He said, "There's something you should know, Ash."

I said nothing, suddenly aware of the thump in my chest.

"Penny... well she was more than just my copy typist."

"More?" I said hoarsely.

He took a breath. "Don't make me spell it out, man."

"I think you should, sir."

"We are lovers."

"Could I have some water?" I asked, delaying for time, hoping my voice didn't betray me. My girlfriend, the one I was desperately trying to help, was seeing another man.

He said some words—I wasn't sure what because of the suddenly oppressive heat and lack of oxygen—I took a glass from his hand and gulped it down, focusing on the water.

When I looked up, he had a mischievous glint in his eyes.

"So she"—I cleared my throat—"came to see you?"

"Yes."

"She was with you?"

"Yes."

I swallowed again as my composure returned. "Are you saying that she stayed with you on the Thursday night?"

"Yes. We checked into a hotel. The Royal. Not our real names of course. Mr and Mrs Smith." He chortled. I didn't.

"And so you saw her on Friday?"

He smiled. "Now it wouldn't have been very honourable of me... yes, of course we were together on Friday too."

"Good," I said, despite feeling anything but good. "You can be a witness."

"Ah," he said.

"Ah, what?"

"I can't be a witness. It's complicated."

I guessed what he was going to say before he said it. There was no ring on his finger, but the naughty-boy expression spoke volumes.

"I'm happily married," he said.

Happily? Did he recognize the contradiction as he said it? I suspected he didn't.

I took another slug of water. "I was hoping you could help."

"I'll do anything I can, Ash. I'm sure you appreciate that. But under the circumstances, I'm not willing to jeopardize my marriage—"

"For the woman you love?" I challenged more forcefully than I intended.

"Hey!" he said. "It's an affair, all right? The woman I love is my wife."

I said nothing. Outside, I could hear horses, and the flash of colour through the window told me that the Royal Lancers were returning to base for the night. I watched them ride past.

Eventually, he said, "If I thought my evidence would guarantee Penny's freedom, I'd provide it, but it won't, will it? I didn't see her get on the bus at seventeen fifteen. I can't attest to the one she caught and the prosecution will see right through that. It's equivalent to the return bus ticket."

I said nothing. The last of the horse-hoof clatter faded away.

I started to rise, feeling like the meeting was at an end. I'd wasted my time coming here. Or rather, I wished I never had, because then I'd have continued, ignorant of Penny's betrayal. Perhaps my mind started to work again because a thought struck me.

"Do you know anything about Kiss of Death?"

"The alleged gang? Trouble with the natives?" He chuckled, clearly far more at ease than me.

"They might be involved. Why do you say *alleged*?"

"Well there's not much evidence, is there? They have only struck a couple of times since I've been on the island. I don't have a great deal of experience, but I always assumed that gangs are like the Mafia. If they were operating here, they'd be everywhere. We'd hear about it almost daily, wouldn't we?"

I didn't know. My experience of gangs was limited to street thugs and religious zealots. Neither type fit the Mafia mould. DS Park had talked about territorial squabbles and smuggling.

I said, "Have you ever come across anything that was suspicious then—to do with land or property?"

He shrugged. "The only suspicious thing I can think of is the cigarette factory." He got up and tapped a map on the wall. "Here, off Nelson Street."

I got up and looked. It was just over a mile to the north. At eleven o'clock, beyond the Nicosia city wall. My eye followed the road west, across the river. A building labelled

"The English Club" sat below a golf course. Not far below this was the Central Prison where Penny lay incarcerated.

He tapped the club building. "I have dinner with friends there often. Including tonight."

"Why's the cigarette factory suspicious?" I asked.

"Because I'm sure they don't make cigarettes there anymore. Cigarettes are all imported these days, but each time I've passed it the factory seemed busy. You know, trucks going in and out. Trucks that don't have cigarette brands emblazoned across them."

"Then what—?"

"Nothing," he said. "At least none that I've noticed. What self-respecting business wouldn't advertise on their trucks?"

"Have you told anyone about this?"

He shook his head. "Look, Ash, you're an investigator, and I'm certain you're a damn good one. You have to remember, I'm just a pen-pusher. I'm not interested in petty crime."

We had continued standing by the map and now he stepped towards the door.

"I'd like to help Penny," he said, offering his hand, which was cooler than mine. "I won't be a witness and I can't do much, but if I can help I will."

*

I pictured the map in my head and drove up to the cigarette factory. Between the trees I saw two long redbrick buildings and two lofty chimneys. Neither had smoke coming out. The sun was low to my left, but I could see no activity beyond high fencing. The place looked deserted.

I crossed the river, went south again and turned into Norman Street. This led me to the prison.

Since they weren't expecting me, the sign-in process took longer than before because there wasn't a warder available straight away. This made me suspect that the prisoners here didn't receive many visitors.

Penny forced a smile when she came into the interview room, but I didn't reach for her as she approached.

"What's wrong, Ash? And your face—it's all bruised!"

"I've spoken to Major Gee," I said, finding it harder to speak than expected. I'd planned my words, but now the sentences jumbled and slipped in my mind. I breathed in and out to calm my heart.

"I met Margie."

"Ash…" There was pleading in her voice, although I didn't know why.

"He told me about the two of you, Penny. You were cheating on me. You told me you were visiting a girlfriend. So you lied too!"

"I haven't seen you since Thursday. That's four days, worrying. And now you accuse me of that! Are we that fragile? I guess we are."

"Fragile? Penny—" Exasperated, I couldn't finish my sentence.

"I didn't lie to you, Ash. You assumed that Margie was a girl. I didn't—"

"You let me assume!"

She raised a hand and I noticed her fingers shaking. "Let me explain, then you can decide how you feel. All right?"

I agreed, although I already knew how I felt. I felt like my guts had been gouged out by the woman I trusted.

She said, "Yes, I came to see Martin,"—I noted the switch to his proper name—"but it was to make sure he understood. I told him about you."

I thought back to my meeting with Gee. He'd given me no indication that he knew about me and Penny.

She continued: "I told him that we were over because I was now seeing you."

"And yet you spent the night with him!"

"I did no such thing," she declared, and I admit she sounded truthful.

"He said you booked into the Royal Hotel under the name of Mr and Mrs Smith."

She shook her head.

"Are you denying it?"

"He booked a room and I stayed in it, but not with him."

I studied her eyes and said nothing.

She said, "He thought I'd change my mind, but I really did come up to tell him our relationship was over. I said I was with you. I stayed on my own."

"Why didn't he mention it?" I asked. "Why did he sound like you were still an item?"

She shook her head. "I don't know, Ash. Is it a man thing? Perhaps he was messing with your head. Maybe it was like two stags rutting."

I said nothing for a while. The background clatter of cell doors waxed and waned. The smell of bleach wafted through the room.

She said, "He won't help, will he?"

"No."

"Because of his wife."

"He said he was just a pen-pusher but would help if he could."

She reached for my hand, I let her hold it and I saw her fear and despair again. This was a dreadful place, better than the military cells but still incarceration. And Penny had no idea when it would end.

We talked about her new lawyer, who had explained the process and seemed confident, but unlike her original military guy, this one didn't talk about finding proof. He just said it was up to the Crown prosecution to prove she was guilty.

"Don't worry, Penny," I said, "I'll get the proof."

She squeezed my hand and nodded and she believed me. Her mouth opened and closed like she was asking a question.

I said, "I haven't found Mrs Johnson yet, but I'm getting closer. I found the parents of the man she eloped with." I said the man's name and saw no recognition in her eyes. But then I hadn't expected any. "He worked at Maxims," I added.

"Oh?"

"But more importantly, I think there is a gang connection. This may be linked to the execution we stumbled across. The Kiss gang."

"Oh?" she said again, and for the first time, I saw hope flicker in her eyes.

"And I didn't tell you about my bruised face"—I raised my shirt and showed the bandages around my ribcage—"I think I met them."

"Oh my God!"

"They warned me off."

"I noticed you were carrying your gun. Is that why?"

"They'll kill me if I carry on investigating or involve the military."

"Then you have to—"

"I have to continue," I interrupted. "They played their hand, and the last thing I'll do is fold."

"This isn't poker, Ash. This is serious. This is life or death!"

"I can handle myself."

She let out a long sigh. "But there is one positive thing. At least it confirms your suspicion. Mrs Johnson did it. Will they release me now?"

When I didn't respond straight away, her face dropped. "It's not enough, is it?"

"No. Like I say, I need to keep digging."

She nodded.

When I'd spoken to Bill Wolfe, he'd expressed concern about me returning home. They'd picked me up outside and would come for me again—most likely during the night. I'd rejected the idea of the army's officers' quarters because that violated their rule. However, Penny's apartment was vacant and a separate bedroom was a more secure layout.

She hesitated a fraction when I asked if I could use her place, but then she agreed.

"Are you sure?"

I smiled. "I'm not giving up, Penny. This is not just for you, but there's a real killer out there, and no one else appears to have the stomach to catch them."

*

I could have just gone east to Nicosia and then around the walled city. But I didn't. Major Gee had said he was eating at the English Club tonight. Would he be there now?

It was probably foolish machismo that made me go north to Nelson Street and then west to find the clubhouse. My jaw clicked and I realized I was making it click. I was angry with Gee. If we *had been* rutting stags then it'd been an unfair fight since I believed everything he'd said.

Even in the dark, I could see the building clearly. Lights blazed both inside and out and I thought it looked out of place, more like an English country mansion than a typical Cypriot property. There were two floors and sandstone brick walls. A grand arched entrance led to dark wooden doors and on either side was a porter or valet in uniform.

There were thirty or so cars outside and I pulled into a space rather than approach the entrance. The men outside looked my way and I suspect they wondered why I hadn't asked them to park it for me.

I sat and watched movement inside and imagined Gee sitting at a table with a bunch of pals. I imagined walking up to him and calling him out. Then I thought that he might be there with his wife and friends. Maybe I'd casually walk up and tell her about Penny. I'd humiliate him and likely ruin his marriage.

Whatever, I couldn't just sit still.

Maybe he wasn't even in the club yet.

He was.

Gee sat at a table with two women and a man. He was still in uniform; the other man was not. They alternated around a circular table: man, woman, man woman, and they talked across one another. I judged that the women were their wives.

No one challenged me. I walked in with confidence, like I was a member. My head was full of questions and lines that I'd deliver.

He saw me coming and I said, "Major Gee."

He stood up. "Lieutenant Carter."

And then I decked him with a powerful left. No explanation, just a punch that sent him tumbling backwards over his chair.

The women screamed and there was a blur of movement as people went to Gee's aid, but I was already turning and walking away.

There were shouts. The two men who'd been outside rushed past me and I kept on walking.

Nobody challenged me.

I got into my jeep and drove away. A big satisfied grin on my face.

I was still smiling as I went past the cigarette factory. Only this time, I could see that it wasn't abandoned. Pinpricks of light speckled the sides beyond the fence.

I turned left into a street called Hilarian. There were trees and more of the high fence. But there was also a gate. And the gate was open.

I sat and watched and saw a van enter. Gee had told me there was no advertising and he was right. The van appeared plain and grey. In fact, it was similar to the one outside Maxims. The one I'd first seen the scarred man driving.

Too much of a coincidence? Maybe, but there were thousands of trucks in Cyprus and I figured many could look similar. Just like army vehicles. Thousands of them.

Like the Land Rover that drove out of the compound and towards me.

An army Land Rover. There were hundreds of those on the island. Although this one was distinctive.

It had *Guard Dog Unit* written on the side.

FORTY-FIVE

Scientists make a hypothesis and then test it. The detective's process can be quite similar, but both disciplines can also lead to the wrong answer. If the tests performed and information gained supports the hypothesis then it will be accepted. But what if the wrong tests were performed, the wrong questions asked? What if you were looking at the problem the wrong way round?

I was pretty sure that I recognized the driver of the GDU jeep: a private I'd seen when I first confronted Mike Ellis at their camp. He didn't look in my direction and I don't think he spotted me.

He just drove around Nicosia to the four o'clock position and then took what people called the 'new road' to Famagusta.

There were no evasive manoeuvres. He just drove straight towards Famagusta and then turned off towards 6GDU.

I kept my distance and watched him go all the way in, acting like it was perfectly normal behaviour. Which it wasn't. No reason for a dog unit man to be up in Nicosia, in uniform, coming out of a cigarette factory.

With my Land Rover hidden, I sat and watched the little camp. People moved between huts and tents. The dogs were fed, and I was bothered by insects. For some reason, they appeared attracted to my scalp. So after an hour of nothing much happening except for me slapping at mosquitos, I headed home.

Keeping a wary eye out for anyone following, I saw none. However, the gang knew my address, so they didn't need to follow me.

Parking in the usual place, I went inside and quickly packed a bag. Fifteen minutes later, I clambered out of the letterbox-sized window in my toilet room, screamed silently as my ribs squeezed through, and then dropped onto the compacted earth below. I waited in the darkness for a few minutes, partly in case anyone was around and partly because of the pain.

Then I slung the bag over my shoulder and zigzagged behind buildings, through shadows and alleyways. I passed close to where Ellis had been murdered and kept going until I reached Penny's apartment.

I waited for a car to drive past before locating the window at the rear of her place. It wasn't ideal, but using a screwdriver, I jimmied the window and climbed inside.

★

An instructor in Mytchett Hutments in Hampshire had told us that there were two kinds of facts: hard ones and soft ones. It was a bit tongue in cheek, but in essence, he meant there are facts and there are things that people either accept or assume are facts. These soft facts are often the result of hearsay or third-party information. The hard facts were evidential. If we didn't convert soft facts into hard ones, then we should be cautious in our interpretation.

What the instructor hadn't explained is that you may discover facts that aren't relevant. Just because it was true didn't mean it helped the investigation. Theory, like science, could be so much easier than real-life detective work.

I believed Mrs Johnson was somehow linked to the gang, because of their threat. The police called the gang Kiss because of the imprint—the Kiss of Death. But what if they were wrong?

Seeing the spotty private from the guard dog unit last night could be my big break. It could solidify some of those soft facts and explain a heck of a lot.

For the first time since my abduction by the gang, I slept soundly, although my gun was still in my hand when I awoke.

After exercising in Penny's room, I slipped out of the window in my casual clothes. If I'd been uninjured I'd have considered avoiding my Land Rover, but I couldn't run without discomfort and I wasn't sure how far I could walk. So I drove to Famagusta, taking a circuitous route and watching for a tail.

No one followed me, and I went into the town from the far side and parked before the commercial harbour. There was a wind off the sea and thunder-blue waves slapped the sea walls.

The first section reeked of fish, although I figured most of the fishermen were out at sea. Maybe it was the old nets and other detritus that smelled rotten.

Then came the main commercial dock, behind which were typical plain warehouses and ugly buildings. These stopped at the black buttress of Famagusta's city wall and Othello's Tower. The land in front of the city had been built upon and acted as another section of dock. The customs house and more long sheds lay across the two-hundred-yard stretch.

I moved from cover point to cover point, scanned and watched for anything of interest.

It wasn't until I was halfway along that I saw what I'd been looking for: the GDU. Two men with two German Shepherd dogs stopped by a ship, talked to someone with a clipboard for a minute and then moved on. Neither of the men was Payne. Neither was the spotty private.

I slunk back, waited for them to pass, and then followed.

They went up and back, patrolling the quay, stopping for the dogs to sniff, stopping to speak to lorry drivers and men loading carts with goods from the ships. The GDU served two purposes, I figured. The dogs were checking for contraband and, in theory, explosives. The men could respond to trouble. They were both armed.

However, from their relaxed attitude I suspected the men expected as much trouble as I did. There hadn't been trouble here in the war, so it was even more unlikely during peacetime. Maybe.

After more than an hour, they got into their Land Rover, dogs in the back, and drove past me. Neither looked my way.

I thought about following but decided to continue my own patrol. I reached the final section. This was south-east of the city, where the Royal Navy had its largest fleet.

I could see masters-at-arms patrolling the quays. MPs wouldn't be here unless troopships came in, and I understood that those tended to dock at Larnaca or Limassol.

The sun climbed high and I cut through into the shade of the old town and found water. That's when I spotted two more GDU men, strolling and chatting. From his height, I knew immediately that one was Payne. Initially, there was no sign of their dogs, but they'd left them tied up in the shade.

Once Payne and his colleague started patrolling, I followed them towards the commercial harbour. When I'd seen them without their dogs, I'd been intrigued, but they did exactly the same as the previous two team members. They'd just changed shift and maybe taken a sneaky break beforehand.

However, towards the end of the next hour, Payne flagged down a truck and spoke to the driver. I wouldn't have thought anything of it, but the other GDU man took both dogs, stepped away and glanced around like a lookout.

Changing position, I tried to see Payne more clearly, but most of his body was shielded by the truck.

Eventually Payne stepped back and waved and the truck drove off. If I'd been able to run I might have raced to my jeep and given chase. Instead, I took note of the vehicle's livery and registration plate and switched my attention back to Payne.

He had a package in his hand: a brown paper parcel tied with string.

With a nod to his colleague, Payne set off walking. I tracked him along the quay to his parked vehicle. Hardly breaking step, he tossed the package inside. I had to duck out of the way as he spun around and trekked back.

As soon as he was out of sight, I strolled over to his Land Rover and looked inside. The parcel lay in the passenger footwell and I quickly retrieved it and walked casually back to the shade of the buildings.

Cigarettes. A tin holding maybe a hundred little white sticks. Specifically, they were an American brand called Lucky Strike. I looked at them, puzzled, before rewrapping the parcel and returning it to the Land Rover.

I saw Payne and the other guy patrolling again and decided to climb the city wall and get a broader view of the extensive harbour.

Once there, I could cover all of the commercial sector and about a third of the naval one.

A large ship docked and the GDU men boarded with their dogs. I wondered if I'd see more unusual behaviour, but they came down the gangplank empty-handed after twenty minutes.

There was plenty of movement with dockworkers and vehicles, but something caught my eye and I squinted towards the naval docks. A Bedford troop carrier stopped and another headed my way.

Redcaps clambered out. I found this curious. Why were MPs on the quays? I looked along the docks in case I'd missed a troopship coming in. I saw none. I also saw nothing resembling a troopship in the bay.

I watched the MPs for a while rather than the GDU men. When I saw a second pair of GDU guys I wondered if something was going down. However, after another tedious hour, I confirmed that the two groups were independent. Occasionally they acknowledged one another but there was no conferring.

An exercise, I decided, although such activities usually involved an objective, and I saw nothing obvious.

The distant Bedford truck turned around and left with the first batch of MPs. Minutes later, the ones on the commercial docks formed up and also left in their truck.

Just me and the GDU teams again.

I watched for another hour and saw Payne leave.

I stretched my legs and came down from the ramparts. I got water and fruit and decided to investigate more of the buildings within the walls.

Goods from the cargo ships came in here as well as to the warehouses beyond.

And that's when I saw an unmarked grey-blue van. I'd seen quite a few during the day, but this one especially caught my attention because it approached the city gate nearest to me. And flagging it down was none other than the GDU private. In uniform, with a rifle over his shoulder, he spoke to the driver.

The driver pointed. The private pointed then signalled for movement.

The van started rolling forward at little more than walking pace. The private followed.

And I followed twenty paces back.

The van came to a set of sky-blue painted doors. The passenger jumped out and took a handle and rolled it back. Then he rolled back the second door before climbing back in.

The van drove through.

The GDU private walked through.

The doors slid shut.

I was close enough to hear the rollers and the final clunk and I was sure I'd heard those same noises before. On the night I'd been driven to someplace and threatened.

I needed a telephone.

No doubt there were phones in some of the premises, but I knew for sure where I'd find one. On the road along the harbour, I flagged a car, flashed my warrant card and hitched up onto its running board.

"Just two hundred yards," I called through the window, and then held on tight as he nipped along towards the naval yard.

With a quick word of thanks, I stepped off. A few paces and I was at a block of naval offices. Up the steps and I was confronted by an alarmed receptionist.

"Sir," he said, standing. "I must—"

"Military police, Special Investigations Branch." I held out my card and he checked it thoroughly before giving me a curt nod.

"Sir?"

"Telephone," I said. "I urgently need to make a call."

★

I asked for DI Dickins, but he was unavailable again.

"May I enquire as to the nature of your call, Lieutenant?" the police operator said.

"Gang-related," I said. "Is DS Park available?"

Two long minutes later, Park grumbled down the line.

"Lieutenant?"

I said, "What if you got it wrong? What if the gang mark wasn't X-I-S?"

"Is this about the Kiss of Death?"

I said, "What if this whole time it was upside down, Sergeant?"

"What?"

He really wasn't getting it, and from his tone I now wondered if he'd been woken up.

"What are you talking about?"

"What if it was six?"

I could hear background noise and figured he was thinking.

"S-I-X," he said slowly, "not X-I-S. Hmm, it could be I suppose. What does that mean though? Six is obviously English and we're dealing with Greeks here."

I waited because I wanted him to keep thinking. Then I said, "Maybe that's the problem. Maybe that's why—"

"We haven't made progress? Hmm. What makes me think this is more than just an idea?"

"Six," I said. "As in 6GDU. Maybe it refers to them?"

"The dog unit?" he said, surprised. "Why in the world...?"

"Sergeant Major Ellis of 6GDU was murdered. I think it was gang-related."

"Would they kill their own sergeant major? Is that what you're suggesting?"

"Gangs kill their own all the time," I said, although I knew there was a problem with my theory. The previous executions had been a bullet to the brain. Ellis had been stabbed through the eye.

"Lieutenant, I—"

"I need your help. I need the police."

A master-at-arms came into the building and spoke to the receptionist.

"If you've a problem with the dog unit, surely you should be calling 227 Provost Company, not me."

"DS Park... Anthem, I need your help, because I can't involve the military." I didn't bother explaining. "And I think this is your gang. There's a compound just inside the city wall at Famagusta." I gave him the address. "I need armed men as soon as possible."

The receptionist caught my eye, and I wondered whether he was suggesting I'd exceeded my time on the telephone. The master-at-arms moved in my direction. I turned my attention back to the handset.

"I'll get men from the Famagusta police. They can be there in a matter of minutes. It'll take me at least forty to get there, so I'll ask them to bar the gates and wait for me, if that's all right?"

"Perfect," I said.

Another pause, and I was about to end the call when he spoke again.

"Lieutenant, you're sure about this?"

"Yes."

The master-at-arms was standing close. Perhaps he needed to use the telephone.

"Police not the military?" Park said.

"Yes."

"I'll be there as soon as I can."

I replaced the receiver and the master-at-arms stepped closer.

I moved aside, but he kept looking at me.

"Lieutenant Carter?"

"That's me."

"Would you accompany me outside, sir?" It was a question, but he said it compellingly.

I followed him thinking it was a little excessive. All right, I wasn't Navy, but surely a short important telephone call hadn't violated any interdisciplinary boundaries.

He stepped outside. I stepped outside into the dazzling sunlight. And I stopped.

In front of me were four men, military police. A warrant officer in the lead looked at me hard.

"Lieutenant Carter? Sir, I need you to come with me. You are under arrest."

PART THREE

"The fox was hiding but its tail could be seen."
- Cypriot Proverb

MURRAY BAILEY

FORTY-SIX

I was back in the Glasshouse, only this time I was behind bars rather than just visiting. The charge was grievous bodily harm of a fellow officer. Although I wasn't given his name, I realized this would be Major Gee.

Punching him had been impulsive and foolish. I had known men thrown out of the military police for similar crimes. I might even get a dishonourable discharge. What was I thinking? Time was ticking, and I was incapacitated rather than helping Penny.

What I couldn't fathom was why Gee would report it. Surely he risked exposing his infidelity. Maybe I'd misread the situation. Maybe he wanted Penny more than his marriage.

What had he said in his office? *It's an affair, all right? The woman I love is my wife.* He'd also told me he was happily married and couldn't be a witness.

That didn't sound like a man who'd report me for GBH.

As soon as I was brought in, I'd asked to see Johnson. In fact, I expected the major to visit me here, but he didn't show.

"He's been out on an exercise all day," the corporal on guard duty said.

"Over at Famagusta?" I said, thinking of the men unloading from the troop carriers.

He shook his head. "No, sir. Actually, I'm sure I can tell you. There's been trouble with the Jews in the detention camp at Pyla."

I said, "We need to get them to Israel."

"Yes, sir."

After a pause, I risked: "What do you think of the major?"

The corporal looked uncomfortable and swallowed. I realized I was putting him in an awkward situation.

"No one can overhear you," I said encouragingly.

He said, "He's not bad. Different, I guess, since he came from the infantry—Johnson and his chief clerk. The men say he's not your typical PM."

I thought about that. Moving from infantry to military police was unusual although not unheard of. I also thought about the photograph of Mrs Johnson—the one where I'd thought her husband was in fancy dress. I still had it in my pocket. Of course, I'd been disarmed and they'd taken my personal effects. But they'd missed the photograph wedged in my breast pocket.

I took it out and showed it to the corporal.

"Seen this before?"

"No sir—" He stared at the picture. "Gracious, the major is wearing a US Army uniform. And he's a Lieutenant Colonel!"

I laughed since the young man mimicked my own surprise when I'd first seen the photograph. I said, "He was assigned to the Eleventh Army infantry and part of Operation Fortitude—the fake US Army."

He nodded, although his eyes told me he knew nothing about the operation or Johnson's role. But that wasn't why I was showing him the picture. I pointed to the tall man behind Mrs Johnson. An incidental character but somehow connected to the other two. It had bothered me before, but now it struck me.

"Is that Graham Crawley, Johnson's chief clerk?"

The corporal squinted at the picture. "Yes, I think that's him."

So Crawley went way back with the major. Johnson had transferred to Cyprus and his man had come with him. *Three in that relationship,* Mrs Marsland-Askew had told me. She said she wouldn't have put up with it, and I wondered how Surena Johnson coped. Maybe she liked it. Maybe it made her relationship with the older husband easier.

"You came from Palestine, didn't you, sir?" the corporal said, breaking into my thoughts.

I stuck the photograph back in my pocket.

"I did."

"Was it as crazy as they say?"

"Probably worse. Terrorists on both sides and us in the middle."

"It'll never happen here," he said, and I grunted agreement. However, I thought back to what detectives Dickins and Park had told me. The British Empire was shrinking, and one day, Cyprus might strive for its independence. They thought that XIS might be a Greek acronym. They thought the gang was Greek separatist.

But surely they wouldn't have a flurry of activity after the war and then go quiet?

The more I thought about it, a British gang made more sense. The voices I'd heard when threatened were muffled but British. Could XIS really be SIX? Could the gang be the 6GDU?

Maybe it was too obvious, but then I figured gangs could be proud and fearless. They could be arrogant, and arrogance led to mistakes.

I needed to get out and discover what was going on. But I was stuck in a cramped cell on an uncomfortable bench. For how long, I had no idea.

★

After my breakfast, a sergeant came to see me. He had the duty guard open my cell. Then to my surprise, he saluted me.

"Sergeant?" I said, prompting an explanation.

"Sir, I'd like you to accompany me to Major Johnson's office."

I glanced outside, saw no more guards and looked back at him. However, no explanation was forthcoming. He just nodded curtly and said, "Follow me, sir."

"Ever heard Major Johnson referred to as *The Man*?" I asked the sergeant as we left the Glasshouse. Soldiers on the parade ground marched in khaki drill and a sergeant major bellowed instructions.

The sergeant with me waited a moment, then: "No, sir, I can't say that I have."

"Anyone else?"

"No, sir."

I saw Johnson standing by his window and I figured he'd watched me walk across the parade ground to the officers' block. The sergeant marched whereas I walked normally. After all, I wasn't in uniform and no close-formation guard boxed me in, like I'd had last night when they marched me into the Glasshouse.

Johnson stretched and clicked his neck as I entered.

"What am I going to do about you, Carter?" his voice cracked, and I thought he looked more tired than the last time I'd seen him.

"Nothing, sir," I said.

"I warned you, didn't I? You're a loose cannon, young man, and I don't like loose cannons." He scrutinized me for a few beats. "First you punch Sergeant Payne outside a cinema and now you attack an officer at his club. Are you going to tell me he deserved it as well? Are you some sort of judge meting out punishments for what you see as wrong-doings?"

I looked beyond him, out of the window.

"You're a disgrace, Carter."

There was a big black crow perched on a fence post outside. I wondered if it was watching the Suffolks on the parade ground doing the drills I'd seen as I walked here.

Johnson continued talking: "And you're lucky he didn't want to pursue the matter."

I snapped my attention back to him. "Major Gee?"

"Yes—the officer you punched at the English Club. He didn't report the matter. That was his dining companion." Johnson gave me the name of an official in the governing administration. I didn't know the man, but I should have guessed he'd be someone senior.

I held out my hand. "I'd like my personal effects back, sir." This was just my warrant card, moneyclip, watch and revolver.

Johnson shrugged and told me where to collect them near the cell block.

I said, "Any news of your daughter?"

Johnson looked at me as though I knew something.

"Have you heard anything, Carter—about my daughter?"

I decided against mentioning kidnapping. "No," I said, "but if I do hear anything…"

"Good man."

He didn't notice the irony of calling me a good man after my dressing down for punching an officer, and I wondered how stressed he must be.

★

Before I left Alexander Barracks, I made a phone call to the police HQ in Nicosia.

"Where were you last night?" DS Park asked when he came on the line.

"I was otherwise detained."

"We expected to meet you outside the bloody compound," he grumbled. "I didn't appreciate travelling all that way. I'm not some floozy you can just stand up because you have other things to attend to."

"I apologize. I really didn't have a choice," I said. "Did you find anything?"

"We looked around but couldn't see anything of interest. No sign of this Six you mentioned. No sign of XIS either for that matter."

"What was in there?"

"It's a distribution business. Water mainly."

I said, "Did you see a small room?"

"There were lots of rooms. Can you be more specific?"

"The ground was earthen. There was a wooden bench."

"Hold on. You're saying it was the place you were beaten?"

"Might have been."

"No," he said. "Certainly didn't register any room with a bench, wooden or otherwise."

I thought it had been a long shot. When I'd been abducted, I'd heard doors rolling back. Most warehouse and similar wooden doors were on rollers. And I didn't even know I'd been held in Famagusta.

Park said, "Tell me you aren't going in there on your own. And if we do go back, we'll need more than a suspicion. Folks don't like the police interfering with the businesses without good reason."

I said nothing for a few seconds.

"Carter?"

"No," I said, "I'm not going back. There's something else more pressing."

*

I hitched a ride and travelled to Famagusta in a truck laden with vegetables. Fortunately, the Turkish driver let me sit up front although he spoke only fractured English.

But he understood enough and kindly detoured until he could stop beside my Land Rover.

He didn't ask for money but I gave the chap two shillings for his trouble.

In the army you learn to leave the keys in the ignition, because, in theory, another soldier could take your vehicle. You also didn't want to risk returning only to find you'd lost the key. However, in Palestine, we'd quickly learned to hide the key in the space beside the steering column, below the dash.

I fished it out from the standard hiding place and fired up the engine.

As I drove along the quay, I was sorely tempted to approach the blue doors where I'd seen the spotty GDU private disappear, but I didn't. I kept on going out of the town, came off the main road and along the dusty track that eventually led me to the sign that read: 6GDU Famagusta Sector.

No time to waste. No more messing about. I needed to tackle this head-on.

Time to confront the private.

FORTY-SEVEN

The private peered at me through his round spectacles and looked sick.

"I saw you," I said, using an inquisitor's trick: make the suspect think you know more than you do. Say little and get him to say a lot.

He nodded. "But I haven't found anything yet, sir."

"Tell me about it, Private…"

"Private Pill, sir."

"Tell me about two nights ago, Pill."

"Two nights ago?"

Oh well, maybe I'm not as good an inquisitor as I thought. However, I brazened it out.

"Start with two nights ago in Nicosia."

He nodded. "The old cigarette factory. I went there to ask questions. But it's not a cigarette factory. They store water in containers there prior to distribution. But I didn't learn anything. When I asked about Sergeant Major Ellis… well, they didn't know anything."

"And yesterday evening in Famagusta?"

"I followed a van—it was pale blue without a company name on the side. I found out they go to and from the place in Famagusta."

I nodded. "And what did you find in there?"

"Same as at the old factory. No one could help me."

"All right," I said. "Let's rewind, back to the start. Why are you investigating?"

"Because of Sergeant Major Ellis."

I waited for more, and he took a gulp of something brown from a tin mug. Based on the bottle of Camp Coffee by a kettle and the smell of chicory, I figured it was that foul liquid.

Eventually, he licked his lips. "I found... I found records. You have to understand that I do a lot of the paperwork around here. In fact, this past year I've probably been the closest person to Mike in this unit." He took a breath after speaking more rapidly. "You see, I don't fit in that well around here. They call me names based on my surname. And Mike—I mean the sergeant major—didn't mix with the dog handlers either."

I looked at the skinny man, who was no more than a boy. He was studious and nervous whereas the dog handlers were all reasonably large, well-built men.

"So you were close to Sergeant Major Ellis then?"

"Er... well, closer than the others, and I found the records."

"Records?"

"Money coming in. You see, I think he was being paid."

I said, "Yesterday on the quay, Sergeant Payne was handed a package by a driver. It was Lucky Strikes."

Pill nodded. "American smokes."

"A backhander?"

"Yes, the men get given all sorts."

I'd seen it before—many times. Guards and Customs men being bribed to look the other way. I guessed full duty hadn't been paid on whatever was in the lorry. Maybe lots of lorries from the same company.

I said, "And Ellis was keeping records of it?"

"No, sir! No, I don't think the CSM approved. In fact, I know he didn't because he'd tell the men off if he caught them at it."

Pill saw me frowning.

He said, "No, I think the sergeant major was doing something else. I think he was being paid off, sir. And that would be a motive, wouldn't it, sir?"

"Indeed it would, soldier," I said. "You called the police. You reported it to DI Dickins in Nicosia."

"Yes."

I nodded. At least I'd tracked down the source of that information. "Why not report it to the provost marshal's office?" That would have been the logical channel.

He bobbed his head in contrition. "I don't know who I can trust. Sergeant Major Ellis was killed and I could be next." He took another gulp of coffee. "Do you think he was killed because of the bribery?"

It seemed likely, but the information took my investigation no further forward. Except for seeing Private Pill leave the old cigarette factory.

"Why the Nicosia factory?" I asked.

"Because Mike—Sergeant Major Ellis—had written down the address in the same records book."

I asked to see the book and Pill immediately pulled it from beneath the desk he was sitting at: a pocket notebook, dirty and well-thumbed.

It had various handwritten notes on the first five pages, most of which I couldn't read because of the scruffy writing in faded pencil. However, I saw *Cigarette Factory Hilarian, Nic* circled and legible. Then the sixth page made my heart pick up its pace. Fourteen entries. Fourteen dates, two weeks apart, starting approximately seven months ago. And an amount.

Initially one hundred pounds, then thirteen entries of twenty pounds.

"Why do you suspect bribery?" I asked, the private watching me intently.

"Well, it's a hell of a lot!"

I said nothing.

"And he was acting like he had money. You know how you can tell if someone's suddenly better off. And he was being more secretive."

He bit his lip and I let the silence grow in the warm air between us.

Finally, I said, "What do you know about Sarah Cartwright."

He swallowed some coffee. "She was one of his girls, right? He had a lot of women... friends."

"He raped her."

Pill swallowed air.

"Private?"

After rapid blinks, he said, "Possibly. I don't know for certain, you understand, but Mike could be er... forceful. He had lots of girls. You know how some men just expect...? And they dated a few times."

I nodded, briefly wondering whether Pill had ever had a girl. Probably not.

"Could the bribes be linked to that?"

"What do you mean, sir?"

I didn't know. I was thinking blackmail but that didn't make sense. Money was coming in.

Pill filled the silence. "Oh you mean the other way around. I don't think so. That'd make him stressed, wouldn't it, sir? If anything, Mike Ellis was cocksure."

"Who do you think was paying him?" I asked, while trying to grasp at a thought, I could sense in the back of my mind.

"I don't know, but I suspected it was linked to the factory."

"You need to stop investigating," I said. "The last person who poked their nose in too far got abducted and beaten up."

His eyes flared in alarm. I wondered then whether his motivation had been to take over the payments rather than investigate a crime.

For good measure, I added: "Sergeant Major Ellis might have been killed for doing the same. Not the bribery, but for investigating a gang."

I flicked through the tatty pocketbook in case there was anything else written. There wasn't.

I thought back to what I'd heard five nights ago with a bag over my head. "Did you ever hear anyone refer to Ellis as *The Man*?"

"The Man?" he repeated. Then: "No, sir."

No, of course, that didn't make sense. Ellis was already dead.

"Anyone else you might have heard being called *The Man*?"

"No, sir."

"One final thing," I said. "Could the other men of 6GDU have been involved… either in the bribery or Ellis's death?"

"No, sir," he said with certainty. "Firstly, because they aren't bright enough in my estimation. And secondly, they might not have mixed with the sergeant, but there was no animosity. He was fairly relaxed, and to be honest, he let them get away with their backhanders. No, sir, they weren't involved. If Sergeant Major Ellis was investigating a gang then they weren't part of his unit."

Damn! I was sure I was onto something with the reversed XIS.

I still had the pocketbook in my hands. When a page is removed from a book, it leaves a fine gap. Did this page have a gap or was it just—

"A page has been ripped out!" I exclaimed.

The private peered at the jagged paper edge I showed him.

I picked up a pencil from his desk and started shading the next page. Lots of indents. I could see the dates and numbers from the prior pages and then I made sense of something else.

CYPRUS KISS

A name.
Surena Johnson.

FORTY-EIGHT

After I turned the page so that he could read it, Pill looked at me, surprised or alarmed; I couldn't tell which.

I waited for him to speak first.

"Isn't that Major Johnson's wife, sir?"

"It's her name. Did you ever see her here, at the dog unit?"

He frowned and shook his head.

"You said Sergeant Major Ellis had a lot of women."

"Yes."

"Did he ever mention Mrs Johnson?"

Pill cleared his throat, uncomfortable. "Sir, yes, sir. But a lot of men did—those who saw her. She's a good-looking woman."

"Did he ever see her—I mean on a date?"

Pill looked shocked. "Of course not, sir!"

"She left the major eight months ago."

"As I understand."

"Have you seen her since?"

Pill thought then shook his head. "No, I don't think I have seen her since I heard she'd left him. There were lots of rumours about her going off with one of the men, probably a sailor. I heard—"

After a moment of silence, I prompted him: "What did you hear, Private?"

He looked awkward again. "Permission to speak freely, sir?"

"Of course."

"I heard she was a goer. You know, she had affairs and... and the major got a kick out of it. But never with any of the men here. Never with Mike Ellis." He shook his head vigorously. "In fact, no one I know of. Just rumours."

Pill was telling me the same as Sister Isabelle Laurent. She'd said *tease*. Pill said *got a kick out of it*. Was it just rumour? But as my Mytchett Hutments instructor would say, it was still a soft fact and I needed hard ones. Mrs Johnson had left with Alexis Velopoulos eight months ago with no sign of either of them since.

Had Surena Johnson been the woman on the night Ellis was killed? I'd had a niggling doubt about bribery. The thought in my back brain finally came to the fore. Was Ellis blackmailing someone? Was that the motive, and if so, was she the one he was blackmailing?

Too many questions and not enough answers. And I needed answers to get Penny out of jail.

*

Major Johnson wasn't in his office and I had to wait an hour for him to show up. He looked even more weary than earlier as he approached along the corridor.

I stood up.

"What now, Carter?"

"Sir, I have discovered something that may be relevant to Sergeant Major Ellis's murder: a motive."

"You'd better come in and explain."

I followed him into his room and closed the door behind me. He sat at his desk and I remained standing.

"So?" he said.

"Bribery."

He studied me for a few seconds. "Bribery, you say?"

I placed the pocketbook in front of the major and pointed to the dates and figures.

"Or blackmail," I said. "Three hundred and sixty pounds over a period of seven months."

"I can add up, Lieutenant. How does that imply bribery?"

"Money coming in like that? What else could it be?"

He pursed his lips, thinking, then folded his arms and looked at me with harder eyes.

"Circumstantial and... But even if Ellis was being paid off, what... for all we know it was that Penny Cartwright who was paying him."

"She doesn't have that kind of money, sir."

He cocked an eyebrow. "And you know that, how?"

"I..." He was right. I knew very little about Penny. Perhaps her parents were rich. Perhaps she was into some nefarious activity that Ellis had found out about. Then I shook my head. It didn't make any sense.

"Ellis raped Penny's sister. There's no way she was paying the man. And for part of this time, she wasn't in Cyprus. She accompanied her sister home before returning and being employed by us over a month ago."

"And you know that for certain, Carter?"

I must have blinked because he smiled at me. He was right of course. That was another soft fact I hadn't checked. However, I had a lead and I was going to follow it.

"Sergeant Major Ellis's post office account," I said. "I'd like to see it. If we can see money going in, at least we'll know for certain that these notes illustrate he was receiving large sums of money. And that could mean blackmail."

Thoughts crowded the major's face for a moment. "All right, Lieutenant. I'll get a list of transactions from his post office account and we'll know one way or the other whether money was coming in or going out." He spread his hands. "But where that leads you, I just don't know."

Me neither, but small things can lead to bigger ones.

I stood for a second, thinking about whether to mention the other thing. Should I tell him about his wife's name appearing in the pocketbook?

"Any news from your daughter, sir?" I asked and saw concern, maybe worry flit across his eyes.

"Nothing."

"But you think she's with your wife?" I asked pointedly.

"Carter, it's not your concern." His eyes hardened again. "I hope you're not still looking for my wife. I told you—!"

His voice started to rise, but I cut him off by turning the pages of the pocketbook and tapping the shaded page.

"That's your wife's name."

"What? Where?" He picked up the pad and studied it closely. Anger bubbled in his voice when he spoke again. "What are you saying, Carter?"

"Just that her name appears in Ellis's notes."

"You think she murdered him?" the major scoffed. "Good God man, you're losing it! You're all over the place. My wife would never kill a man"—now he genuinely laughed—"she would be more likely to…"

He cut himself off and cleared his throat. I thought he was about to say "sleep with him", but he didn't.

I waited and saw thoughts pass behind his eyes.

When he finally spoke, he said, "She's an attractive woman and much younger than me. Lots of men found her attractive, Lieutenant. I expect Ellis was the same."

"Sorry to have to ask, sir, but did your wife have a relationship with him."

"Of course not. Preposterous!"

I said nothing in case he would say more, but he didn't.

FORTY-NINE

I went back to the office on Pine Street, checked for messages and went through the post. There was nothing of interest except the operator told me I'd missed a call from DI Dickins.

When I was put through to him, I apologized for wasting police time in Famagusta.

He said, "Yes, DS Park wasn't too impressed."

"Unfortunately I was otherwise engaged."

"Detained," he said. "Park told me."

"Overzealous provost marshal. I'm sure you understand. Did your sergeant tell you my theory about six?"

"No, but we've been ships passing in the night. It's been very busy up here."

"I wondered if X-I-S was an upside-down S-I-X. I then made the leap assuming that six referred to the military—to 6GDU."

He made a guttural sound that I figured meant he understood the logic.

"But I was wrong. It's just coincidence," I said. "As you know, Sergeant Major Ellis of 6GDU was murdered. Then I saw one of their men was acting suspiciously up at the old cigarette factory near you."

"I never like coincidences," he said.

"Me neither, but this time it looks like I made a mental leap too far. I've spoken to the suspicious chap and it turns out that he was also investigating. And he's the one who tipped us off—the one who called about bribery."

"Ah!"

"There may also be a link to Mrs Johnson."

"Oh," he said, his tone going from relief to concern. "That's not good."

"But it could help my cause."

"But seriously? The major's wife!"

"Ex-wife. I found out who she eloped with. He was a waiter at Maxim's nightclub called Alexis Velopoulos."

"Not a name I've heard."

"Here's my current thinking," I said. "The Kiss gang is a mix of Greeks and Brits. Velopoulos is one of the gang and Mrs Johnson is with them. Ellis knew something about the gang—after all, the guard dog unit see an awful lot of what goes on in and around Famagusta, and I've seen first-hand how they can be paid to turn a blind eye."

"Why am I not surprised?" he said.

"Ellis was being paid to keep quiet—until they'd had enough."

"And she killed him?"

"Yes."

He blew out air. "Major Johnson isn't going to like that theory."

"That's why I haven't expressed it to him. And it's also why I'm talking to you rather than the provost marshal." I paused before continuing: "Have you ever heard Major Johnson—or anyone else for that matter—referred to as *The Man*?"

"Doesn't ring any bells. Should it?"

"The night I was abducted and threatened, I heard the gang use it. It's how they referred to their boss."

"The Kiss gang's boss? I'll let DS Park know."

I explained I'd already mentioned it to Park and that he hadn't heard it either.

"Perhaps that's their first mistake," he said.

I thought their first mistake was to involve me, but I didn't say so. Instead, I switched back to the conversation about Ellis's pocketbook.

"DS Park will want to see it," Dickins said.

"I'll pop in," I said. "I'm about to travel up to see Penny Cartwright again. It might not be great news, but at least I'm making some progress."

What I didn't mention was that I would be taking a bag of tools with me, including bolt cutters.

*

When I got to the police HQ in Nicosia the sun had gone down and I wondered whether Dickins or Park would have finished for the day, but the sergeant was still there.

"I hope you didn't go charging into that compound in Famagusta, Lieutenant."

I grinned. "No, just into 6GDU. Did Dickins appraise you?"

"He told me you have a notepad that may have been Sergeant Major Ellis's. He said it suggested he was being paid off by someone."

I nodded.

"He also said you had a theory about Mrs Johnson, but he didn't like to say too much. I decided to wait for you so you could tell me yourself."

So DI Dickins had been sensitive about what I'd suggested. I could understand that. Making accusations that had implications for the provost marshal were serious. Possibly as serious as they could get.

Dickins had struck me as someone who stuck to the facts rather than encourage tittle-tattle. But as far as I was concerned, this was not gossip, and I showed Park the entries in the pocketbook, the missing page and the shading.

"Surena Johnson," he said, nodding slowly. "What's your next step, Lieutenant?"

"Well, after updating Penny Cartwright on my progress, I thought I'd take another look at the old cigarette factory."

"Why's that?"

I turned to the page where the address was circled.

"Interesting," he said. Then: "But it's a red herring."

"Oh?"

"Because we raided it this morning based on an anonymous tip-off about illegal goods." He pulled a face. "Bogus. Nothing illegal there as far as we could see."

"They're connected to the operation in Famagusta."

He shook his head. "And there was nothing untoward there. Someone is yanking your chain, Lieutenant."

"Maybe," I said. "How are you getting on with the Verity Johnson disappearance?"

For a second I thought he looked surprised.

"Is that connected?"

"Maybe," I said again.

"Too many maybes for me." He shrugged. "To be honest, we're nowhere on the Verity Johnson case. All forces have been given her description, but without more information, I don't know what we can do."

So I told him about the possible kidnapping, although I refused to say that Sister Laurent had told me. I finished with, "It could be the same gang, Anthem."

"Another maybe, Lieutenant." He reached for Ellis's pocketbook. "Can I keep this?"

"Not just yet," I said. "I prefer to keep hold of it for now in case it's useful. And I want to match the dates and amounts to Ellis's post office account."

He shrugged. "Well, all right. Thanks for coming in."

"If there are any developments—"

"I'll be certain to involve you, Lieutenant. You can count on that."

★

The melancholy atmosphere in the prison seemed to have seeped into Penny. She could only force a smile when I arrived and it felt like she was just happy to have a visitor rather than who it was.

She said, "I thought you'd come yesterday as well. Not beaten up again, I hope?"

If there was sarcasm in her voice, I ignored it. "Bloody Johnson," I said. "He had me thrown into the Glasshouse for the night."

She blinked her surprise. "Oh, why?"

I didn't want to confess that I'd been a rutting stag with Major Gee so I said, "Just some trumped-up charge." I quickly followed this with my news about the possible link between Mrs Johnson and Ellis, but she merely nodded like it was inevitable.

"Ellis was being paid and had written her name in his pocketbook."

"But it's nothing like enough, Ash. You said you'd prove I didn't do it."

"I'm making progress," I said, trying to encourage her, although her eyes told me she thought I'd fail. "What does your lawyer say?"

"The first news," she said with a quaver in her voice, "is the charge isn't theft. They're going for murder."

It's what I'd expected. The suggestion that there would be a holding charge of theft was just a ruse. Johnson had always intended to charge Penny with Ellis's murder.

She continued: "The second thing is that the initial hearing will be this Friday at three."

It was now Wednesday evening, so that gave me less than two days to find the evidence. To find the real killer.

She said, "He's focusing on the mistaken identity—the time gap between the witness seeing her go into the alley with Ellis and me running down the street, plus the hair colour issue—that should be enough to raise enough reasonable doubt. They can't convict... evidence works both ways."

"I agree," I said.

"I wish I had your faith in the legal system."

To be honest, I didn't have great faith in the law. I'd seen and heard of enough miscarriages of justice to know that judgements didn't always go the logical or reasonable way.

DI Dickins was waiting for me at the front desk as I left the prison.

"Thought I'd come with you to see why you're so interested in the old factory. And it'll give you the chance to update me on the way."

FIFTY

"How is Miss Cartwright doing?" Dickins asked me as we walked towards the factory gates. I was carrying the bag of tools I'd brought with me. We'd parked side by side in the trees and his breathing sounded loud in the night.

"Not well. I feel like I'm failing her."

"Prison is a dismal place, and I would expect it's even worse if you're innocent."

"And she *is* innocent."

We peered through chained wire mesh gates. I couldn't see any lights on, although I could see a lorry to the right.

From my bag I removed the bolt cutters and raised them against the chain.

"Ash—" he started to say, but I'd already chopped through metal before he could tell me to stop.

"I'll pay for a new one," I said, pushing the left-hand gate ajar.

He grabbed my shirt. "We need a warrant. I assumed we'd be able to walk in and speak to someone."

"Did you never do this in the Met, George?"

"Breaking and entering, you mean?" He looked at me and I could see uncertainty in his eyes.

I said, "Due cause?"

"If we think there is a crime being committed…"

"Hear that?" I asked. "Sounds like someone calling for help." Of course, I'd heard nothing, but he accepted the lie.

"If you're certain, then all right."

We took five or so paces, looked around and listened. Apart from the inspector's breathing, I could hear the cicadas and another, sawing noise.

"What's that sound?" he asked.

"Metal creaking," I said. "I couldn't say what though."

As I'd seen from outside, there were two red-brick buildings with chimneys at the far end.

There was a door directly in front of us, but to the right was what I assessed as a loading yard. That's where the lorry was parked.

We shone torches and headed that way.

Dickins put his hand on the vehicle's bonnet.

"Cold," he said.

I examined worn tyres and corroded metal. "Not been used for a long time, I'd judge. Probably abandoned."

"Probably."

We switched our attention back to the buildings. In front of us were double doors. They reminded me of the doors to the compound in Famagusta, but then that wasn't surprising.

I tried them and found the chains resisted movement.

"No, Ash," Dickins said as I pulled out the bolt cutters again.

"Can't you hear the cry for help?" I asked.

"Not yet I can't." He signalled for me to put the tool away. "Let's walk around first... and hope we don't have to resort to more criminal behaviour."

I chuckled, but he was being serious and we started circling the building. We tried all door handles, and as we came to each window we shone our lights inside.

I saw rooms, boxes and crates but couldn't gain entry until the second building. This had an unlocked side door and we slipped inside.

It smelled of dust and tobacco and we could hear the metallic grinding noise more clearly now. The source turned out to be a door to a furnace. Air was coming down the chimney and causing the metal door to move just enough to creak.

Shapes moved rapidly across the floor and Dickins's torch picked out a scampering rat. Then we saw more open packing cases with components for making cigarettes, I guessed.

Benches ran the length of the building and I figured it was for some kind of processing from raw materials to final product.

At the end of the room we found broken windows where the air came in.

When Dickins spoke, his voice echoed off the factory walls.

"Like the lorry, this hasn't been used in a long while."

"But I saw lights on before," I said, thinking also of Private Pill coming out. "And people."

"Then they must be using the other building."

We went out through the unlocked door and circled the first building. We came to a toilet block and took a quick sniff. It was rank and possibly fresh.

We continued.

"No broken windows or open doors this time," said Dickins.

"But these double doors aren't locked after all." Before he could stop me, I'd snipped through the chain and added: "I keep hearing someone call for help."

We took a handle each and slid the doors back. They ran on rollers, and I imagined I was in the car boot being taken by my captors. Was this the place?

Inside, our torches showed a wide clear space with a row of offices. Dickins tried the light switch but nothing happened and we moved forward.

I pointed out marks on the floor: squares, circles, drag marks.

"There were crates and barrels here," I said, sniffing the air. "Can you smell alcohol?"

"No."

"Me neither."

We went into the first office. There was a desk with a drawer and a filing cabinet. Both were empty.

The next room was larger, with a trestle table and metal chairs. Marks on the walls suggested posters or the like had been stuck there but were now gone.

And then we came to the final room at the far end.

My torchlight showed a broad storeroom with a sawdust floor, I could smell wood and earth and a hint of alcohol.

However, what made me catch my breath was not the smell, but a wooden bench. I sat on it and closed my eyes and I was back in this room with a hood over my head, expecting to die.

"Ash?" Dickins shone his torch on me. "Are you all right?"

"This is where they brought me. This is where I was threatened before being dumped out on the road."

"You're sure?" He sounded relieved.

"No question."

"Then we have our justification," he said, and I could see that our entry had been troubling him. "I'll arrange for fingerprinting—"

A sound made us exchange concerned looks.

"Sir?" a voice called. "Lieutenant Carter, are you in here?"

"I am," I said, leaving the storeroom.

A man stood in the doorway and I could see he was in uniform. A young policeman hopping with nervous energy.

"You're not...? Sir!" the man said, breathlessly as he spotted the inspector with me. "Sir, I didn't realize you were here too."

"What is it, Constable?" Dickins asked. "And relax."

"Sir, Sergeant Chadwick sent me."

"Right?"

"I'm to take you right away. Sir, we know where the Kiss gang are hiding out."

FIFTY-ONE

When the constable checked, we both confirmed we had our service revolvers with us. The policeman fetched a rifle from his vehicle and we all piled into Dickins's car. We were in the back with the young man up front, driving.

Dickins asked where we were going and the policeman gave a name I didn't recognize.

We went north, over a rail line, and then picked up the road to Kyrenia. However, before we got to the mountains we turned left. Despite the darkness, I could see their outline on our right against the night sky.

Between five and ten miles later, the driver turned right, down a lane, and we were soon in the foothills. Trees closed in.

Another turn and we were on a bumpy track. Stones crunched under the tyres and the car jolted.

"This isn't an off-road vehicle!" Dickins said, alarmed.

"Not far now, sir," the young man called over his shoulder. And he was right. Two seconds later, the headlights picked out someone in the road.

We stopped and the man outside leaned in.

"Chadwick?" Dickins said.

"Sir, I wasn't expecting you." The other man looked into the car and nodded a greeting to me. "Lieutenant."

I'd seen the man before. Not a detective but a larger than life police officer. His bulk made him look more like a bricklayer than a policeman, in my opinion.

"What's going on?" Dickins asked as we both got out. The air was cool and smelled strongly of pine.

"We've traced the Kiss gang to a farmhouse in the woods." He pointed into the darkness. "It's half a mile down the track."

"How many of them?"

"Not sure, sir. DS Park is coming back with armed men."

I said, "Any sign of a woman and a girl?" thinking of Mrs Johnson and her neice.

"I scouted around while I've been waiting. It's possible… yes, I think they have hostages."

"Hostages?" Was Surena Johnson being held against her will?

"There are bars against some of the lower windows," Chadwick said. "Like a prison. I was thinking there may be someone held down there."

"Let's take a look," I said, and started down the track. Although I still had my torch, it stayed off. The sky was clear and speckled with stars but I could barely see the road beneath my feet.

Chadwick instructed the young policeman to wait by the car for DS Park before following a step behind Dickins.

"We didn't expect you, sir," the sergeant said again, repeating what he said when we arrived.

We came to a gate with a stone wall each side. Hunkering down beside it, Chadwick pointed to where I could see spots of lights.

"They're in there."

"Thanks for bringing me along," I said. "If there *are* hostages…"

"Yes, DS Park said you'd be keen."

I could hear night-animal noises and the occasional rustle in the undergrowth. Were there snakes out here? I don't like snakes but my logical brain told me snakes need heat and it would be unlikely they'd be out at night.

"I'm going closer," I said after a minute.

"We should wait for DS Park," Chadwick suggested, but I was already clambering awkwardly over the wall.

Dickins started to follow.

"Sir, I don't think... We should wait for the armed backup or it could turn to shit slime in no time."

Dickins hissed back, "Wait here then, Chadwick!"

"No, no, I'm with you."

They came behind me. All three of us had our revolvers out, walking beside the track towards the house. I could see it's slightly lighter bulk against the dark trees. Lights were on inside, but not bright. I figured they were from internal rooms, not from the windows we could see.

Chadwick said something else, but I wasn't listening. My back brain was processing something. I was in the storeroom again, the hood over my head. Waiting. Listening for any clue.

It could turn to shit slime.

I swung around, raising my gun, but I was too late. Chadwick must have been ready for the movement. He was already aiming at me.

Instinct made me dive as his revolver fired.

I yelped from the pain in my ribs, but I rolled and turned. Chadwick was there. Dickins was not. The junior officer was standing over the other man and I barrelled into him, again ignoring my injury until the electricity of pain went through me.

A blow from my gun stopped Chadwick fighting. His head jolted back and then he didn't move.

I shone my torch at Dickins on the ground. He was alive but in shock. There was blood on his shirt and a hole in his right jacket shoulder.

Pulling the jacket off, I could see the bullet had caught him. It didn't look too bad, but he couldn't move his arm.

More lights went on inside the house. There was movement inside and I thought voices carried on the breeze.

"Can you walk?" I asked.

"Yes," he said through gritted teeth.

"Let's get out of here. Help me drag Chadwick."

We looped an arm under his shoulders and made a rapid retreat to the gate. Once on the other side, Dickins sank down.

"What the hell's going on, Ash?"

"Your man here is one of the gang," I said. "When I was a prisoner I could hear them discussing what to do—before The Man arrived. One of them said something I'd never heard before. He used 'shit slime' to describe the situation. Chadwick did it just before he shot you."

"I didn't mean to shoot the inspector," a groggy voice said and I realized Chadwick had regained consciousness. "I didn't know what to do. I wasn't expecting him. Then you got in the way, sir."

Dickins slapped handcuffs on the man and I gripped his collar. Tight, but not so tight that he couldn't speak.

"How many men are in the house?" I growled at him.

"Ten."

I squeezed harder. "Now tell the truth."

"Six."

Maybe he was being honest this time, I couldn't tell, but I decided six was more likely than ten.

Dickins said, "Who's running this?"

Chadwick looked away. No answer.

I stuck my revolver under his chin.

"Who's the one they call The Man?"

Chadwick snorted. "You aren't going to shoot me!"

I clicked back the hammer. "I'll count down from three."

"Three."

Nothing.

"Two."

He said, "If I talk, I'm dead."

"That's a possibility. Play the odds, Chadwick. Don't answer and you'll be dead for sure," I said. Pause. "One."

He spat at me and Dickins lashed out with his pistol butt. Chadwick's head jolted away from my gun. Probably deliberately to stop me shooting, although I wouldn't have fired. Not because of the man, but because of what might come later.

"Let's get to the car," I said, and we heaved Chadwick up between us again.

Dickins had his gun ready. I put mine away.

"What about the constable?" he said.

Chadwick said nothing.

I said, "He's not involved." If he had been then the two of them would have walked with us. Leaving the young man at the car meant that he didn't know what Chadwick had planned.

Dickins looked at me as we walked and then nodded, probably figuring the same. We came around the corner and saw the cars. The constable was using Dickins's car door as a shield. His rifle poked over the top.

"It's all right," Dickins hissed in the dark. "It's us."

The constable stood. "Oh thank God!" Then as we approached he stuttered, "Sir... sir, what's wrong with the sergeant... and sir, have you been hit?"

I said, "Take them back, Constable. Make sure Sergeant Chadwick is locked up and that DI Dickins gets medical attention."

Dickins said, "What are you going to do, Ash?"

"I'm going to wait for the cavalry," I said. "I'm sure DS Park won't be long."

FIFTY-TWO

I doubted DS Park was coming. He didn't know about this little ambush that Chadwick and the gang had set up for me. If Dickins guessed my intentions, he didn't say anything.

Before he was driven away by the constable, I checked Chadwick's pockets and found the key to the other car.

Dickins's car disappeared down the track and I was left alone in the eerie night.

Back through the gate, I jogged-walked down the track to the house. The lights had gone off, which was sensible. They'd heard a gunshot and then nothing. Had Chadwick killed me or not? They didn't know.

That was why I couldn't shoot Chadwick earlier. If they heard a second gunshot they were more likely to suspect I was alive.

However, more than fifteen minutes had passed since the shot and they must have been suspicious. Lights on would have given me a target. Lights off meant they could see better in the dark. They'd be looking out across the field.

Eighty yards out, I cut left, off the track. The rough, lumpy ground made me tread carefully. My ribs hurt like hell and slowing down meant I could breathe more easily.

Forty yards out, I went onto all fours. Dirt and stones bit into my hands and knees but I scuttled closer, scanning all the time. I could see the outline of windows and the front door. Close by was a parked car. I couldn't see the make but it wasn't as big as Dickins's and I guessed it was a small Morris.

There were eight windows at the front of the house and I expected at one of them was a sniper. Probably two. I stopped for a second and tried to guess where they were.

In the dark, if you look straight ahead, you can see less than if you look slightly away. Something to do with the retina. I looked directly at each window and then a few feet away.

Got them. Two windows were open a crack. One on the top floor one on the ground floor by the door. There would be a man with a gun behind each of those.

I moved on, reached trees, and stood to catch my breath before continuing until I was all the way behind the house.

The ground dropped away and I could see more windows on this side covering three floors. None of the windows were open on this side, as far as I could tell, but that didn't mean there was no one behind them.

I kept going until I was at the far corner and then I closed in, approaching at an angle.

There were bins out here. I could smell the garbage before I saw it. I came up behind a large hoe of some kind. The sort that was pulled by a tractor. Its cold metal felt old and rusty. There was a piece of metal—an oblong sheet—and I propped this up as a small shield as I assessed the house and then gave the hoe a wide berth, avoiding any sharp bits I couldn't see.

When I reached the corner of the house, I stopped and breathed again before moving. There were two downstairs windows. There was a door between the windows with rubbish piled outside. The windows were small with bars.

It's possible they have hostages.

So Chadwick hadn't been lying. These could be prison cells. Mrs Johnson and Verity could be behind those windows.

A night creature scurried under my feet as I tiptoed to the second window and looked in. Total darkness on the other side and I couldn't make out a thing.

I moved around the trash and listened at the door.

Nothing.

Could all the gang members be at the front? I doubted it.

Retreating to the hoe, I picked up an egg-sized stone and flung it in the direction of the door. I missed, but the ricochet luckily hit a garbage box and created as much noise as I'd wanted.

A middle floor window opened a crack.

"Chads, that you?" a nervous voice hissed.

I said nothing, and the window thudded shut after a moment.

As I waited, I got an idea. I unbuttoned my shirt and removed the bandages around my chest. Then I pressed the cold metal sheet against my flesh and bandaged it up again.

Five minutes later, I saw movement outside. A figure came around from the front, hugging the wall. He went down the side and then edged towards the door.

Just as he reached it, I threw another stone. It clattered against the wall and the man dropped out of sight, presumably behind the boxes of rubbish.

I threw another stone and it whacked into the trash. The man dived and fired wildly.

The window above opened again and I saw what I figured to be a rifle barrel poke out. Lying flat, I prayed that I was as invisible behind the hoe as I believed.

"Carter? Is that you, Carter?" a voice from the window called.

I breathed in dry dirt.

"Carter, you're outnumbered. You're a bright man. Raise your hands and we'll talk. Maybe we can come to an arrangement."

I kept quiet.

The man at the window said, "Tosh, you out there?"

I couldn't see him, but the man behind the rubbish whispered, "Yeah."

"Get back inside."

I was moving, getting closer, ignoring the agony in my chest.

The man called Tosh got up and appeared by the door. I saw him pull the handle. And then I fired.

An instructor had once told me that the chances of hitting a target with a pistol decreases exponentially with distance. Unless you're a sharpshooter. Mathematically I doubted he was right, but the principle was correct. It's hard to hit a target at distance with a pistol.

I was no pistol sharpshooter, about thirty paces from Tosh and it was dark. But my bullet not only hit the target but the man went down with a grunt and a gurgle.

A shot, then another, rang out from the window as the man upstairs tried to get me, but neither seemed close.

"Tosh, you all right?"

The man outside was no longer making any sound.

The window closed.

I scuttled back to the hoe and then out and round. I was going to the front of the house, hoping another brave gang member would appear. No one did.

The car was close to the front door and I could now tell it was a Ford Deluxe. Nicer than a Morris.

With a fist-sized rock, I closed in on the nearest window, smashed it and listened briefly as I hugged the wall beside it. I hoped this would draw people to the front of the house.

After a count of five, I scuttled around to the back door. I could see Tosh on the floor blocking it. If anyone opened the door they'd be restricted by his body, so unless they'd moved him back, no one else was out here.

I checked his pulse and my hand came away wet. The bullet had taken him in the throat. He was a solid man like Chadwick and the exertion of lifting him made me wince. I kept him upright and managed to get the handle turned then used my foot to open the door.

Immediately, Tosh's body jolted and I pushed him forward as a gun fired. Another shot, and this time I felt like I'd been punched in the solar plexus. But I'd seen the shooter clearly in the muzzle flash and returned fire.

Two shots silenced him and I let Tosh topple like a felled tree on top of the second man.

Wasting no time, I stepped over the bodies. This was the basement. Two rooms down here that I knew of and stairs rising to the ground floor.

Get the woman and girl out or face the gang?

I'd got two men. I guessed there were no more than four based on Chadwick's likely exaggeration and the small four-seater outside. That left two gang members. If I was right. There could be eight more if Chadwick hadn't been lying the first time he'd answered.

So far, I'd fired three shots, which left me with three.

Not great odds for someone who isn't a sharpshooter. But gang member number two had used a rifle. I located the gun and slung it over my shoulder before opening a basement door. The room smelled of mould and there was nothing but boxes and barrels. An alcohol store.

I tried the door to the second room. It was locked. After rapping on the wood, I listened. I could hear creaking floorboards above, but apart from that, nothing.

Beyond the cellar stairs, I found another door. It opened easily. A quick flash of my light and I saw what looked like a games room: a table tennis table and billiards table, a dartboard and a pub-like bar with stools.

Retreating into the hall, I could hear footfall above me. I aimed the revolver up the stairs, but no one came down. They were positioning, waiting for me.

Back to the locked door. No time to waste. A front-kick broke the lock and I burst in.

An armoury, guns in racks: military-looking rifles, pistols, Sten and Bren guns. And a cage.

A prison.

An empty prison.

FIFTY-THREE

I recognized the smell of gun oil, but there was another smell in here: the scent of fear. The cage had been in use recently, I was sure. Had Surena Johnson been in there? Had Verity? If so, where were they now?

No more sounds came from above, and after a pause I retreated quickly and stepped out into the darkness by the trash.

Now I had a moment to breathe, I pulled the metal sheet from my chest. It had a dent where a bullet had passed through Tosh and struck me. The sheet had saved my life. A lucky escape.

I circled the house and went to the broken window.

Once there, I passed across it, close and fast. The theory being that if anyone was looking they'd react but I'd be out of the way before they got off a shot.

I waited and listened.

Let's hope they aren't too clever, I thought, before I rolled back around and reached in through the hole I'd made earlier with the rock.

My fingers found a catch, and the sash window came up easily. Pain from my ribs again reminded me of my poor condition—climbing through a confined space was definitely against doctor's orders.

I found myself in a comfortably furnished room, at least the amount of furniture made me suspect a comfortable living room. The floor was wooden with a rug, and once I was on the carpeted section, my feet made no sound.

My heart stopped.

Unmoving, in a corner, I could see a man. I dropped behind a sofa, pointed my gun, my heart now pounding. But I didn't shoot.

The shape hadn't moved at all.

I risked bringing up my torch and flicking it on. The shape wasn't a man but a mannequin in an American Army uniform.

Flashing the light around the room, I saw that this was some kind of museum. The walls and tables were covered with memorabilia from the war. Army photographs, maps, flags, shell casings and bits of uniform.

I switched off the torch and crept to the far door. Once there, I pressed my ear against the wood and listened.

The imagined layout in my head had a wide hall on the other side of this door with a staircase going upward. The front door was to the left and there would be a descending staircase to the right.

If I were one of the gang, I'd be waiting at the top of the basement stairs, probably behind a protective wall. I'd have one eye on the front door.

No point in waiting here.

I crouched, gun ready. With a gentle turn of the handle, I eased the door open and prepared to shoot. Anyone on the other side would aim higher and miss, giving me a split second advantage.

Nothing.

I could see a rising staircase ahead and figured my layout plan was about right. But how to step into the hall without being shot?

There was a stunt I'd heard Wolfe pull in Palestine once. He'd partially unscrewed the bottom of a torch so that the contact was broken. Then, with the torch upside down, he'd switched it to the 'on' position without the light coming on.

I did that now. Then, tossing it like a German stick-hand grenade, I threw the torch down the hall beyond where my presumed assailant hid.

The torch *thunked* on the floor and flashed. Not the contact that Wolfe had achieved but enough to show a gun and arm. At the same moment, I crabbed out into the hall and fired. Two shots.

A grunt told me I'd made contact with at least one bullet. But it wasn't good enough. The other man fired back, although he hadn't judged my location well enough and the muzzle flash gave me an easy target. One more shot and he was down.

I dropped my empty gun and swung the rifle up, aiming for the first-floor landing.

Once my ears had stopped ringing from the exchange, I listened. Could that be it? Just three men?

I repositioned to the bottom of the stairs and the floorboards creaked underfoot.

Then the idiot from above called out. "Pete? Kiddo, you all right?"

"Pete's dead," I called back. "It's over."

The man upstairs didn't respond.

"I've killed your three mates. The police are on their way. Give yourself up while you have the chance."

"All right."

I found a light switch and the hall and stairs lit up.

"Come down," I called. "Hands in the air."

He stepped out onto the landing, arms wide, a revolver in his left hand. I recognized the guy. The tall man with the scars around his eyes. The one who'd followed me from Limassol on a motorcycle. He'd made the mistake of staring at me for too long now and I figured he wasn't the brightest of the bunch.

"Drop the gun, soldier," I shouted.

He dropped it but didn't step forward.

"Come down the stairs slowly," I said.

"You're going to shoot me."

I shook my head. "I want answers."

He stood on the top step. "Lower the gun. Just don't point it at me. I know how these things can happen—just go off. You might not mean to shoot me but—"

I aimed slightly away. "Happy? Just start walking or I'll shoot you anyway."

He stepped down, one at a time, painfully slowly. His eyes never left mine. When he was halfway, his right arm dropped.

"Arms up!"

The speed of his movement caught me by surprise as his right hand flicked forward. A blade flew towards my face and I just managed to avoid it.

But he wasn't waiting. Even as I looked back, he was diving on me. I went backwards and yelled as his bulk crushed my ribs.

I managed to jam the rifle under his chin, which eased the weight, and for a second I thought I could press him up, but he had another knife. He used the distance to gain momentum and stabbed it down.

I twisted and my knee came up, connecting between his legs just as the blade struck my shoulder. The power went out of his strike and I kept my momentum going, leveraging him over. I rolled too and swung the rifle towards him. The barrel pressed into his chest.

"Stop!" I yelled, but he still had the knife and flashed it at me.

I pulled the trigger.

He didn't die straight away, just glared at me through hateful eyes set in those awful scars.

"Where's Mrs Johnson?" I said standing over him as he bled out. "Where's Verity?"

He laughed. Although dying, he laughed. Then his eyes rolled back and I thought he was gone, but he started muttering.

"Half a league, half a league, half a league onward, all in the valley of death rode the six hundred."

The poem by Sir Alfred Tennyson. What the hell?

"Soldier," I said, desperately gripping him, "tell me where I can find Mrs Johnson?"

"Forward, the Light Brigade! Charge for the guns! Into the valley of death..." Blood bubbled on his lips, which moved silently now.

"Mrs Johnson?" I pressed.

His eyes rolled back and looked through me. "Did I serve with honour?" he mumbled, coughed, spluttered blood, and then died.

FIFTY-FOUR

I found DI Dickins in the hospital after driving Chadwick's car back to Nicosia.

"Good God, man!" he said, shocked.

Tosh's blood that had splashed all the way down my front. "It's not mine," I said.

"Except for your shoulder," he said, pointing at my left arm.

It was just a nick and looked worse than it was. Certainly not as bad as the bullet wound to his shoulder.

I told him what had happened and that there were four dead soldiers in the house.

"If this bullet had gone through my left shoulder, I might have two useless hands," he said. "We've both been lucky tonight."

"Not as lucky as I needed to be. I'd hoped Mrs Johnson was being held there. Someone has been, I'm sure."

"We'll get answers from Chadwick."

I nodded.

He said, "You called them soldiers. Dead soldiers."

"I'm sure they were all ex-army."

"Isn't everyone?"

He was right, of course. Most men of a certain age had served in one way or the other, although Dickins himself had been in the police at home.

Before I'd left, I'd searched the whole house in case Verity or Surena were being held. I found no one. Finally, I had returned to the war memorial room. I told Dickins.

"It's full of memorabilia," I said, "especially stuff about the Eleventh Cavalry, including a flag. One of them started reciting 'The Charge of the Light Brigade' as he died."

"Tennyson's poem?"

I nodded.

"Eleventh," he said slowly. Then he got it. "XIS!"

XIS wasn't Greek. It wasn't an upside-down six. It was the Roman numerals for eleven. XI and an s.

"Elevens," I said. "It looks like the gang called themselves the Elevens. Four dead at the house, and Chadwick in custody. There will be more of them."

"I expect so."

"Look at the war memorial. There are lots of photographs. They might be out of date, but I think you might recognize people if Chadwick won't give you names."

"What are you going to do now, Ash?"

"I'm going to sleep," I said, "and then I have a phone call to make."

*

It was four in the morning by the time I got back to Larnaca. With no idea who or how many Kiss gang members there were, I remained both alert and cautious. I parked outside my lodgings and went inside. It had been turned over. Properly this time, with no attempt to hide the fact. Again, nothing had been taken. They'd found the cash in the suitcase but left it. They'd even broken open my hiding place in the wardrobe but not taken the money. Now that I was carrying my gun, the cash was my only thing of value.

As previously, I slipped out and made my way to Penny's, where I climbed in through her rear window.

My ribs had been re-bandaged in the Nicosia hospital and I could see new bruising on my chest when I looked at myself in the morning. It hurt like hell and seemed fitting for my mood. I felt like a deflated balloon. Being lured to the gang's house last night, I really thought I'd find Mrs Johnson. And my gut still told me she was crucial to this case and crucial to Penny's release from jail.

Looking half-human, I went to the office and sorted through the post before making the call I was dreading.

"Good morning, sir," I said when put through to Major Johnson.

"What is it, Lieutenant Carter?" he asked warily.

"I'm sorry, sir but I haven't found your wife or Verity."

"What are you blithering about, Lieutenant?" He took a breath. "You carried on searching?"

"Yes, and I thought…"

"What?"

"Last night, working with the police we found the Kiss gang's hideout."

"But you weren't… I've told you before, Carter that my wife is not involved with the gang. She did not kill Sergeant Major Ellis. Penny Cartwright is the killer."

I cleared my throat, buying time and staying calm. "Sir, I have some bad news, I'm afraid."

"What?"

"I think your wife or Verity or both were held in the house. There was a cage… a prison cell in the basement. It had been used recently."

Johnson said nothing and I let him process the information.

He said, "Who are they… this gang?"

"It was X-I-S after all," I said, spelling it. "They appear to be ex-army and called themselves the Elevens, as in the Eleventh Cavalry."

"Eleventh," he said quietly. "How…?"

"One of the men recited 'The Charge of the Light Brigade' before he died. I suppose they associated with the heroism. There was a whole room of military ephemera."

"Military? You said ex-army. Are you sure?"

"Am I sure—?"

"They are ex-army." A pause, and I could imagine him thinking. Then: "Any left alive?"

"Four of them died in the house. But we have another of them," I added. "One of the police sergeants from Nicosia is a member. He's still alive and being questioned. Sir, your wife and Verity… if"—I almost said, if they're still alive but stopped myself just in time—"if he knows where they are, we'll be able to find them."

"Right," Johnson said tersely, and I imagined him standing, looking controlled: stiff upper lip and all that. "I'll call the police for an update. Thank you for letting me know, Carter. And Carter—"

"Sir?"

"Well played."

★

I checked with the switchboard and learned that Captain Wolfe had called again. And in the post was a letter marked 'Eyes only' from the War Office for his attention.

"Any progress," Wolfe asked me when we connected. "Have you found Mrs Johnson?"

I gave him a summary of what had happened, and he cursed. "You'll get Penny out," he said.

He couldn't see me shaking my head at the telephone, but I said, "I remain hopeful."

The silence grew between us as I thought about my failure.

Then he said, "I have disturbing news of a different kind, Ash. Remember I mentioned I'd seen Dave Rose?"

"Yes."

"And I said that our operation here would be buggered if he recognized me. Well, he fuckin' has recognized me."

As he moaned about having to move outside the border, my eyes alighted on the War Office letter.

"Before you decamp just yet, it looks like you have new orders," I said. "There's a letter here for you."

"From the War Office? What does it say?"

"Marked for your eyes—"

"Just open it, Ash!"

I tore open the thick manila envelope and read it out. It contained information about British Army deserters in the new state.

"The Engineer," he said excitedly.

I recognized the name. The man was believed to be a bomb-maker and terrorist. There were terrorists on both sides, Arabs and Jews, but there had been a group of British soldiers who hadn't left with the rest of us. They'd been deserters who were probably guilty of terrorist activities against Israel.

"There's information about the Killing Crew," I said.

"Tell me," Wolfe said, excited.

I read the instructions about finding these deserters.

Then I said, "But isn't it the Israelis' problem now?"

"Optics, Ash. They were our men and our problem." He paused. "At last, a proper Branch job, rather than this snooping around without a clear objective."

I had to admit he was right.

"I need you here, Ash."

"I can't—"

"Let me rephrase it. It's an order."

"Give me four days. Penny's case is tomorrow afternoon and it may run over to next week. I can't abandon her. Not now."

He thought for a moment then said, "I want you here on Saturday then, Ash. And when you get Penny off, of course we'll need a secretary in Israel."

Except for the day touring villages in the Mesaoria Plain, I rarely drank coffee. However, I made myself a mug and hoped it would ease the ache that was blossoming in my right eye socket.

Last night, I'd felt like a failure. It seemed like the solution to Penny's release had been within reach. If only Mrs Johnson had been at the house. Had she been there? Where was she now?

I tried to give focus to my spiralling, negative thoughts by writing down what I knew. Sergeant Major Ellis had been murdered by someone who looked like Mrs Johnson—and Penny. Penny looked guilty because she seemed to run away from the crime scene. But she had caught a later bus from Nicosia.

She had a return bus ticket but I'd been unable to find a witness to confirm that she'd caught the late bus. Because of the timing, Penny didn't have the opportunity, but I had no proof.

What about the means to commit the crime? Ellis had been stabbed through the eye with a stiletto blade. Penny didn't have such a blade, I was sure. And the murder weapon hadn't been found.

Motive? Well, Penny had a motive because she accused Ellis of raping her sister. But Ellis was being paid off by someone. I'd asked Johnson to obtain Ellis's post office records but forgotten to chase him about them. If they showed the large sums coming in and stopping before Ellis's murder, then that was reasonable doubt. I hoped.

Within Ellis's pocketbook, I'd seen Mrs Johnson's name and also the address of the factory. The factory was undoubtedly where I'd been held. It seemed a logical assumption therefore that Ellis linked Surena Johnson to the Kiss gang.

Verity Johnson had been kidnapped. Her adopted father thought she'd gone to be with Surena, but Chadwick had confirmed hostages. And I was sure someone had been held prisoner lately.

I stared at what I'd written.

I'd been too close to this to see the obvious.

FIFTY-FIVE

Dickins was in the office and in a bad mood when I checked on him.

"You won't believe it!" he said, but I did. I not only believed his news but it disgusted me to the pit of my stomach.

Minutes later I was on the telephone to Lieutenant Colonel Dexter and then raced over to his office.

"Major Johnson has taken over a police case I was involved in last night," I said, barely controlling my anger.

Dexter listened intently as I told him what had happened with the gang and the news this morning that the military police had cordoned off the property and were investigating the gang.

"Johnson is compromised!" I said, concluding my summary.

"Serious allegations, Lieutenant," Dexter said with a crease on his forehead deep enough to wedge a sheaf of paper.

"His wife is involved in this crime, and if she's being held against her will, then—"

"Hold on, son, are you saying that Johnson is in league with this gang?"

"Not necessarily, sir. I suspect there's a link between Surena Johnson and the man she eloped with."

"What's his name?"

"Alexis Velopoulos."

"And he's a member of the gang?"

I winced and he saw my uncertainty. "I don't know the connection, but it's likely. Velopoulos worked with and around the military. He could be one of them, sir."

Dexter shook his head. "So many questions."

Desperate, I said, "I may not know everything but Johnson is compromised and should be off Penny Cartwright's case."

"Because you want the case dismissed."

"That's true, but—"

"Ash, I can't go up against the provost marshal based on what you've told me. Your only real link to Mrs Johnson is the pocketbook. True?"

I nodded. He was right, and it was the biggest weakness in my argument. I had no proof that it was Ellis's writing or that her name connected her to the gang.

Dexter said, "I think you should reassess your opinion of Major Johnson because he wants this gang brought to justice and he even mentioned there may be a link to Ellis's murder."

I shook my head. Johnson didn't believe the gang had killed Ellis. Nothing would change his mind about Penny, except for hard proof from me.

Dexter said, "Look, Ash, I understand, but he's right. If there's a military link it could be that some of the gang are still in the army—"

"Then it's an army issue," I finished for him. I stared out of the window thinking of the similarity between this and Israel. The Killing Crew was believed to be ex-British Army and so the army wanted it resolved. *Optics*, Wolfe had called it.

★

Dexter warned me not to, although he must have known I'd storm over to Major Johnson's office anyway. But Johnson wasn't there. I left a message for him to call me urgently.

"At your office, sir?" Crawley, his chief clerk asked calmly, as though unaware of my anger and frustration.

"Try me first at the police HQ in Nicosia," I snapped. "Ask for DI Dickins."

Then I tore north, up the road to Nicosia.

Dickins wasn't available either. Park met me and said that his boss was back in hospital. The wound was worse than they'd thought.

"And how are you, Lieutenant?"

"I'll survive," I said. "But it hurts to laugh."

"Not much to laugh about. I suppose you heard?"

"About 227 Provost Company taking over?" I shook my head in disgust. "Bloody Johnson."

He looked at me enquiringly. "What about him?"

I put my head in my hands. The headache was coming back and I figured it was the frustration as much as tiredness.

Park was looking at me, waiting for an explanation, but I wasn't about to have the conversation with him. I could complain to Dexter, but not to some detective sergeant.

I shook my head. "I was hoping this wouldn't be a military issue. Has Chadwick said anything?"

"He's not saying much. Won't admit a thing."

"Mind if I try?"

"Be my guest," Park said, and took me into the basement, where stale, warm air clung like a woollen blanket.

Chadwick was asleep in a one-man cell and sat up when Park rattled the bars. He didn't make a move to open the cell door, but it was fine. I could speak through it.

The prisoner looked from Park to me and back again.

I said, "You only have one option."

He looked at me with dead eyes.

"You shot the inspector and intended to kill me. You're part of the Kiss gang. The Elevens. You're a criminal and murderer."

A smile flickered on his lips. "Is that supposed to make me talk, Lieutenant?"

I said, "Tell me where Mrs Johnson is."

The dead-eye stare returned. "Who?"

"You said she was a hostage."

He shook his head. "No, I didn't. You must have heard what you wanted to hear."

"Rubbish!" I said. "I saw the cage in your gunroom. Someone had been there. You'd had a prisoner."

Chadwick folded his arms and looked at Park. "Are we done here?"

"Help me and it'll help your sentence," I pleaded.

He looked back at me and shook his head. "I didn't have anything to do with the girls. You can't pin that on me."

I waited for a few beats.

"If not you, then was it the one you call *The Man*?" I knew Chadwick wasn't *The Man* since he'd said the expression 'shit slime' while they were waiting for the boss to arrive.

He gave me a knowing smile but said nothing.

"Who is he?"

Nothing.

"Who was in the cage, Chadwick?"

"I didn't have anything to do with the girls," he said again.

"Who was in the cage?"

"Don't know her name."

"Where is she now?"

He breathed in, long and slow, and looked at Park. "I want protection."

Park said, "You can have protection if you tell us something useful."

"They're buried out back, behind the clubhouse."

So they called it their clubhouse.

"They?" I asked.

He grinned like a tiger about to devour its prey.

"What about Mrs Johnson?"

"You're such an idiot." He chuckled. "Do you know that? I'm messing with you."

"Sir?" A voice interrupted us. A constable had come down the stairs.

"What is it?" Park snapped at the new man.

"For Lieutenant Carter, sir. An urgent phone call."

"We'll continue this," I said to both Park and the prisoner then left them both down in the basement and followed the constable to a telephone.

"Yes?" I said into the mouthpiece. "Lieutenant Carter here."

"Carter, it's Johnson."

I took a deep, controlling breath. "I heard you'd usurped the investigation."

"What?"

"Are you at their so-called clubhouse now?"

"No, Carter, I'm not. I'm at the detention camp near Pyla."

He paused, and I wondered what he was doing there. Was there trouble again? Was this about the release of the remaining Jews?

Johnson said, "You're looking for my wife."

My heart stopped. "You've found her?"

"No," he said, "but I think I know where she is."

FIFTY-SIX

I gave DS Park a quick update and he looked confused.

"So you don't want to carry on interrogating Chadwick, sir?"

"Maybe later."

"I'll come with you. Near Pyla, you say?"

I shook my head. "Stay with Chadwick. The priority should be to find out who else is involved. See if he can tell you more about the Elevens."

"Elevens?" He said it slowly with uncertainty.

I realized I hadn't had this conversation with him and maybe Dickins hadn't been well enough to give Park a complete update.

"Your Kiss gang call themselves the Elevens or something similar. It's based on the Eleventh Cavalry."

Park frowned at me.

"Never mind, Sergeant. After I've met with Major Johnson, I'll come back."

Pressing my foot to the metal, I raced out of the city heading back to Larnaca. Following the road around the bay, I turned inland before Dhekelia onto a single track. Dust billowed behind me as I drove through the low hills.

Eventually, I passed through a smattering of houses that was the village of Pyla, then a sign for the Roman ruins. I saw the army sign for the detention camp, and after a switchback that crossed a river, I came to the perimeter fence of the camp. Faces stared dumbly at me as I continued. Misery eked out of the encampment.

The track continued past and I could see a Land Rover parked further up by the tree line.

"Major Johnson?" I asked a guard at the detention camp gate.

"You Carter?"

"Yes."

He pointed at the distant Land Rover. "In the woods, sir."

The Land Rover had been modified like one of the GDU jeeps with a cage in the back.

I stopped beside it and shouted, "Major?"

After a minute of listening to nothing but a low whistle of wind through the trees, I started walking into the woods.

Where was the major? He could have given me more specific instructions. I looked back at wires I'd driven under and wished I had a field telephone. All I'd need to do was throw a wire over the line and connect to the operator. But I didn't have a field telephone.

"Major Johnson?" I shouted into the woods.

"Down here!" a voice called back.

I couldn't see him, but he couldn't be far ahead. I went further into the trees.

"Carter, down here!" I heard him shout again, and then I saw him fifty yards ahead, Johnson's German Shepherd at his side.

I came down the slope between the trees and saw him more clearly.

Not Major Johnson. His chief clerk, Crawley.

"Crawley?" I said, approaching. "Where's Johnson?" Then I saw the spade and hole in the ground.

Crawley watched me approach. His eyes were deep wells of sadness.

"What is it, Crawley?"

He looked down and in a quiet voice said, "I've found her. I've found Surena."

I looked at the ground and understood.

"Would you mind taking over the digging?" Crawley asked. He tied the dog to a tree as I picked up the spade and prepared to dig. Then I stopped, thoughts crowding my mind. This didn't make sense. Johnson had called me because he thought he'd found his wife.

This wasn't Surena Johnson, this was just a hole.

"How do you—" I began as I turned towards him.

Crawley raised a hand like he was saying it doesn't matter. But in his other hand was a gun. And it was pointing at me.

FIFTY-SEVEN

Instinct kicked in and I did two things. Almost simultaneously, I lashed out with the spade and dived away. The spade made contact and Crawley howled.

I didn't stop. I rolled, came up onto my feet and scrambled for cover.

With my right arm hugging my wounded chest, I stood behind a tree and drew my revolver. Then I stepped out and we stood face to face, about twenty yards apart. My gun pointed at him, his at me.

The German Shepherd barked at me, straining, his chain taut.

"Quiet, Caesar!" Crawley snapped. The dog stopped barking and sat obediently.

I kept my eyes on the other man. "What the hell's going on, Crawley?"

He took a breath. "I thought you knew."

"Where's Johnson?"

Crawley laughed. "That was me," he said in a Scottish accent. "I fooled you, didn't I?"

So it had been Crawley on the phone telling me to come here. "You said you've found Mrs Johnson," I said, looking at his gun and thinking. "Why, Crawley? Why lure me here?"

"You got Ellis's post office book. You knew he was a blackmailer."

Shadows beneath the trees were enough to hide my surprise at this news. Blackmail not bribery. I'd asked Johnson to obtain the post office transaction records and I'd begun to suspect that Johnson was the one paying Ellis. This new news explained why my rooms had been broken into but nothing taken.

"You thought the records were in my apartment," I said with a smile. "You didn't find them."

"No, I didn't."

"Why break in twice?" I asked, thinking back to the time before I'd asked for the post office records. The time when my room had been disturbed but not turned over.

He shook his head and I read that he knew nothing about the first break-in. Then who had that been?

I wanted him to confirm he'd killed Ellis, but I wanted him to talk more before he admitted what he'd done.

I thought about the gang and what I'd learned. XIS. The Elevens. Or Eleventh. I thought about the photograph of Mrs Johnson I'd seen. The man behind. Crawley. The First US Army Corps.

I said, "You were with Johnson in Operation Fortitude. You were in the Eleventh Army…" And then it struck me. Why had I felt something unusual about the photograph? Surena Johnson wasn't with her husband—not just her husband.

He liked the tease. He liked to watch his wife with other men.

"The three of you?" I said.

His gun didn't waiver but he smiled. "It's more common than you think. The French even have a term for it: *ménage à trois*. Which is quite romantic I think."

I didn't comment. I didn't truly understand.

He said, "The major liked to watch more than anything. He liked to see two young, fit people making love."

"So you followed him to Cyprus."

He said nothing for a moment then nodded. "If you want an explanation then you drop the gun."

"Not a chance."

"I'll put mine down at the same time. Then I'll tell you everything."

He directed the gun away, started to lower it, and I copied the motion until we both laid our weapons at our feet. He must have trusted that my instinct as a detective—the need to know the truth—would outweigh anything else.

"All right," I said, "so explain."

"It was the other way around. John Johnson followed me. Back then, I was in control. I wanted the move and it worked well for both of us—for all three of us."

From the expression, I could tell things had changed. "You aren't in control anymore."

"Over time I found Jonny didn't care who it was. I suppose I lost my good looks. Perhaps I didn't give him the same level of excitement anymore. So they sought new partners."

I thought about Lazzell and Lewis, the naval officers; good-looking men. I thought about what Lazzell had said to me. *Johnson scared me off. He said he'd kill me if I carried on with her.*

It didn't make sense if Johnson encouraged his wife to have relations with other men. He didn't scare anyone off.

"It was you," I said. "You threatened the other men. You wrote to them and let them think you were Johnson."

"Yes," Crawley said, and the smile returned. "Jonny encouraged Surena to flirt with other men."

"At Maxims."

"And other places, like the OC in Nicosia. Good pickup places for officers. I knew what they were up to because they'd go out without me."

I nodded. Crawley wouldn't be able to dine at an officers' or officers-only club.

"What did they do with Verity when they were out? Surely they didn't leave her at home?"

"What?" He shook his head like I was on the wrong track and asking the wrong questions. "Verity often stayed with a school friend."

Sister Isabelle Laurent's daughter.

I thought about what the neighbour, Sophie Cay, had told me. She'd heard Johnson arguing with Surena, said the major's voice had sounded different. Hazel Marsland-Askew had mentioned the flirting with other men, but I now knew that Johnson liked it. He wanted more partners. It was Crawley who'd been jilted.

I said, "You argued with them."

"Frequently."

"The neighbours heard."

"But they had no idea what was going on. Not really."

"Did Ellis realize? Is that why he was being paid off by Johnson?"

It was only as he laughed that I realized my mistake. It wasn't Johnson paying Ellis. It was Crawley.

He said, "I told Jonny it was because of our connection to the gang. You see, there had been another murder less than a year before. We knew who was doing it. We knew who the Eleventh were. I didn't care and Johnson was too preoccupied and ineffectual to act."

I bluffed: "So Ellis worked out it was you who did it." I was starting to form a picture but it wasn't complete. Fortunately, Crawley wanted to talk about it. I think he was proud of what he'd done.

Crawley said, "Ellis was working at the detention camp the night I brought Surena's lover here. He saw two men go into the woods and only one come out. He was a natural investigator. Missed his calling. Should have been one of you chaps."

"The Greek boy, the waiter at Maxims."

"I don't think Jonny suspected anything. I don't think he could countenance Surena being with someone who wasn't an officer. God, the man was just a wog!"

"What happened, Crawley?"

"I had a girl call the boy, pretending to be Surena. Left a message to meet me and that I would take him to her. The boy had packed suitcases and everything." Crawley laughed. "He really thought... anyway I buried him here. Then I called Surena."

Despite the humidity, I felt a shiver go down my back.

"Is Surena buried here too?"

"I wanted her to come to her senses. I thought she would see how much I loved her. And that she would come back to me. But she went berserk—attacking me with whatever she could get her hands on. So I hit her on the head with the shovel."

"When?" I asked, and my voice suddenly lost its force. "When did you kill her?"

"Eight months ago," he said with pride. "Everyone believed the story that she'd run away with the chap."

Eight months. My chest collapsed. Surena Johnson was dead. My only real hope of getting Penny off the murder charge and she was long dead.

"Is Verity buried here too?"

He shook his head. "I don't know where the kid is."

I heard a squirrel scamper along a branch above my head. The wind whistled through the valley.

"The Eleventh—" I started to say as a distraction, but dropped to my knees and snatched my gun.

"Don't!" he said, and I saw a pistol in his hand. Not the one on the floor. Crawley had a second gun.

"But I'm not going to shoot you, Carter," he said. "I'm going to let you walk away."

I started to stand with my gun in my hand.

"I said drop it!"

The gun fell from my open fingers.

I stepped back and back again. His gun was levelled at me but I sensed he really was letting me go. I started walking with my head turned so that I could watch him.

When I was more than thirty paces away, Crawley shouted.

"Hey, stop!"

I stopped and faced him. He was holding the dog's collar like he was trying to lift the beast off his front paws.

"Caesar," Crawley commanded. "Take him down!"

As he let go of the dog's collar, the German Shepherd leapt forward, barking. I flashed back to the training ground at 6GDU. The dog had gone for a limb. I'd watched the big guy called Payne knocked over by a dog called Jasper. Payne had been wearing a padded jacket protecting his body, arms and legs. I had nothing of the sort.

Caesar pounded towards me and I imagined evil intent in his black eyes. Perhaps if I'd had a gun I'd have shot the dog. Could I shoot a dog? Perhaps in this situation, but I didn't have a gun.

Ten yards away and I snatched a broken branch from the floor and held it out with my right hand. Did it look like a gun? I hoped so.

Five yards out and Caesar's eyes were on my arm and the supposed weapon. I could see the saliva on his teeth.

The dog leapt, his jaws ready to clamp on my arm.

I swivelled. I'd seen a Pathé News clip of a bullfighter once and imagined the stick was his red cape.

As my right arm pulled away, my rotation brought my left arm around. *Forget that this was a vicious animal about to rip my arm off. Imagine an opponent in the ring.*

The connection between my left fist and the dog's skull didn't feel like any boxing contact I'd ever made. It was bony and sharp and weirdly light. But the blow crashed him into a tree and he looked up at me, stunned.

With a rapid movement, I whipped off my belt, and before Caesar could regain his senses, I'd looped it through his collar and fastened it around the tree. Then I started moving away as fast as I could. Crawley had a gun and I had nothing.

But he was a fit man and I was injured. Each time I glanced back, I could see him closing on me. I was scrabbling up a slope, dirt clumping in my fists when he fired the first shot.

I slipped and stopped.

"One more question," I said, breathless.

He aimed the gun and closed the gap.

I asked, "Where did Ellis fit in? Did you kill him?"

Crawley shook his head with derision on his face. "No, someone did me a favour. I was paying Ellis because he thought I'd killed the Greek kid."

"But you had! And Surena."

He laughed. "You know, it actually felt better than I expected. She didn't love me and she wanted to be with that dirty local boy. I don't think she ever loved me. She just went along with the arrangement for—"

"For the sake of Verity?"

He pulled a face, like he was thinking: "Who knows?"

Caesar the dog came through the trees and I thought it must have pulled free of my belt somehow. The way it sat next to Crawley made me realize it wasn't just Johnson's wife who was close to Johnson's chief clerk.

Crawley's finger flexed on the trigger.

I stood up and faced him. I wasn't going to die lying in the dirt.

Then I looked over Crawley's shoulder. Past him.

"Mrs Johnson didn't die after the first blow, did she?"

"No, it took half her face off." Crawley blinked as if remembering a dreadful image. "I had to hit her five times before she finally died."

"Don't shoot," I said, again looking past Crawley.

Crawley gave a twitch of his head. "That old tr—"

But he would never finish the sentence. He'd never declare my words were a ruse. Instead, he first looked surprised as a hole blasted through his forehead, then he keeled face-first into the earth as a second shot was fired.

The dog bolted. Major Johnson stepped forward and emptied the rest of his gun into Crawley's jerking body.

FIFTY-EIGHT

Johnson's head was down and I could hear a guttural sound: a visceral moan that came from deep inside the man.

Although his gun was empty, he held it out to me and I took it.

We walked in silence out of the valley and woods and onto the track that led to the detention centre. At some point, Caesar joined us, because he came padding along behind us as though nothing had happened.

There were now three Land Rovers on the track. Johnson had parked behind Crawley's modified one. I thought about taking that because of the dog, but Johnson lifted Caesar into the back of my jeep and then sat in the passenger seat. He was breathing hard and seemed lost in his thoughts.

After the village, I eventually said, "Did you know?"

A rumble in his chest became words. "No. I thought she'd really run away with another man. I wanted her back, I wanted our life back, but at the same time, I couldn't face her. Do you understand that, Lieutenant?"

"Yes," I said, although I didn't. "Crawley told me Ellis was blackmailing him. Did you know?"

His eyes told me that he considered lying, but he said, "Yes. Graham told me that Ellis had worked out our connection to the Kiss gang."

I said, "I think Ellis was working on it, but Crawley paid him because Ellis guessed he'd killed the Greek boy. Maybe he suspected Crawley had killed your wife too."

Johnson nodded mutely.

I said, "Tell me who killed Ellis."

He looked at me with thousand-year-old eyes. "I think Penny Cartwright did it. You're blind, too involved. Just like I was blind to what Graham did."

"Where's Verity?"

"They have her. They have her so that I won't betray them."

"Who's the boss, the one they call *The Man*?"

He looked at me again. "I thought you'd worked it all out. The Eleventh Army Corps."

"You were in Fortitude," I said. "Were you from the Eleventh Army too?"

"Operation Quicksilver. After recuperating I was assigned to FUSAG, the fake US Army. They were the Eleventh—mostly from 55 West Lancashire. Graham Crawley was one of them too. No, I had been in the 51st Infantry Brigade. The Highlanders. I wasn't one of the Eleventh, but of course, I knew who they were."

"So X-I-S were ex-55th?"

"Yes. A few of them came here after demob. Graham persuaded me the change would be good for us."

"Tell me about the one they call *The Man*."

"He came up with the plan. Water rights," he said. "Water is the most valuable commodity on this island. Control that and you're sitting on a gold mine. And all legitimate."

"Legitimate?" I said with disbelief. "Men were executed!"

"Only in the early days when they were establishing themselves, and they were all small-time crooks anyway—and wogs."

I tried to hide my disgust at his attitude. He was talking and I needed him to keep talking.

"Who is *The Man*?" I pressed.

"I can't tell you that."

"Why not, for God's sake? It's over, Major."

"He has Verity!" His voice broke.

I waited a moment as he collected himself. Then: "Tell me and I'll get her back."

He looked at me with those ancient, weary eyes. "I can't do anything. I can't say anything. He'll kill her if I betray him."

★

I drove into Alexander Barracks and told the guards at the Glasshouse to lock up their provost marshal. At first they thought I was joking, but Johnson took himself in, signed the register and sat in a cell.

After leaving Caesar with them, I went to Jim Dexter and told him the news.

"Good God!" he said when I told him that Crawley had tried to kill me and that he'd been shot by Johnson. "Good God!" he said again when I told him about the murders. "I'll arrange for the bodies to be collected."

I told him where I thought Surena Johnson and her boyfriend were buried, and when I finished speaking he told me to write up my report.

"Later," I said. "There's something much more pressing." The Man had Verity and would know that I'd arrested Johnson. I was sure her life was in imminent danger. However, I didn't know who I could trust. Soft facts, I kept telling myself. I've accepted what people had told me rather than checked.

I used a clerk's desk and made two phone calls. My first was to London and the Department of Energy in Whitehall. I gave the operator my father's name and waited.

When I finally got through to him he answered, "Hello, Ash. I hear you're in Cyprus. How is it?"

"Better than Palestine."

"Right." He paused. "It wasn't your fault, you know." Despite the lack of explanation, I knew he was talking about my mother's death.

I took a breath and then another. Maybe I did harbour a sense of guilt because I hadn't been there for her. But she didn't take her life because of that. My actions hadn't been the cause.

He said, "She had mental issues, Ash. You should understand that."

My chest constricted and I couldn't talk. I wanted to shout down the telephone that it was his fault, but I needed his help and I didn't have much time.

"Not now," I said, swallowing the lump in my throat. "Not now. I need a favour, sir."

My father had a lot of contacts in high places, including the Metropolitan Police. "We have a Detective Inspector here called Charles Dickins. He claims to have been transferred here within the last two years. I need to know if that's true."

"Give me ten minutes," he said and ended the call.

I waited until my pounding heart had eased before I placed my second phone call. This one was to the Nicosia police HQ.

"Get me Sergeant Park," I said more tersely than intended.

"Sir, he's accompanying the prisoner to the Central Prison."

"Is DI Dickins still in hospital?"

"No, sir, I believe he's on his way back to the office."

"Right," I said. "Hold him. I'm on my way. Don't let the inspector go anywhere."

But I wasn't on my way. I had to wait for my father's phone call which took slightly longer than the ten minutes he promised. Human after all, I thought.

We spoke briefly and he confirmed what I needed to be sure of. I dropped the telephone and dashed for my Land Rover. As I drove north, I did a lot of thinking, going back over what I knew and what had happened. Fifty thumping minutes later, I slammed to a halt outside the police station and hurried inside.

I had the answer and kicked myself for not seeing the clues earlier.

"Dickins?" I said to the desk sergeant.

"In his office, sir, but—"

I didn't wait for the rest of his sentence; I was already past him and hustling down the corridor.

Dickins's door was open and there were four other officers with him.

"We have a problem," he said to me as I barged in. Although his skin was pale he looked uncomfortably hot, and I wondered how strong his painkillers were. "There's trouble at a storage unit in Famagusta. The one you were interested in a few days ago."

"Could I have the room?" I interrupted. "Just you and me."

He waved the other men out and I closed the door behind them.

"What's going on, Ash?"

"The first thing you need to do is work out who you can trust. The Kiss gang may well associate with the Eleventh Cavalry, but they were in the Eleventh Army Corps, principally the 55th Infantry Division—the West Lancashires."

"What about the trouble in Famagusta?"

"Let the local police deal with it. It's probably a distraction anyway."

Dickins paused then picked up the telephone and asked someone to compile a list of previous military postings.

When he replaced the handset he said, "How do you know you can trust me?"

"Because you weren't army, you were civilian police. I confirmed your story about being at Scotland Yard during the Blitz." This was the confirmation my father had given me. Dickins could be trusted.

He nodded.

Ten minutes later, a policeman came in with a list and Dickins underlined the names of policemen connected to the Eleventh Army.

Chadwick was listed along with two others.

Dickins looked at me and I pointed to a name.

"He's *The Man*," I said. "He's got Verity Johnson and we need to stop him."

FIFTY-NINE

DS Anthem Park had told me he'd been injured in the Battle of Greece, but he'd been nowhere near. He'd said he was part of W Force, which had been a tank command. He'd lied. Park had been an infantryman. He had been in the 55th. Eleventh Army.

"Anthem," I said to Dickins. "I should have seen it. *The Man* is an anagram of Anthem."

The inspector picked up the phone and asked to be put through to the Central Prison. As he listened, I saw the colour drain from his face.

"DS Park and the prisoner never arrived," he told me after putting the telephone down.

I nodded. "They're on the run."

Dickins picked up the phone again, and a moment later the men who'd left his room came back in.

"Powell," Dickins said. "You're under—"

Before he finished, the man I'd guessed to be Powell swivelled and reached for the door, but I stepped in his way and two of the others grabbed him.

"You're under arrest for being part of the Kiss gang," Dickins said.

It didn't take much for Powell to talk. Under interrogation, he told us that the clubhouse was a retreat, a reward bestowed by DS Park. He also said they'd used the old cigarette factory until recently and that the place in Famagusta was part of the legitimate operation.

I said, "It's not about alcohol, is it? It's water and water rights."

"Yes."

"Where's Park gone?" Dickins asked.

Powell had been beaten and my watch now showed we would be coming up to half an hour of interrogating soon. The man's face was bloodied and dejected.

He's not going to tell us, I thought.

"Don't know," Powell mumbled.

I stopped him being slapped and conferred with Dickins. We gave the prisoner a drink and waited for him to raise his head.

I knelt before him. "Help us, please. I just want to save Verity Johnson."

He blinked and his eyes finally focused on me. I read confusion in his face.

I gripped his arms. "Help us, for God's sake! It'll look better for you."

He considered it but still didn't speak.

Dickins said, "Come on, man, where has Park gone?"

"I don't know."

"He must have had somewhere he'd escape to. Somewhere special."

Powell hung his head. "All I know is there's a place up north."

"And?"

"His family used to own it. It's where the water operation started." He took a ragged breath. "And I know he kept arms up there, said there was a future in arms dealing. Better than alcohol and nightclubs. Better than water."

I said, "Tell us what you know."

He looked at me, wearily. "The family had or have a farm. Oranges, lemons, that sort of thing."

I shook my head. That could be a thousand places.

Powell said, "He called it the castle. Apparently, there is a tower or turret or something."

"Come on, man, give us the address!" Dickins said.

"I don't know it," Powell said pleading. "It doesn't have a wall."

Castle, I was thinking, flashing back to my brief time away in the north with Penny.

"Does it have a fence?"

"Yes. And I think it had—"

"A red rose!" I exclaimed, suddenly picturing the red flower on the stone marker beside the gate on the road to Lapithos.

"Yes, a rose—the Lancashires," he said.

I grabbed Dickins's good arm. "I know it. Let's go!"

★

The light was fading fast as five police cars raced north out of Nicosia. I was with Dickins and we had ten armed men, none of whom had been in the Eleventh Army.

We reached the mountains and the lights of five police cars washed backwards and forwards behind me on the winding road. Powell was in one of those cars, handcuffed to a policeman.

"I should have guessed it was Park," I said to Dickins beside me in my Land Rover.

"You?" he said, scoffing. "The man worked under me and yet I had no idea."

"He was in charge of the gang investigation. He could control everything—like the execution I stumbled across. It happened at night and I disturbed them. There should have been a shell casing, maybe even fragments of the bullet."

"Park made sure nothing went into evidence."

I said, "And I saw him coming out of Major Johnson's home after Verity went missing. He let me talk and then used my comments to reinforce my opinion. And then you didn't know he'd told me he was looking for her."

"So he was there to tell Johnson they'd kidnapped Verity?"

I nodded. That's what I believed. "And then, of course, there was his name."

"I'd never heard anyone call the Kiss gang boss *The Man* until you mentioned it."

"And that's why it's not your fault."

"Don't beat yourself up about it, Ash," Dickins said. "We'll find Park and we'll rescue the girl."

I drove faster. The moon was bright and high, and the air fresh. We cut through to the far side of the mountain range and began a winding descent towards Kyrenia and the north coast.

"How long?" he asked.

"Another half an hour, maybe." I'd been thinking about the gang picking me up, bundling me into the car and making me wait in the factory storeroom until Park arrived and gave me a warning.

I thought about what Wolfe had said, about me being Flynned. The *Palestine Post* reporter had been flailed and dismembered. His eyes had been gouged out.

The Stern Gang hadn't needed to kill Tom Flynn. They got what they wanted, but they brutalized him anyway.

That could have happened to me.

That could happen to Verity.

"Do you have any hostage negotiation training?" Dickins asked me.

I wished Wolfe was here. He'd handled hostage situations before. I hadn't.

"No," I said. "Have you?"

"No. In all my years in the Met, I never had a criminal take a hostage. Can't be too hard though, eh?" he added without conviction.

*

I led the police convoy west just before Kyrenia and I kept a lookout for the fence and the post with the red flower. I had a niggle of doubt about the location and prayed my headlights would find it.

However, we spotted the fire before we reached the place with the castle-like turret. There was an orange glow through the trees where there oughtn't to be one.

If I could have driven faster, I would have, but my foot was already pressed down hard.

I passed the red rose marker and turned off the road. The Land Rover lurched and bounced and Dickins gripped the door handle harder.

Flames were coming out of the turret and grey smoke spiralled with sparks into the night sky.

The gates were open and a group of people milled around, half watching the fire, the other half focused on us.

I stopped and heard the other vehicles thumping down the track and stopping behind us.

"Get out of the way!" I shouted at the crowd, and gradually they parted so that I could drive closer. Forty yards out I stopped again. Now I could see the whole place was burning, but the airflow drew the flames up and out of the tower.

I hustled towards the door.

"Ash!" Dickins shouted a pace behind me.

"Verity—she might be in there," I said.

"It's too late if she is."

I pulled up and stared, disconsolate. He was right. It would be an inferno in there. Then I realized there were adjoining buildings that weren't alight yet. In front of them was what I first thought was an oil truck. It had a tank on the back and a hose. Not oil but water.

I grabbed Dickins. "Water," I shouted. "We can fight the fire!"

Whether or not Dickins flashed back to losing his hand in a burning house, I don't know. However, he showed no fear as we hurried to the truck's hose. Another policeman ran with us, only he was faster and two paces ahead when I saw a thin line in the dirt ahead.

It flashed briefly as the house flared.

"Stop!" I yelled, dragging the inspector down. "Stop!"

Too late. Two more steps and the other policeman ran through the tripwire. The truck exploded. Hot air blasted over us, and for a second the world seemed nothing but heat and percussion.

It took a full minute before the ringing in my ears subsided.

I'd seen the same thing in Palestine. It gave me nightmares, and I guessed this one would too. Dickins and I were fine. The other policeman had disappeared, blown to pieces.

But there was no time to dwell on it. After the first explosion, there was a series of random small bangs, like someone was shooting at us. Then I remembered. Powell had said they stored arms here.

Dickins was shouting, "Retreat, retreat!" But we were already hurrying away.

As I slammed the Land Rover into reverse, the house erupted with a shower of bangs and flashes. I heard bullets ping and whizz through the air.

We got back to the gate, breathless.

"My God!" Dickins gasped.

I sucked in air and breathed cordite over the smell of burning wood. "If anyone was alive before," I said, "they aren't now."

The crowd was still there, workers from the estate I supposed.

"Anyone speak English?" I shouted, standing up and addressing them above the noise.

A man in overalls and flat cap stepped forward. He removed the cap and bowed.

"I am the manager here," he said with a Turkish accent.

"What happened?"

"The fire started just after Mr Park left with his friend."

"How long ago?" Dickins asked.

"More than an hour, sir."

"Where—which way?"

The man shrugged and shook his head.

I said, "Did they have a girl with them?"

"A girl, sir?"

"About eight years old with long dark hair."

"No, sir."

I looked at the fire. The explosions were quieter and intermittent now. Was Verity in there?

The man said, "Sir, there hasn't been any girl here—of any description."

I looked back at him with hope, and read sincerity in his eyes.

"Powell!" I shouted, and hurried to the car, where the prisoner remained cuffed in the back seat.

I opened the door and looked at him hard.

"Tell me about Major Johnson's daughter," I said.

He looked at me and a smile played on his lips.

"What?" I said.

"You got it wrong."

"Explain, Powell, or by God, I'll wipe that smile off your ugly mouth!"

He shrugged. "We never took Johnson's girl. It was you who told Anthem she'd been kidnapped. All we knew was she was missing."

"Hold on," I said, gripping his shirt. "Be honest with me. Spell it out. You never kidnapped Verity Johnson?"

"No."

"So who was held in the cell at your clubhouse?"

"Some wog who needed a lesson. We didn't need to kill most of them, just the ones who refused to hand over their water rights."

I shook my head. "Tell me where Verity is!"

"I have no idea."

I stared back at the burning farm. Was Verity in there? I didn't think she was. Powell was telling the truth. I'd told Anthem Park that Verity had been kidnapped and he'd used that to silence Johnson.

I'd been taught to find evidence, but as I watched the flames lick the night sky, I knew my mistake. There was one more crucial soft fact that I'd taken as gospel.

SIXTY

It was the middle of the night. The small hours of Friday morning, the day of Penny's hearing. I wanted to visit Penny and give her an update. It was both good and bad news. Bad that Mrs Johnson was long dead and therefore couldn't have killed Ellis, but good that Crawley had a motive. Matching his post office account records to the blackmail payments would be enough to raise reasonable doubt.

He'd denied killing Ellis, but he was no longer alive to defend himself.

I'd see Penny and her lawyer in the morning and we'd stop the case.

Driving back to Larnaca only to return in a few hours didn't make sense so I asked Dickins if there was a comfortable cell available that I might use.

"No such thing, lad," he said. "And I won't hear of it. You're coming home with me."

Dickins had a large house to the west of the city. I was mildly surprised to find a plump and rosy-cheeked Mrs Dickins at home. I hadn't asked, but Dickins later explained that he'd met an old girlfriend and remarried after the war.

Despite the hour, she fussed over us, warmed dinner that she'd made hours earlier and insisted I take a bath.

"Because look at the sorry state of you!" she said jovially.

I awoke to the smell of fried bacon and demolished a large breakfast before thanking my hosts and heading for the Central Prison.

But Penny wasn't there.

"Released ten minutes ago," the man at reception told me.

"Where?" I said, before realizing how foolish the question sounded. However, he acted like I'd been reasonable.

"An MP collected her on orders of the provost marshal."

I shook my head. This didn't make sense. Major Johnson was being held in the Glasshouse.

"Who?" I said again, showing my command of the English language.

Now he looked at me curiously before checking some documentation. "Major Gee," he said. "Major Gee is temporary provost marshal. And going back to your original question, I believe I heard the MP say he was to drive the young lady home."

Major Gee had taken over from Johnson? With doubts about the unit, I'd assumed that Lieutenant Colonel Dexter would take temporary charge. However, Gee was military police, so it made ironic sense.

After driving like a maniac, I arrived outside Penny's apartment to find her driver still sitting in his vehicle.

I ran up the steps and Penny almost died of shock as I burst in.

"Ash?" she said.

I reached out to hug her but she turned and went into the bedroom. She plonked a large suitcase onto the bed and immediately started throwing clothes into it.

"What are you doing?" I asked.

"Leaving."

"Leaving?"

She didn't stop packing as she spoke. "I thought a lot about it, Ash. I want to go home. I can't stay here any longer. There's a boat leaving for Blighty this afternoon. Martin—"

"Margie!" I snapped, and then regretted the tone of my voice.

She stopped for the first time and turned. Her face darkened. "Yes, Margie. He came through for me, Ash. Unlike you."

"What?"

"You lied to me. You said he wasn't going to do anything, but look—he got me out of prison!"

"He did—"

She cut me off. "While you were focused on finding out who the Kiss gang were, he actually did something for me. He got Ellis's post office passbook and he was receiving large amounts of cash each month. That's evidence he was blackmailing."

So it had been Gee who had got the passbooks. Crawley had searched my place thinking that I had them.

Before I could comment, she continued. "What's more, Martin has temporarily taken over as provost marshal of 227 Company and dropped the case."

"Penny—" I couldn't get the words out. She'd got it all wrong. No way could Gee have taken over and dropped the case without me arresting Johnson. Yes, I'd been distracted at the end, but I was worried about Verity.

"And," she added, "not only did Martin arrange for me to be driven here, but he's paid for the ticket home too. So I'm going."

I sat in the lounge and waited and tried to think of the best way to explain without making it sound like I was criticizing the man she saw as her hero.

When she appeared at the bedroom door with the case, I jumped up.

"Let me carry your bag."

She thanked me and let me carry it to the door.

"I'll take you to the dock. Which one?"

"King George's at Famagusta, but I have a driver."

We were on her steps now and she pointed at the MP who was still outside.

She headed for his Land Rover, but I hefted her case into the back of mine.

"No," I said firmly, "You're coming with me."

She hesitated, thought and then nodded.

Once we were on our way, she said, "Sorry if I seem awful and ungrateful, but I'm confused."

"It's all right," I said. "You've been through a lot."

"It's been hell, and I'm grateful to you for all you did for me."

I said, "Martin Gee—"

"He did a lot too, and I realize I'm confused."

I smiled over at her. "You said that already."

"I have feelings for you, Ash, I really do."

"But?"

"I realized I still have feelings for Martin." She sounded tearful. "So I need to get away. Not just because of the horror of being in prison with a potential death sentence on the cards, but because of you and Martin."

I could have criticized my rival, I could have pointed out that he was married. I could have clarified what I'd done and that Gee hadn't done much at all. He wasn't even seeing her off.

We arrived in Famagusta and I drove past the naval dockyards and parked at the civilian dock where a steamer was being prepared.

A porter took Penny's suitcase and we watched it being wheeled away.

She looked at me and a tear rolled down her cheek. "No long goodbyes," she said, and then kissed me.

"I'm going to Israel tomorrow. New orders."

"A change for both of us then," she said, forcing a smile. "That's good."

"There's a job for you," I added hastily. "If you change your mind, Wolfe and I need a secretary."

She kissed me again.

"Take care, Ash Carter."

"I'll miss you," I said, but she was already walking away and I don't know whether she heard me. She disappeared up the gangplank and I never saw Penny Cartwright again.

SIXTY-ONE

Sister Laurent wasn't at BMH Nightingale, and I obtained her home address, a private villa outside of the Dhekelia cantonment.

"I wondered how long it would take you to realize," she said, walking to meet me by the road.

The soft fact that I'd accepted.

"You lied about the kidnapping."

She nodded. "Something needed to happen. You weren't making progress."

I got out of my Land Rover and looked at the sea. It was a great location, out of town, beyond the garrison, but not too remote.

I said, "Did you send the photographs?"

"Yes. Maria's cousin cleans for me as well. We let you think the messages came from Verity, but I arranged it. Verity was even more worried than me, and when she heard you were an investigator who didn't work for Johnson—well, you were the ideal candidate to find Surena."

I took a long breath of the clean sea air. "It's bad news about your friend I'm afraid."

When she spoke her voice was stoic. "I guessed. I knew Surena wanted to get away, but no contact didn't feel right. It wasn't like her. Despite her problems, she loved Verity." She bit her lip, then: "Did John kill her?"

"No, it was Graham Crawley."

"Give me the details."

I decided she was a strong woman so I told her everything, including the six blows to kill her friend. However, I left out the bit about Surena's face being half off.

When I finished she said, "Where's John Johnson now?"

"In a cell."

"Will he be charged with Crawley's murder?"

"Unlikely," I said, and I heard the sound of girls laughing somewhere behind the villa. "He'll be charged based on conspiracy to commit and cover-up criminal activity—the gangsters from his old army group, the Eleventh."

I suspected he'd get a good lawyer and argue that he acted under duress. Maybe the belief that they had Verity would help his cause. Maybe he'd get away with an Other Than Honourable Discharge and no prison time. I hoped not.

"Is Verity all right?"

"She's happy here. As happy as can be expected under the circumstances. She knew too. So I'll fight to keep her. John Johnson may not have killed Surena, but—"

For the first time, her voice broke, and I waited for her to regain composure.

"—but he may as well have."

I said, "The 227 are looking after Caesar."

"I'll take the dog as well," she said, and then forced a laugh. "People keep telling me I should have a man around the house. A guard dog seems like a good alternative."

A driver came over from Alexander Barracks as I was finishing up, mothballing the office until we came back. And we would be back, I was sure. The operation was in Israel but this was our bolthole.

"As soon as you can, Lieutenant Carter, Colonel Dexter would like to see you in his office. Full dress."

"I've packed," I said, more to myself than as an excuse to the driver.

"Sir," he said apologetically. "The colonel insisted."

Fifteen minutes later, I was in uniform and being driven to Dhekelia. I stared fixedly ahead, trying to suppress the wild thoughts in my head.

Was there one final twist? Had Mrs Johnson turned up alive? Had Johnson been released? He might change his story and claim I'd killed Crawley.

Alternatively, Gee might have changed his mind. Maybe he'd decided to press charges against me for punching him after all. But if so, wouldn't I have been arrested at the office rather than be taken to see Dexter?

When I saw the colonel's face it gave nothing away.

I saluted him.

"At ease, Lieutenant," Dexter said.

I said nothing. My palms began to sweat.

Dexter walked around his desk and stood an arm's length away.

"I've been told about your new orders," he said. "And this morning I spoke to Major Wolfe."

Captain Wolfe, I thought. Dexter had made a mistake about Wolfe's rank, but I didn't correct him. Instead, I gave a small nod.

"I know you're off to Israel today. Going after those deserters."

I said nothing.

"It's not going to be easy, Ash. The politics are all over the place. Back into the lion's den, and without a team this time."

He was right. Normally we'd have a good sergeant and some junior ranks as well as support staff.

I said, "I'm not afraid of the action, sir."

He chuckled. "That's an understatement if ever I heard one! You were only here five minutes and... well that's not why I asked to see you. You and Wolfe will be alone out there so you're to keep in touch—not just with HQ, but with me. And if there's any trouble, we can be there in a day. A political nightmare, I'm sure, but we'll let others worry about that. Got it?"

"Sir."

He said nothing for a moment and I wondered if we were done, but then he looked serious again.

"There's another matter." He picked up a piece of paper. An official letter.

"Your senior officer Bill Wolfe has picked up his majority. The new role requires status—so that the Israeli authorities show the appropriate respect and provide access to the highest levels."

I nodded. So Dexter hadn't made a mistake earlier. I admired Wolfe, and his new rank of major was a well-deserved promotion.

The colonel paused and then nodded. "Similarly, it gives me great pleasure to inform you of your promotion to captain."

I looked at him, surprised. Promotion to captain was usually automatic, assuming you didn't make a cockup, three years after graduating from Sandhurst. I had more than nine months to go.

"Your role requires planning and decision-making as well as tactical nous. You've shown those qualities in spades, Ash."

He saluted and handed me the formal letter, a copy of a signal to the manning and records office, before giving me a third pip to be added to each of my epaulettes. Then he shook my hand warmly.

I never worried about status or rank, and if anything, I knew I could be guilty of not showing the appropriate respect—Major Gee being a case in point. However,

Captain Carter had a certain ring to it, and I left Lieutenant Colonel Dexter's office with a wide grin on my face.

♣

SIXTY-TWO

Park and Chadwick were still at large. They might have left the island or they might not. When I looked at the door to my lodgings, I decided that to stay there tonight would be tempting fate. In the morning I would finish packing everything and put into storage what I didn't need to take to Israel. There wouldn't be much, we'd been here just five weeks and appeared to have done little of use except get my secretary arrested and then try to clear her name.

Someone had murdered Sergeant Major Ellis. Ellis had been blackmailing Crawley because he suspected the man had killed Surena Johnson's Greek lover. The notes in his pocketbook suggested a link to the Kiss gang, but it seemed he was just a natural investigator and on their trail rather than spotting a link between Mrs Johnson and the gang.

The gang had a good motive to kill Ellis—if the killer hadn't been Crawley. However, the Peeping Tom witnessed a woman entering the alley with Ellis and then running from the crime scene. He'd checked the body. If there had been someone else, surely they would have killed the witness. No, I thought, the auburn hair meant it was a woman who looked like Surena Johnson.

After eating, I sat on Penny's sofa and thought about the fun we'd had. I would miss her vivaciousness. I remembered our passionate kiss outside Maxims. I remembered her shouting and laughing into the wind as I drove back through the night with the roof off the Land Rover.

I remembered our weekend escape in the north just before she'd been arrested.

And most of all I remembered her sitting on the apothecary coffee table looking sexy. We'd sat on the Famagusta city wall and talked a lot of nonsense. I'd shown her how a straw could be strong and penetrate an apple skin if jabbed fast enough.

We'd come back with the talk of hot cocoa. I could imagine her sitting in front of me on the table, her hands behind her, her knees high.

Her skirt had ridden up and I remembered how she'd made it slip further until I could see her white panties.

I took a shuddering breath. My God, she was so sexy!

She'd be out at sea now, probably nearing Sicily. And yet I kept flashing back to that night. I'd had only a few hours' sleep at the Dickins home in Nicosia and I was tired. The last thing I needed was the sexy image of a lost girlfriend teasing me all night.

With one foot on the table, I pushed it so that the alignment changed. Psychologically I guess I was pushing her away. Letting her go.

And that's when I noticed her bag. The one she'd been carrying when she'd come back from Nicosia.

She'd walked in and flung it towards the sofa. It must have slipped and gone under the table. Did she forget it? I thought back to that night. She'd seemed uncomfortable and wanted me to leave. I'd stayed with her and then we'd left for our nights away.

She hadn't come back here until this morning. And again she'd seemed awkward, like I was disturbing her. Was it because of Martin Gee or was it something else?

I picked up the bag and my hands tingled with nerves as I opened it.

I hadn't turned on the main light in case anyone was outside looking for me. However, there was enough light to see something dark and hairy inside the bag.

I pulled it out.

A wig. An auburn wig cut in the style that Surena Johnson wore in the first photograph I'd received. And shown to Penny.

I held my breath as I pulled a second item from her bag: A skirt.

The woman who had met Ellis had worn a skirt. Penny had arrived home in slacks.

The final item in the bag was Penny's pencil case. I already guessed what I'd find inside. But it wasn't a stiletto knife, it was a knitting needle.

The pathologist had got it wrong. It had been an innocent-looking knitting needle that had killed Sergeant Major Ellis.

Penny hadn't been on the late bus.

She'd arranged to meet Ellis outside the pub and disguised herself with a wig. Maybe Ellis thought he was meeting Surena Johnson, but the disguise had been deliberate because the major's wife was missing.

I'd shown her the colour photograph. I'd said they looked similar.

Someone had searched my apartment the first time, while I was with Maria touring the peasant villages. Not Ellis looking for a passbook, but Penny looking for my gun.

She'd made the arrangement the previous week to meet with Ellis. She'd probably bought the disguise in Nicosia and maybe had intended to shoot the man. Instead, she'd lured him into an alley and stabbed Ellis through the eye. God! I'd even told her about how that could kill a man. Penny had got revenge for what had happened to her sister.

I didn't sleep after all.

I spent the night fretting about what to do. But in the morning, I closed up the office and boarded the ship in Larnaca and set sail. Leaving a land where trouble was just brewing, and heading for the Promised one.

Acknowledgements

I would like to recognise Richard Callaghan, curator of the Royal Military Police Museum, and Phil Ellis, SIB Branch Secretary for their support in answering my questions. Any deviation from historical fact is due to creative license rather than any mistake on their part. I am also grateful to John Christiansen for advice on military matters in general.

Thanks as usual to my official editor, Richard Sheehan, and my unofficial ones, Pete Tonkin and Richard Lipscombe. Your help and support is appreciated.

The next instalment:

THE KILLING CREW

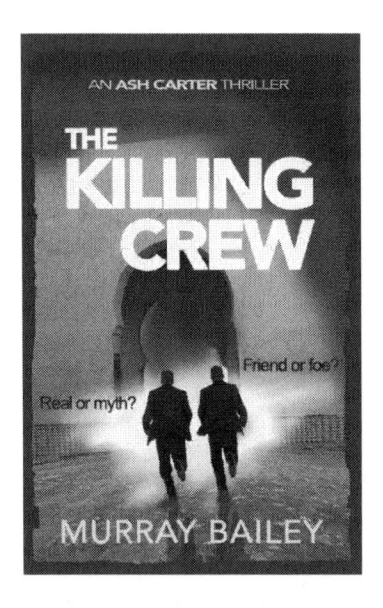

Ash Carter and Bill Wolfe are in Israel hunting a group of British Armey deserters known as the Killing Crew. Some people think they were a myth, others believe they were the most hated of British soldiers.

In the newly formed state that's at war with the Arab nations, hated by Jews and despised by Arabs, the two SIB officers think they face an uncomfortable task.

But when they become targets they start to realise this is more than just a job. It's life or death.

BLACK CREEK WHITE LIES

One night, Jade Bridger takes a dead-end path by the creek, and vanishes. Eighteen months after being wrongly accused of her murder, Dan Searle returns to Cornwall to rebuild his life and forget. But others won't let him forget.

He is quickly drawn back into the case and a dark and violent mystery; one that involved another girl years before. As the lies begin to unravel, Dan uncovers startling truths about his family and the past.

With dangerous people trying to keep their secrets safe, he must save those he loves - before time runs out...

I DARE YOU

Why was Kate's boyfriend snatched off the street? People said she couldn't trust him. They said he was a liar. But a year later she discovers a photograph that makes her question everything she thought she knew.

As she investigates, people start to die and Kate is left wondering who she can trust.

She follows clues from England to the Czech Republic and finally to the US. All the while a killer is on her tail.

Kate just wants the truth.
But is the truth worth dying for?

THE SINGAPORE
ASH CARTER THRILLERS

murraybaileybooks.com

IF YOU ENJOYED THIS BOOK

Feedback helps me understand what works, what doesn't and what readers want more of. It also brings a book to life.

Online reviews are also very important in encouraging others to try my books. I don't have the financial clout of a big publisher. I can't take out newspaper ads or run poster campaigns.

But what I do have is an enthusiastic and committed bunch of readers.

Honest reviews are a powerful tool. I'd be very grateful if you could spend a couple of minutes leaving a review, however short, on sites like Amazon and Goodreads.

Thank you
Murray

Printed in Great Britain
by Amazon